DOG WALTZ

Michael Donovan was born in Yorkshire and now lives in Cumbria. A former consultant engineer, his first novel *Behind Closed Doors* won the 2012 Northern Crime competition.

By the same author

Praise for Michael Donovan's writing

www.michaeldonovancrime.com

DOG WALTZ

MICHAEL DONOVAN

CHAPTER ONE
Nothing illegal, I assume

It was a decent day for early June. There were pools on Bishop's Bridge Road but they reflected blue sky and blinding sun, and the damp office workers heading for their buildings were cheerful, the way you are when the forecast's way up. I pushed up the pavement for fifty yards then crossed to the station side, dodging buses and cabs. Progress took muscle on account of Herbie, my brindle Staffie, who was in sea-anchor mode, oblivious to the sun or the people or the buses, pulling all ways to check for intruder smells. Paddington Station's a little outside his territory but who knows? Could have been one of his old haunts. He probably knew the area better than me. I gave the leash a tug to get his attention and he gave me a grin and desisted. We continued, heading for a nine-thirty appointment on the station concourse.

Neutral territory.

Some clients insist on stations and hotels and bars, public buildings. Sometimes it's an authority thing, sometimes it's just nerves at the idea of a P.I.'s office. And sometimes it's because the client's come in by train and can save time and a taxi fare, which was the case this morning. The guy on the phone last night said he'd be in after nine. Told me to look for a concourse table.

We went in and pushed through the tail end of the rush hour to the fast-food area to check the tables. Of which there were plenty. So the first trick: before we talked we needed to find each other. We'd neglected to agree on carnations in buttonholes, or top hats – which I'd have favoured in honour of the station's builder – so what I did was zero in on the only table occupied by a lone guy deep in thought. His thoughts were interrupted and his head lifted as he clocked me. He raised a hand and I dodged potted plants and dividers and arrived at his table.

He was in his early sixties, a business professional in a sharp woollen suit and sober sky-blue tie. Something of a military air in the hollows of his cheeks, his buzz cut widow's peak. Eyes reflecting a cold glint, suggestive of steel. Someone used to giving orders.

I confirmed my ID and he gestured to the other seat.

I sat and tied Herbie to the table pedestal. My canine associate had clocked the fact that we'd arrived at an eating place and his street-dog instincts were on full alert. I got the leash secure and my foot on the pedestal base then held my hand out across the table. The prospective client, whose name was Locke, leaned sideways to stick his own hand over a leather document wallet and grasp mine horizontally, his atop, a short get-it-over-with formality.

Then he sat back to watch me.

In control.

Though not fully: he wasn't controlling whatever had brought him searching for a private investigator. And the brief compression of his lips before he spoke revealed an inner tension as he struggled to conceal the fact that the last thing he wanted to do this morning was sit here talking to me about the content of the leather folder.

But he was going to have to do just that.

So he breathed in and pulled himself upright and kicked things off by dropping his hand onto the folder, flat out, fingers splayed, protecting whatever was inside.

'I've come a fair distance,' he said, 'based on your reputation.'

I smiled. I presumed that the reputation he referred to was the one for getting results and not the one created by the media last year which covered various other aspects. We hadn't got ourselves into the news over routine jobs – the ones that went smoothly. If you'd read the papers back then you'd have thought we were an entertainment company or some kind of reality show offshoot.

But that was then. Today was today and I assumed the guy knew what he was looking for.

I wondered just how far he'd travelled.

We once had a prospective client from El Salvador, though he never signed the contract due to someone catching up with him in his Bayswater hotel the evening before our meet. I guessed Locke's journey was a little shorter. The arrivals screens had trains in from Basingstoke and Weymouth and Portsmouth, though if he'd come in on the Heathrow Express the planet was his Oyster Card.

Turned out he was from closer to home.

'I'm over in Bristol,' he said.

A hundred miles or so. Not far on a global scale but quite a distance as an alternative to flicking through the local yellow pages. And quite a bill if his job took me out of town. P.I.s don't travel cheap, even if we end up in cheap hotels eating at cheap restaurants. A local firm will always give you a better rate. So our reputation must really have impressed the guy – sufficiently to warrant a two hundred mile round trip even to discuss the job – though Locke didn't look the type to be over-impressed. I folded my arms and looked at him. Waited for him to tell me what was up.

Crowds eddied around us, a bubbling white noise of voices bouncing from the iron and glass arches. Indecipherable conversations. A comfortable din to blanket a confidential chat.

'You perhaps know who I am,' Locke said.

He sounded serious so I stayed neutral which he interpreted as a negative though it didn't make him unhappy.

'Bernard Locke,' he said. 'Avon and Somerset.'

A copper. And high up, was my guess.

'Chief Constable,' he elaborated.

See?

I smiled. A Chief Constable was a first. Though not so strange: chief constables have straying spouses just like anyone. But why he'd come so far wasn't clear. Unless his wife had been taking trips up to London.

Turned out she hadn't. It was something else.

'I want you to find somebody,' Locke said. 'With maximum discretion. A quick in-out.'

I pursed my lips. Dropped my arms discreetly to anchor the table and stop it sliding. Herbie had radared in on some savouries on a nearby table and my leverage was insufficient. I shifted my leg to get more pressure on the base. Progress stopped but the tension held.

'Who?' I said.

Locke sat back. He hadn't touched his coffee. The drink was just a prop to get him a seat.

'You may have heard of my daughter,' he told me.

I waited again since the logic behind his assertion was weak. I hadn't heard of him so why would I have heard of his daughter? Unless she was head of the Metropolitan Police.

'Sarah Locke,' he clarified.

And that was it. The picture came clear

I should have known.

The name was sufficiently well known for even me to recognise.

Though I couldn't say exactly *what* she was.

Celebrity didn't quite fit, and TV presenter was too narrow. I recalled a regional show she'd hosted, maybe news or talk, and a consumer affairs programme then a stint on *Crimewatch*. Nowadays she fronted an investigative series for an independent production company called TownGate. I'd seen an episode that had torpedoed a scam involving NHS equipment suppliers. I'd watched it with my former girlfriend eighteen months back, and though I hadn't been focused on the TV I recalled Sarah: a bright, bouncy, intelligent personality who had a way of connecting through the camera like the pair of you were chatting at the bar.

'What's the problem?' I asked.

Locke lifted his hands and opened the document case and pulled out three sheets of photo paper. Inkjet prints. He rotated them and lined them up on the table.

The one on the left was a guy coming out of a corner pub on a busy road. The quality wasn't good but there was enough definition to make out the face. Late thirties, early forties; a ragged fringe of dark hair topping a lean face; a goatee wrapping his thin mouth. The eyes were intense, like he was pondering a tenner he'd just dropped on a horse.

The centre photo was the same guy in amongst pedestrians on a shopping street. The entry arch of a shopping centre rose ahead of him and a church spire marked the background. The guy was easy to spot in the crowd because he was dead centre in the picture and because I'd just seen him in the first shot. Definition not too good again but you couldn't miss the same intense look, the dark hair, the goatee.

But not someone you'd remember when he passed you a second time.

The third photo was more interesting.

I recognised the face this time, though it wasn't the guy's. It was Sarah Locke: her trademark smile and layered blonde hairstyle. The photo looked like a still from a location shoot, somewhere out in the sticks. Sarah smiling to camera between takes.

But what was interesting was the guy standing behind her.

He was smiling too but this one wasn't pretty.

Because all that was visible was the smile. The top half of his face had been digitally obscured to leave just the thin goatee'd mouth leering at the camera. The leer was a screaming contrast with the natural smile on Sarah's face which was the smile of someone unaware of anything wrong.

Which she was.

Because the goatee'd guy wasn't really there.

He'd been Photoshopped in.

The work was sufficiently competent that you'd have to look twice to spot the fakery but the light across his face wasn't quite right, and the smile on Sarah's face wouldn't have been there if she'd sensed the guy or the big ugly knife he was holding blade-forward to almost touch her neck.

A tight, ugly message.

The juxtaposition was fiction, care of our brave new digital world, but the effect was powerful. The message clear.

The message said: I'm right beside you. Just *this* far away.

I looked closer but with the obscured eyes there was no way to tell if this was the same guy as the other pictures. Lots of men wear goatees. The build was similar to the previous photos and the black hair was the same but there was nothing positive except for Bernard Locke's stare when I looked up.

'He's been following her,' he said.

I waited for him to explain. The guy had been Photoshopped in so he wasn't anywhere near Sarah, and he wasn't following anyone in the other two snaps, assuming they were him.

Locke leaned in over the table to make himself heard above a PA announcement about signalling delays.

'Sarah's *Exposed* series brings her into conflict with some unpleasant people,' he said. 'People who might hold a grudge. And she gets nutcases like any celebrity, the ones who think she's in love with them because of a look she gave to camera. Sarah lives with the risk. It's part of the job. But she's smart enough to know when a threat is real.'

'And this is real?'

'Yes.'

'So who is this guy?'

'We don't know. Sarah reported a character showing up at locations a couple of months back and more recently she's spotted a guy near her house. He ran off when she approached him but then was there again a few nights later, hiding in the shadows as she drove into her driveway.'

Locke paused. I kept my foot planted on the table base. Things had escalated. A scrap of food had dropped from a nearby plate. Herbie was focusing.

My own focus was still on trying to see the connection between Locke's story about someone watching his daughter and the images on the table in front of me. And the connection between the Photoshopped image and the others. I guess Locke was coming to that.

'Did you check the watcher out?' I said.

'To a very limited extent. I take my entitlements like any civilian. Made Central aware of the prowler. They sent a car round to Sarah's house a few nights but didn't spot anything.'

'Maybe he spotted them and backed off.'

'Possibly. Things went quiet for a week or two. No further sightings, though Sarah might not have told me if she spotted his face at a shoot. She still tends to shrug things off. But I can't forget Jill Dando.'

He spoke the name then stopped and looked at me to see that I got it.

Which I had.

Because I'd seen the resemblance.

And this was his fear.

That his daughter looked a hell of a lot like Jill Dando. The Nineties TV presenter. It's what had been on his mind since the goatee guy first popped up.

Jill Dando. At the top of her game. National news anchor, morning show host and one of the *Crimewatch* team, the show that went after the bad guys. But someone had been watching *her*. Someone who turned up on her doorstep one day with a 9 mm semi-automatic and terminated her career. The case was never solved. Was it a lunatic fan, a hit-man or a foreign assassin? There were as many theories as pundits. I came within an inch of involvement myself after a request for extra manpower pulled out my name but my guv had his own unsolved caseload and declined the invitation. If I'd joined the Dando investigation I'd probably be on it still.

So TV personalities had been looking over their shoulders in the decade since. All it takes is one stranger to step out of the shadows...

And Sarah Locke's similarity to Dando didn't stop at her looks. Sarah's *Exposed* series must have netted her a few resentful watchers in the shadows. Locke's unease at stalkers and night visitors and a guy Photoshopping himself into a picture with a knife made sense. Though he still hadn't explained the connections.

I pushed things along. Tapped the knife photo.

'How did you get this?'

'Sarah received it two days ago. Hand-delivered to her house.'

'And you think he's the guy who's been following her?'

'I'm sure of it. And whether or not, he's still damn scary.' He tapped the photo himself. 'This is not the product of a rational mind.'

I looked at it again. Didn't disagree. Looked back at the other two.

'You only see half the face in the Photoshopped picture,' I said. 'I'm still not clear how you're linking it to the guy in the street pictures.'

Locke answered by pulling another picture from the folder.

'This is Sarah's front door security camera. It caught the guy delivering the photo.'

I looked at the new snap.

And got the link.

A night-time porch, a guy holding a manila envelope, about to push it through the letterbox. Quality not so good but it was the same face as the street guy. The link.

'I'm not free to use police resources for a personal situation,' Locke said, 'but the doctored photograph is a clear indication of criminal intent so I asked one of my civilians to run an exercise yesterday using the door camera image, see if the same face had been caught anywhere on CCTV around the city. It was a case of two birds with one stone: a good test of the system's capabilities and the potential prevention of a crime. We've got face recognition software in the experimental stage and my guy ran a quiet training exercise with his council contact. They auto-scanned stored images for the last fortnight and got these matches: the shots at the pub and on the street. It's the same guy. He's there in the city.'

'But it's not within your privilege...'

'...to use police resources. The guy's committed no overt crime so far. But damned if I'll wait until my daughter's been hurt.'

'Why come to London? A local agency would be handier to get eyes on the streets. You could get two or three times the coverage for your money.'

'The hourly rates aren't the issue. The issue is that I want a result, fast. Which brought me here. We've heard about your firm even in the provinces.'

Anywhere that tabloids are read, I guess. We'd been national news twelve months ago even if it was for the wrong reasons, with my own face plastered under some less than complimentary headlines. Though by the time the story signed off the words had turned more kindly. That later coverage might be interpreted as positive publicity by clientele looking for miracles. I didn't picture Locke as a tabloid reader but I guess crime stories that went national caught his attention.

'Truth is,' I repeated, 'I'd go for a local crew and spend the change on a bodyguard.'

'I've already put people with Sarah. Twenty-four hours. She's safe for the moment.' He tapped the photo again. 'So what I want is this guy finding.'

'What happens then?'

'I'll have words with him. Educate him. If he goes near Sarah again he'll regret it.'

'No threat of illegalities, I assume?'

Locke looked at me. His cheeks looked gaunter. The light in his eyes glinted with a new frost.

'Give me credit,' he said.

'I do. But I'm wondering whether professional ethics will hold up in the heat of a threat to your daughter.'

Because they hadn't entirely held up when Locke opted to use police resource for his street cam. search, even if the resources were limited and the reasons understandable. It made you wonder about the Chief's judgement. Running a face-recognition exercise was a tightrope walk. It would be a pretty big trawl even with the smartest software. And the software had to be state of the art. I'd never heard of face-recognition used this way. The nearest equivalent was the live monitoring when the services were looking for someone specific at a specific location, say a terrorist heading into the House of Commons. The facilities over in Bristol must have been pretty advanced. And Locke must have some close personal connections with the local council to talk them into co-operating on the quiet. If it was me I'd never have imagined that I could get away with it. But I was never chief constable material.

'Full disclosure,' Locke said: 'if I catch the guy in the act of assaulting my daughter I'll kill him. Policeman or not. But it won't get that far. I'll make sure he sees the lie of the land before things escalate. Make him understand that we'll be watching him twenty-four seven until he leaves the area. It won't be true – not on an official basis – but I can call a few favours outside the force to give him periodic reminders.'

Which also sounded a little illegal – like harassment. But harassment was minor on the scale of the murder threat I'd just heard from the chief constable's lips.

I sat back. Took a breath.

The station buzzed. Crowds flowed. Cups and cutlery rattled. The station PA told us that the nine-forty-eight was now the ten-thirty-five. Destination Cardiff. Maybe Locke could make that one. He just needed to hear a response.

I thought about it. Murder and harassment. Coppers who'd overstepped the mark in the past.

And thought about an unknown assassin living in a villa in the sun on the back of the Jill Dando paycheque.

I made my decision. Pulled out a card.

'Give me a fax or email,' I said. 'We'll send the contract through. One week fixed fee plus expenses. If I get nothing by then you can decide whether we bring more people in. Which is when it will get expensive.'

Locke fished out a card of his own. Held it up to show me his name under the Avon and Somerset Police logo. Their Valley Road HQ address. Then he flipped the card to reveal his private number and email, inked on the back.

'Send it here,' he said. 'Don't use official lines.'

He tapped the envelope and pictures.

'Keep these. I've written the locations on the back of each picture. Which means you've got everything I've got.'

He pushed his chair back.

'When will I see you?' he said.

'You won't. But I'll be in Bristol this afternoon.'

His face relaxed finally. A knot loosened. A burden sliding off his shoulders with the knowledge that things were moving. The threat to his daughter scared him. He needed to push back. And now he was.

The first step in taking back control.

He stood and looked down.

'What's your dog's name?' he said.

'Herbie.'

He nodded.

'Good boy, Herbie,' he said. 'Good boy.'

Herbie's attention was on the dropped food. He ignored him. Locke walked away and disappeared round the barriers.

Herbie strained towards the discarded scrap.

I pushed the photos back into the envelope and untied his leash. We exited and left the concourse clean.

CHAPTER TWO
Hallway Mona Lisa

I called back at Chase Street and got Lucy to email the contract. Left Herbie sitting on her desk. She'd drop him off later with my neighbour Henrietta Hutt who acted as sometime babysitter. Herbie knew the handover routine. Knew it included a Lunch Stop. As I walked out he pined for two seconds then went back to grinning at Lucy and watching the clock.

The Orbital was flowing steadily and the M4 west was clear. I made Bristol by one p.m. and found a cafe down on the docks with tables in the sun. Ate lunch whilst I snapped copies of Locke's photos onto my phone and located TownGate Productions at an address over the river. Seemed Sarah Locke's company was doing well enough to plant a foot in the city in lieu of a cheaper out of town rent. The company had been operating for three years and had sold two of their prime time *Exposed* series to national TV. I guess they were looking at a steady income stream. I finished my lunch and drove round.

And adjusted my image of their high rent HQ.

It was a radically different landscape across the river. The facade of Edwardian terraces lining the Avon's southern bank hid an inner-city patchwork of residential and commercial properties, shabby-old mixed with characterless-new. Walls, fences, wire, weeds and trees lifting paving flags, suspension-killing potholes. TownGate's building was as nondescript as any other, a two-storey brick and concrete structure with their name alongside two others by the steel and glass entrance doors. I pushed through into a dark and empty space. Took concrete stairs to the upper floor. This wasn't *Thames Television*. But things improved upstairs where TownGate had put the money in. Glass doors slid open automatically to invite me into a reception that was bright and modern, with a hum of activity beyond a back wall of opaque tinted glass. The space was all pastels and colourful comfy chairs arranged with designer carelessness. All empty apart from one occupied by a guy in a leather jacket reading a magazine. A single receptionist sat behind a desk, busy at her screen.

I asked for Sarah Locke. Mentioned her father.

The receptionist offered to check. Pressed buttons.

The name-dropping worked. Sarah would be out in a sec.

The name-dropping also worked out here in the lobby. Five seconds after I'd settled into the nearest chair the magazine guy came over and sat down next to me.

'Hi,' he said.

I nodded back.

'Can I ask who you are?' he said.

The guy was thirtyish, six feet two, solid build, probably muscle under his jacket. He had the confident look of a guy who has the edge.

'Depends,' I said. I held my smile. Watched for signs of Sarah coming through.

'On what?'

'Whether you tell me who you are.'

'Sure.' His own face stayed serious. 'I'm Ms Locke's security advisor.'

'Well,' I said, 'that means we're probably here on the same business. Watching out for Ms Locke.'

'I don't recognise your name. Does she know you?'

'Not yet.'

Security Advisor was beginning to tense up. His head cocked and his shoulders hunched up.

'It's cool,' I told him. 'When I talk to Ms Locke everything will be explained.'

'All right,' he said. He stood and crossed his arms. 'We'll talk to her together. Check she's happy to see you.'

'That's fine by me. But once the formalities are over our talk will be private.'

'That's for her to decide.'

'Naturally,' I said. 'But that's what I'll tell her.'

Security Advisor stayed close, standing over me, blocking the light. If I made a move to pinch the potted plants he'd be ready.

Then a section of the tinted glass slid back and Sarah Locke came out. Instantly recognisable. Striking as her TV image. She was wearing a navy trouser suit, maybe ready for a piece to camera. Or maybe just a smart dresser. I stood and she came over with a smile that looked genuine even if its wattage was low. We shook hands.

'Mr Flynn! So my father's been as good as his word.'

'I'm not sure what his word was,' I admitted.

'He said he'd find my nutty fan.' Her eyes had mischief in them. 'I assume you're with a detective agency. Or are you on a foreigner from CID?'

'Private agency,' I said.

'Of course. Father's a stickler for the rules. But I'm a little concerned that he's spending money on a private investigator. He found Gary here to look after me and that's probably enough.'

Gary Here waited beside us and looked mean. He was pretty good at it. If I was a nutcase I'd consider nutting elsewhere. But you need to take into account the nature of nuts: they're not necessarily rational.

'You can't be looking over your shoulder indefinitely,' I said.

'I realise that. But I'm not so sure I'm in any great danger.'

'Your father prefers not to find out the hard way.'

Sarah nodded. Held her smile. 'I know. And I hate to be impolite now you've called but you've caught me on a hectic day.'

'Your father didn't ask me specifically to come and see you,' I said. 'But it would be useful to know what you know. If you could give me ten minutes I'll be out of your hair.'

She looked hesitant about even a quick natter but had the good grace to put a game face on it. She invited me through. Asked if Gary should come with us. I said we'd get by. Gary kept his gaze locked on me but she nodded to him and he turned and went back to his magazine.

She took me through into a small room with slatted blinds hiding what had to be an unglamorous view. A rectangular, shiny table filled most of the floor space and the six chairs round it were functional rather than boardroom plush. Sarah gestured to a chair and came to perch on the table, clasped her knee in her hands.

'So what can I tell you, Mr Flynn?'

'Eddie,' I said. 'No need for formalities.'

'Eddie.' She smiled. A twinkle had appeared, though it was hard to interpret. 'What do you need to know?'

'Anything you know about whoever sent you that doctored photograph. Your father has supplied me with a couple of CCTVs of

13

a guy who seems to match the image on your house cam shots. But Bristol's a big place to spot a face. So if there's anything we can pick up from this guy's behaviour when he's approached you...'

'There's no behaviour to describe. I've only seen him a few times. If it was him.'

She detailed the same instances her father had described. A face in the background at a few location shoots, the impression of a youngish man, possibly with a beard though she wasn't sure even of that: just some kind of facial hair. And a guy loitering near her house, jogging away when she walked out to challenge him. And last week the figure she'd spotted as she drove in late one night. Maybe the same guy, maybe not. The house incidents made her uneasy but she was in the business, was used to over-zealous fans. She spotted faces wherever she worked. There was nothing to say that any of them were a threat. The sole difference this time was the knife photo.

'But you were concerned before the photo: you called your father after you spotted the guy outside your house.'

'My father happened to call me and I mentioned it to him. I guess I was a little concerned but it was really just conversation.'

'Does the photograph worry you?'

'Sure. The photo's pretty scary,' she said. 'But let's not forget that it's a fake. The guy hasn't been within a mile of me with a knife. It's a Photoshop fantasy played out on his computer.'

The distinction between a guy faking things on a computer and getting himself into a real shot with Sarah didn't seem so great at face value, but there *was* a difference and my hope was that it worked in our favour: the serious nutcase would be satisfied only with a real snap, the two of them together. Harder to set up but ten times the kick, and ten times as effective if you want to scare the subject. More likely, a truly serious nutcase would have turned up and used the knife. But the symbolism in the doctored photo was powerful. The stance with the knife would scare anyone.

But Sarah was sticking with downplaying things.

'I think he's just some sad case who'd never act in the real world,' she said. 'When you're in the media business you touch all kinds of people.'

'Have you had much of this before?'

'Not photographs. But I get people – fans – who show up at

shoots. Keep begging autographs. Two of them have knocked on my door on occasions. It's not welcome but it goes with the job.'

'And you've never felt directly threatened by them?'

She thought about it. Shrugged again. Locked her fingers tighter about her knee.

'No. It can be unnerving sometimes but I've never felt that someone was out to do me harm.'

'Your father had Jill Dando in mind. I suppose she didn't sense anything until the guy stepped up with the gun.'

I sensed a shiver go through her this time. More inside than out. But the twinkle had dropped from her eyes.

'I never do forget Jill,' she said. 'I'd just started with Westcountry at the time. The news came in on our feeds whilst we were setting up for the evening magazine. And yeah, I actually look like her. So her killing affected me. But we have to move on. I'm no more at risk than any other media personality.'

'But your *Exposed* series – investigating illegal businesses and criminal activities – might make you more enemies than most. And you own the company. So if someone wanted to hurt TownGate you'd be the perfect target.'

'Of course. But I don't see our exposé targets lurking in the bushes or developing fixations.'

'Maybe the lurking in the bushes is separate. But the knife photo could be a threat from someone you've injured, or someone you're threatening.'

'It's possible.'

'Have you anything controversial in the pipeline? Anyone you're after?'

She smiled. Slid off the table and walked over to adjust the blinds and take in the view.

'I like to think all our investigations are controversial,' she said. 'We go after people and companies who need exposing. We've gone after rogue loan companies, car-repair shops, scam marketing companies, illegal dog breeders and a hare coursing organisation. And an organised burglary ring here in Bristol.'

'What's going on right now?'

'Right now we're investigating an art theft that's part of an organised operation.' She let the blinds fall and walked back. 'Have you heard about the Bardi Stradivariuses?'

The name rang a bell. Some kind of violin fest, maybe. I take an interest in classical music when I'm not listening to jazz but the particular term had passed me by.

'The Bardi Strads are a pair of original Stradivarius violins owned by the Marquis of Lenbury,' she told me. 'The "Bardi" refers to the original owners who were an Italian aristocratic family descended from the Florentine Bardis. Lenbury's family acquired the pair in the early nineteenth century and they've been displayed at Lenbury House in Wiltshire ever since. The pair might be the most valuable set of Stradivariuses in the world.'

'I guess we're talking a few bob?'

'The last estimate was forty to sixty million. The pair were made in 1702 and '03, right at the start of Stradivari's prime period of instrument making.'

Memories were starting to surface.

'Nicked a couple of months back?'

'That's them. The Marquis has an estimated hundred millions worth of collectibles behind his high tech security but the security didn't help when two masked raiders barged in and held his family at gunpoint. They took the Strads and vanished. It was all over in ten minutes.'

'Was anything else taken?'

'No. It was a targeted raid.'

'And you're onto the thieves?'

'We followed a few tips and found that we were looking at more than a single theft. We're gathering evidence that points to an international art theft operation. A steal-to-order service. And right at the centre of the operation is an art dealer called Pauline Granger who's based right here in Bristol. We've no hard evidence that she was involved in the Strad theft but things are pointing that way. So we're still notionally looking for the Strads but the Granger lead is opening out fast. We'll soon have enough to blow her operation wide open. It will go out in the current series. *Exposed* is going to sink a multi-million pound theft business. Paintings and artefacts, musical instruments, any kind of collectible.'

'Is Granger a legitimate operator?'

Sarah pushed herself back onto the table.

'She does exactly the same thing in her day job: facilitating artwork acquisitions, including stuff not in public auction. The difference with the day job is that the buyer negotiates with the seller and pays. But some artefacts will never be for sale. So there are collectors who are willing to take other routes to acquire them and that's where Pauline Granger's night job kicks in. She's the go-to woman if you want the Mona Lisa in your hallway.'

'Got it. And if these people knew you were onto them they might push back?'

'Conceivably.'

'And *do* they know?'

'Probably. We've been asking a lot of questions, digging all around Pauline Granger. She must have picked up a whisper.'

'Would the knife photo be her style?'

'I don't know. But if it was her or her people I'd have expected a more specific message. And we have had one message recently that we think's from them. The sender didn't identify themselves but they stuck to the practicalities, less drama.'

'A threat?'

'Against my business partner Mark Sewell. Mark and I formed TownGate together. He's responsible for research and production. I cover additional research, script and camera-front.'

'What was the threat?'

'A letter. A straight up warning to stop our investigation or they'd stop us. More specific than a Photoshopped picture but it still didn't identify the aggrieved party. They didn't say which investigation they were talking about.'

'I'll need to take a look at the letter. Is your partner available?'

'He's out setting up for a shoot. I'll ask him to call you. Though I'm still not sure that the guy who's been following me around or the knife photo are related.'

Maybe they weren't. But now we had two threats not one, and I wasn't about to ignore that. The kettle was starting to bubble.

Sarah glanced at her watch and smiled to dampen any offence.

'Eddie... I've got quite a schedule here.'

I stood and smiled back to show none taken.

'Fine,' I said. 'I'll be in touch.'

I handed her a card and she handed me one of her own and we

were done. We walked back to the glass doors and I let myself out through reception. Gary watched me go but didn't jump up to open the outer door. I threw him a salute as I passed. He threw back a "watch it, pal" and returned to his magazine.

CHAPTER THREE
Fishing

I drove back across the river and parked behind the docks. Took a walk up the High Street past the Markets entrance where Locke's CCTV annotation had located the goatee'd guy. When you're searching for someone it helps to get a sense of their world, tread the same streets, drink at the same bars, view the same faces and taste the same hopes and fears. Put your feet on the ground and walk in their footsteps and your quarry's world will give something. The trick is to tune in to free up the worthwhile from the wispy impressions, the half-imagined ghost of a life. Sometimes you get nothing and sometimes you get a subtle direction that steers you where you need to be going. Back in the practical world the walk gave me time to think, to help refine my plans. In a city of half a million I wasn't going to spot the guy from a casual stroll, and those wispy impressions might never come. I could be here ten years and not spot him. Realistically, I was looking for someone who recognised his face, and I wasn't going to find them in the anonymity of the city centre. If I wanted to get nearer the guy I needed to move closer to home – which might be near the pub where Locke's CCTV had spotted him. Locke had annotated that location as an area called Bishopston.

That's where I'd start.

I cut through the Markets and picked up a local A-Z. Checked the route and drove out through streets busy with commerce and contrasts, old merchants' houses jostling with concrete and glass, crowded pavements and chaotic traffic. Bristol is a city that likes to spring surprises: the merchants' buildings had barely faded before the road swung me beneath the massive wall of a six-storey Soviet era apartment block that blended into the city's character like a Stetson on the Archbishop of Canterbury. Out the other side the tone dropped to dingy as low-rise modern chaos sprouted and then decayed.

Traffic was chaotic. I hit the brakes fifty times for wandering vehicles and pedestrians. Breathed dust. Stopped, started, rolled. Hit a red light and another contrast: a Polish church with Corinthian entrance columns and a nice cupola up top. A good landmark if my search stayed in the area. The lights changed and I cruised on, rolled under a railway bridge and spotted the pub from the CCTV up on a bend ahead. The pub was called The Pig and Poke. I turned off and parked on a quiet residential street and walked back down. Roads radiated away at all angles, a mixture of retail and residential, vistas softened by a profusion of trees. Commerce stuck to the main road as it snaked out north, and the quieter streets angling off were all residential, nineteenth century upper middle class dwellings on the city limits: accountants', merchants', clerks' and shopkeepers' homes, reincarnated in the late-twentieth century as flats and maisonettes. The streets were too narrow to call avenues but the lines of trees made a mosaic of sun and shadow that gave the perspectives a dusty permanence. A place to attract the new professionals.

I took a tour, searching for a sense of the place that might home our mystery guy. Walked a hundred tiny front gardens enclosed behind tiny walls. Dodged in and out of pavement-parked trader's vans. Renovations and scaffolding everywhere. The walk delivered nothing. No sense of whether this was our mystery guy's territory. The only clue that it might be was Locke's CCTV of him exiting the Pig and Poke.

I arrived back there. The place was a town pub, stone-rendered at street level, sky blue brickwork above. The paint job was recent. Suggested gastro rather than drinkers' den. I went in.

Not gastro. Just a traditional lounge and pool room at the back. Eating limited to a rudimentary bar menu. The lounge was almost empty. Just two tables occupied by afternoon drinkers and a guy polishing glasses behind the bar. The drinkers were an elderly couple and two young women with a baby. Not promising as witnesses. If anyone recognised the CCTV face it would be someone in the evening crowd. I walked over and got the bar guy's attention. He had the portly, put-upon look of the owner looking after the shop in the lull. Took barely a moment to shake his head at my phone screen. Didn't recognise the face. So maybe the guy wasn't a regular here or maybe the landlord just didn't notice.

I repeated the routine at the tables and got the same result. The face in the CCTV image wasn't known.

I needed to get amongst the evening crowd.

Might even spot the guy himself.

I nodded to the landlord on the way out. He returned disinterested. Understandable. I stopped in the doorway to check a cork board. Notices and local events. Four of the notices were for club meets in the pub's upstairs rooms. Maybe our guy had come from up there. The first of them was a flyer announcing a daytime mothers' and infants' club. The second was a Pilates class running Saturday and Wednesday. Then a badly photocopied sheet promoting a monthly tabletop sale – bring your old stuff for a straight £2 charge. The fourth sheet announced weekly meets of something called the Livingstone Club. Tuesdays at 7 p.m. The notice didn't detail the club's business. If you were interested I guess you knew. But the date stamp on the mystery guy's CCTV image was Tuesday, which was interesting enough to send me back in to talk to the barman. His face lifted for a moment, thinking I was returning to order a drink. I disabused him. Asked him about the Livingstone Club. He shook his head with a scowl. Knew nothing about them. He had all kinds of clubs up there.

Four by my counting but I couldn't expect him to remember them all.

I thanked him again and went out. Called the Livingstone number. The call went to voicemail. I left a message expressing a vague interest in membership. Requested a call back. Pushed my phone away and I went to walk up the main road. It was three forty-five.

The route took me away from the city. I moved fast. Called at convenience stores and newsagents, all-day takeaways and a bookies. Covered a quarter of a mile and twenty retail businesses in forty-five minutes before I hit the end of the drag. Crossed the road and worked back. Another twenty businesses. Another blank. Our guy wasn't a regular shopper or fast-food junkie and didn't lay out on the horses. I passed the Pig and Poke and walked citywards. Traffic intensified. Rush hour coming on. Dust and din. I hit three mini-markets, two phone shops, another bookies and four burger and kebab bars. Then commerce faded again. Residential up ahead and the gleam of the Polish church in the distance. End of trail. I crossed the road and worked a final leg back. Nothing. They guy wasn't recognised on the street.

Six p.m. My shoe leather was wearing thin and I was no nearer the guy. But I hadn't expected miracles. Maybe the guy was from elsewhere, hopped into the Pig and Poke for a quick drink.

I quit. Drove back into the centre. Cruised under the Moskva Apartments and found a Travelodge just off the Harbour with rooms that were tiny but clean and bright. Tiny included shower stalls modelled on phone boxes, but the water was powerful and warm and did the trick. I changed, left my crash bag and went down. The hotel had an in-house eatery that wasn't my thing but the student on reception had outside recommendations and I found an Italian by the water and replenished the footslog calories with pasta and Peroni

Then I drove back out under Little Moscow for the evening shift on the Bishopston drag.

I parked at the city end and trekked towards the Pig and Poke as dusk came on. Traffic had thinned but people were out. I stopped passers-by, hit evening takeaways and a workingman's club on a back street behind the arches. Called in at five eateries and a laundromat. The bookies were still open but it was the same punters and the same answers.

I reached the Pig and Poke. Went in.

The pub was alive this time, lounge and bar buzzing, pool room clattering behind. The landlord had assistance, looked almost happy, though he hadn't spotted me yet. A young guy pulled me a pint of the local cask and checked my pic. Shook his head. I hefted the beer and circulated. Flashed the phone photos.

Nothing.

No-one knew the goatee'd guy.

Not a regular.

The landlord finally spotted me as I held my phone over the bar to one of his girls. He gave me the evil eye and came up. Shook his head. Wagged a finger. I held my glass up as proof of good intent and he backed off but the girl had already said no, she didn't recognise the face.

I repeated my routine in the pool room then left.

Dark was coming on outside.

I turned northwards on the main road. Crossed and re-crossed through the traffic. Hit the open businesses. Got nothing. Collared passers-by, though that was just fishing: the chance of bumping into

22

the guy's neighbours or pals on the street was minimal. If anyone recognised his face it would be indoors, in businesses and bars, places people spent time enough to remember a face. By ten I'd reached the limits of my search area and stood looking at a pub just off the main street called the Mason's Arms. I'd bypassed it on my afternoon hike but the evening crowd was worth a shot.

The place was a fifties build atop whatever German bombs had pulverised a decade earlier. A curved facade, post-Moderne shout to the thirties, toned down by stone cladding in place of concrete. I went into a big open lounge floored in patterned tiles. A bar long enough for a pub crawl ended in curves that mimicked the exterior. Thirty or so people in, mostly younger, a few students. Buddy Holly playing on the speakers. A decent buzz for a Monday. I strolled the bar end to end looking for something palatable. Spotted the flaw in the place. The taps were all cheap kegs and Fosters, Heineken bottles and lemonade taps. Then I got lucky and clocked London Pride on the end curve. I held my phone up as the barman pulled a pint. The guy was cheerful but non-committal. Didn't recognise the face. I sipped froth and strolled back along the bar, showing my phone screen.

Got nothing.

I diverted to the tables. Worked my way back towards the door, picking up nervous looks from students fearful of council age-checkers or evangelicals. When I put them right they co-operated from relief but the co-operation was all head-shaking.

I circulated doorwards. The speakers thumped out Buddy Holly yelling for Peggy Sue and my Pride tasted fine. The beat moved me along.

I was two tables from the door and holding a near-empty glass when a grey-bearded forty-something in a bob hat and tee-shirt raised his eyebrows and looked more closely at the screen. Glanced at his two pals.

'Yeah,' he said. 'Reedy! He's in sometimes.'

Buddy ended on a crash.

I grinned.

Planted my glass and sat down.

CHAPTER FOUR
Exotic fragrances

I exited the Travelodge into bright early morning sunshine. Deployed shades and walked east past the cathedral and onto an unfashionable shopping street that ran up from the Harbour. Howling busses and early morning traffic din ricocheted from the buildings. I dodged shopkeepers pulling out awnings and trudged up the hill in the direction of the Law School's gothic tower, looking for an eatery. Spotted a place with a bright facade called the Coffee Stop. Lights and movement inside. I went in. A homely ten-table interior with three customers eating breakfast. I ordered at the counter: scrambled eggs and toast. Coffee with a kick by way of a little chit-chat with the girl, queries about just how *strong* their brew was. Turned out it was *strong.* Her assurance came with a grin and I spotted four espressos going in, a light touch on the milk. The shots did their work and I ate my eggs under speakers broadcasting local radio jingles and forecasts of heat. I pushed a fiver into the tip jar on my way out which got a truly bright smile and invitation to call again from my hostess. I promised and exited. Continued up the hill. Turned past the Law School and Museum and was presented with another of the city's quick-change acts: the grandeur of the Museum buildings ended with a patched-tarmac one-way street running through twenties commercial properties homing the unfashionable end of the business spectrum. Flaking facades, meshed-over windows, tarnished door plaques, shutters. Up top, neglected office windows. Jobbing firms drawing reliable profits and seeing no incentive or spare cash to shift nearer the centre or move out to the industrial parks. A litter of letting signs marking the firms that *had* moved on or folded.

I spotted what I was looking for: a shop front in a three-storey terrace with poster-blanked windows and a tired perspex fascia with the name ValuAd across it.

My lead from the Mason's Arms.

What my informant had said was that the guy who'd delivered the knife photo to Sarah Locke went by the name Reedy. Which might be a surname or nickname or first name. The bob-hatted forty-something who talked to me didn't know. All he could tell me was that the guy showed up at the Mason's now and then and was on nodding terms with a few of the regulars. They'd nattered occasionally if they'd rubbed shoulders at the bar. More often, Reedy drank alone. Never came with company and never stayed long. Just an early evening pint then he was gone. Bob Hat couldn't tell me anything about the guy except that he was in advertising. Then one of his pals piped up and said that Reedy worked for a company called ValuAd.

Which was the place across the street from me now.

Google listed their business as design and branding, display posters, shop signage, printing. No reference to more modern fields: web support and social media management had either not arrived in this street or had long departed.

I found the doorway of a closed-down shop and waited. Traffic was heavy. A one-way flow. Right to left. Around eight-thirty businesses started to open their doors. Shutters rose, delivery vans mounted the kerbs. Packs and pallets went in and out. At nine ValuAd's door opened and I counted seven people going in over the next thirty minutes. None of them had a goatee or short dark hair.

I waited.

The street warmed and settled into a workday hum. Traffic eased. Delivery vans came and went. Lorries tail-lifted cartons and crates. A few visitors went in ValuAd's door. None of them was Sarah's stalker.

I wondered about rear parking spots. Had the guy gone in the back way? If he had then I could be here all day.

I shifted my weight. Tensed muscles through a routine of stationary calisthenic moves. Kept my circulation going. Waited.

Surveillance is an art built on patience.

It's like a ticket on the horses: mostly you get nothing back, sometimes you get a ten-to-one winner. The P.I. sheds hours like the punter chucks used tickets, always eyeing the next chance. The next minute that might bring payoff. More likely, ten hours will just bring aching legs.

I took a turn up the street every half hour, also for circulation. Never out of sight of ValuAd. If this had been a discreet surveillance I'd have been stuck in the doorway. But no-one was watching for observers. If Reedy appeared I'd be nothing to him.

At twelve-thirty people started coming out for lunch. A group of two and then of three came out of ValuAd's door and disappeared towards the Law School. Reedy wasn't amongst them.

By one-thirty the same ValuAd people were back in and if Reedy was expected on the afternoon shift he was late.

I crossed the street and went in.

My preferred option would have been to confirm the knife photo guy's ID and address without him knowing. Locke would decide when to open that can. But Locke needed a result. And if the guy had taken the week off or if he'd quit or if he'd never worked here then it was better to know now. And worst case: if word got back to Reedy about a stranger searching for him it might at least hold him back from further shenanigans whilst Sarah's father reviewed his options.

The shop behind the poster-covered window ran back beyond a rudimentary reception into stock and work areas. Stairs ran up to first floor offices, and since reception was unmanned and movements at the back were vague I opted for that route. Arrived at a veneer door with "Authorised Personnel Only" pasted across it. I pushed it open and went in. Found eight or ten work pens in a dingy open plan office. Four of the pens were occupied. The woman at the nearest jumped up to apologise for the empty reception and offer help. She was thirtyish with a broad, friendly face that you'd notice as soon as you'd pulled your attention back from her blue-streaked hair and Snow Bunny tee-shirt. Something about her had me thinking of Lucy.

The woman returned my smile. Snow Bunny looked perplexed.

'I'm looking for Reedy,' I told her.

Now it was the woman who looked perplexed.

A guy in a Jurassic Park sweater near the street window raised his head.

'John,' he clarified.

The woman's face cleared.

'Of course!' she said. 'John Reed. He's not in today. Can I help?'

'I'm just digging for a little info.,' I said. 'We're looking at a posters and flyers campaign, maybe an image makeover. John said he might be able to help.'

That got a grin with a head shake.

'John doesn't actually work for us. But we can talk about your needs.' She held out her hand. 'I'm Sue.'

I shook it. Acted surprised.

'John doesn't work here? I thought he said...'

I held back on revealing what I thought he'd said since I hadn't a clue what would make sense here. ValuAd knew the guy but vague information from a pub table is always apt to go haywire. Maybe Reed had left a decade ago.

But Sue's head shake was more of a misunderstanding thing.

'John's one of our bill posters. He's freelance.'

'Bill poster? With a ladder and bucket?'

'Sure.' She held her grin. 'Our street business is still poster. Though we don't use paste. We manufacture with adhesive. We manage twenty boards round the city. Used to be more but the electronic displays have pushed them out. John's a dying breed. Like our street business.'

I got it.

Reedy: in advertising.

John Reed: bill poster.

I backtracked.

'John wasn't so specific,' I said, 'but he recommended you. So I thought I'd touch base. Is he around?'

'Tomorrow,' she said. 'But I'd be the one to discuss our services. Whatever your line of business we can give it the facelift you want.'

I held my grin. If Sue knew my line of business she'd be less breezy. And we'd be talking more about sand-blasting than facelift. Putting a shine on private investigating would be a challenge for any company, though they manage it with lawyers and funeral firms so I guess anything's possible. But revealing the nature of my business might trip alarms so I pulled out one of Harry's generic cards. He has a range. Some have my real name and number but vague business names to match a variety of stories. You just tag on the spiel to suit.

The card I pulled out had my real name under a company title I'd never heard of, which was 'Fishhook and Bates Ltd'. I handed it across and Sue read it and looked at me for enlightenment. I pointed out the small writing.

'Exotic fragrances. We're small but we're leaders in the infused scents business.'

'Really?' Her eyes widened. 'I've never heard of that. But come through. Let's get an idea of what you're looking at.'

She gestured towards some rooms at the back but I stopped her.

'Truth is I was just passing. Thought I'd say hello. I'd need to clear my diary for a sit-down.'

Disappointment clouded Sue's face. No sale. But she kept up the patter.

'No problem. Anytime, Eddie. We're absolutely keen to help with exotic fragrances. I think you'll be impressed by what we can do.'

'I'm convinced of that.'

I took the card she offered me. Sue Jones. Design Executive.

'Soonest opportunity,' I said.

'The soonest,' she said. 'It's not often we meet executives from the fragrance industry.'

Her smile was bright, brighter than it would have been if she'd known exactly what kind of *fragrances* we were talking about.

I repeated "soonest". Hesitated for a second on the consideration of whether a discussion over dinner might not be too soon. Then pulled myself together. Why mess up this woman's life? I slotted her card into my wallet, flicked a salute and left them to it.

CHAPTER FIVE
You can't take the heat...

John Reed. Freelance bill-poster. Sometime celeb-stalker and Photoshop whiz-kid. Working elsewhere today or maybe snatching a day off – busy with his hobbies. I wondered if those hobbies involved hanging around places linked to Sarah Locke. Decided it would be a good time to check out her house.

I retrieved the Frogeye and folded the hood down. Drove out from the centre looking for the property her father had described. A distinctive white house across the river, three floors, corner turrets. Easy to spot.

The instructions steered me west and across the suspension bridge to an exclusive area on the far side of the Gorge. Detached properties in the two to three mill. bracket protected by twelve foot hedges and old stone walls. TownGate might operate from a downmarket base but the business was clearly paying. The lane narrowed. Getting Mercs and Jags past each other would need concentration. I spotted Sarah's house through the open corner gateway Locke had described. Complete with the turrets. I continued past and found a shaded grass verge two hundred yards on. Hopped out to make a tour of the area on foot. I'd not spotted anyone loitering as I drove in, seen no cars that didn't fit, but maybe Reed knew how to stay out of sight. The lane marked the edge of the residential territory, dropped away through steep woodland to a valley running out towards the Gorge. I opted for the cover of the slope. The vegetation-choked ground was hard going but kept me hidden below the lane, the way it might keep a guy with bad intent hidden. I followed the slope back past the houses. Didn't spot anyone. Just trees and brambles and an empty lane above me. No sign of Reed.

I continued along the slope until the lane turned above the Gorge, then climbed back up to the tarmac and followed the road out. Worked my way round until I found a side lane that ran back to Sarah's house. A twenty-minute trek. Nothing unusual. Sarah's house wasn't visible through the thick foliage until I was almost back at the gate, and the few vantage points near the corner were unoccupied. If Reed was nearby he was good.

I walked into Sarah's drive and lifted my shades to survey the gardens. Half an acre, mostly lawn, behind twelve foot hornbeams. Deserted. But a black Jeep Cherokee was parked in front of the garage and made me wonder if someone was home. I walked across and pressed the front porch bell. Better to talk to whoever was in there than the police. I spotted the porch camera that had recorded Reed's postal visit. Threw it a grin.

No-one came out.

I stepped back into the sunshine and listened to the distant hiss: the river down in the Gorge or the traffic on the city side, or maybe just the breeze. I couldn't say. I quit listening and walked the garden. Checked shrubs and hedges and outhouses. Satisfied myself that John Reed was nowhere around. Not that it was likely. If the guy was fixated on Sarah he'd show up when she was home. Other times he'd either be out tailing her on her shoots or living some kind of life. Or maybe he was at home, working at his computer.

I found a lawn bench and sat down. Phoned Sarah. She picked up after a delay.

'Eddie.'

Slight impatience. Unscheduled calls probably weren't welcome.

'I'm at your house. There's no-one around but I may have a name for you.'

A pause.

'Okay. That's good...' Though nothing in her voice suggested great enthusiasm and she didn't ask what the name was. Had probably opened distance between herself and her prowler. In the light of day, in her office, surrounded by people, there'd be no sense of danger. Only the nuisance factor of a private investigator pestering her.

I asked where she was and she told me she was at her desk. Would be leaving around six.

Maybe Reed knew that. Maybe I'd spot him this evening. Meanwhile I had a few hours to fill.

'Is your partner around?' I said.

'He's out setting up a shoot. We've a closing piece to camera tomorrow for one of our stories.'

She described a location on the outskirts of Bath. I rang off and walked back across her lawn, out and down the lane.

I drove over to Bath. Found a group of people down on the towpath of the canal cut that bypassed a rough bit of the Avon as it flowed out of the city. Six of them. Busy with clipboards and a camera and boom-mike. Checking levels, framing shots. A stand-in walked up from the locks and the camera followed her for a while then panned away across the canal to an industrial site where something dodgy was going on. Something the country would soon know about.

TownGate were selling prime time programming but they were still small. No convoy of trucks and mobile canteens back at the road. Just one van with their name on the side and a few private cars parked behind it.

I stood with a few onlookers and watched a guy waving his arms at the stand-in, slowing her pace and yelling at the camera guy to pull *out, out, out* and *pan for Chrissake*. A wild guess said this was Sarah's partner, Mark Sewell. I waited until the stand-in had stood down and Sewell was huddled with his camera guy then went over and butted in. Introduced myself. Mentioned Sarah.

Sewell grimaced. An actual wince. Something you don't often see. But probably the guy grimaced a lot. His manner screamed moody. *Artiste*. Mid forties, slim, faint olive skin, spiked black hair and forty-eight hour stubble. Thick framed glasses. Bulked up with a hoodie sweater over denim despite the sun. Maybe hoodies and denim were the vogue for the arriving producer.

The grimace dissolved into a scowl. He looked round and shook his head. Nervous energy.

'Bad time,' he said. 'No can talk. I'll be back in the office in an hour. Catch me there, bud.'

In an hour I wanted to be holed up *outside* the office waiting to see if John Reed showed up to wait for Sarah.

'Two minutes,' I said.

'Can't, matey, can't.' His hands were flapping. More nervous energy. 'C'mon, pal. Later. Back at base. Shift back. I need the path.'

I'd walked down under the misapprehension that the path was public. But maybe all public places have an ordinance giving media crews priority. Like those car chases round New York. Streets closed; barricades up; city taxpayers detouring round Hollywood's latest real

31

estate stake.

'Two minutes,' I repeated. 'That's better than five minutes arguing.'

I jabbed my hands in my jacket and stood legs akimbo. Tried to look permanent. Annexing the place for myself.

Sewell swore and threw in some religious profanities but then walked me away, flapping his hand behind him, yelling to take a break. We got clear and he turned to face me.

'You're the detective guy?'

'Investigator. Flynn. I guess Sarah told you I'd be around.'

'She told me her old man's panicking about some guy following her.'

'That's right. I'm taking a look.'

'How can I help? In, like, two minutes.' He looked at his watch to start the clock. Right wrist. Some kind of fashion statement, like the watch itself which was an ugly Cartier with a transparent mess of a face that had you squinting for thirty seconds before you got a sense of the time. More concentration than Sewell would give it, but that wasn't the point.

'Do you know about this guy?' I said.

'Yeah. And he's not the first, nor the last. You get these people, know what I'm saying?'

'Part of the business.'

'Part and parcel. Everywhere you go. They're drawn to any little action.'

He waved his hand at the onlookers to dismiss media shoot action as nothing any sensible person would notice, though if nobody did notice he'd be damn upset. Simple fact: for him to be on the *inside* you needed a public watching from the *outside*.

'This guy seems to have taken a personal interest in Sarah.'

'It happens. She can handle it. If you catch the guy, kick his arse for me. Fucking hard. We'll have one less parasite on our backs.'

'I'll note that. But my priority is to find out if he's dangerous.'

'He isn't. Just another fruitcake. He'll lose interest eventually.'

'You hear about the photo?'

'Seen it. Like I said: fruitcake. A piece-of-shit nobody hiding behind amateur digital tricks.'

'But it's a nasty message. The knife at Sarah's neck. Don't you worry that someone will act out one of their fantasies some day?'

He shrugged, twitched. Looked at his watch again. It was still on the same wrist. Different time. Sixty seconds on.

When he'd finished his act he looked at me and grinned and opened his eyes wide behind his frames.

'We're in the media business, matey,' he said. 'Hello? We're here to get noticed? Goes with the territory? Don't worry about it. One of these days maybe a real lunatic shows up. But we're not gonna hide under the desk. You can't take the heat, get out of the kitchen. Sarah knows how to look after herself.'

'She seems fairly relaxed. It was her father who called us in.'

'Exactly. Old man's over-reacting. A guy sending pics isn't the same as a guy confronting her. The real world scares this shit-bird. He lives in his virtual world. Photoshop. Dirty movies.'

I said nothing. Experience said the opposite. When a guy starts to include you in his fantasy, starts to wrap it round you, there's a chance he won't stop. Once the momentum's built he may not be able to.

'One interpretation is that the photo is a warning from people you're investigating,' I said. 'Does that sound credible?'

'Credible as anything else. But that's the business. We're not out to make friends. But the photo's from the guy who's been getting near Sarah.'

'He could be acting for an aggrieved party.'

'Yeah. Sure. Theories. Who knows? If I listened to everyone who threatens us I'd never make TV.'

'I heard you received a threat yourself recently.'

'I did. A letter. Anonymous. Could be from any of the groups we've burnt. Or from someone we're chasing now. It could have come from right over there.' He gestured over the canal. I looked. Saw only trees. Maybe the squirrels were getting aggressive.

'Scam recycling business,' he elaborated. 'Watch the show.'

'So the threat doesn't worry you?'

Sewell spat out a laugh. Checked his watch again. Yelled back to his crew. Break over.

'Course it worries me. But here I am. On the job. I don't pull my investigations every time someone warns us off.'

'I hear you're looking into a high value art theft operation. Linked to a Stradivarius theft.'

'Yeah. The letter could be related to that. But not Sarah's Photoshop nutcase. Friend, I'd love to talk more but our two minutes are *gone west*.'

He raised his right wrist to prove it then finger-shot me and walked away.

I watched him go.

The guy didn't share Sarah's father's concern. Didn't seem concerned at all. But maybe he was just too far up his own backside to believe that the real world would ever be permitted to threaten him. Confident about that glass wall round his media world that kept out the nobodies, the envious, the fruitcakes. I watched him pushing and waving to make up the wasted two minutes. Get things wrapped.

I looked across at the trees and back up the path, checking again for anyone who might be about to shatter that glass wall.

Saw nothing.

~~~~~

I drove back to Bristol and rolled slowly down past TownGate, looking for signs of anyone watching. Spotted no-one. Found a surveillance spot in the entrance to a tyre dealer's yard fifty yards from the building and settled in. Forty minutes later, Sewell and his crew arrived in convoy and drove round to the small parking yard behind TownGate. Filed back round and in through the entrance. Then five minutes later they were back out in ones and twos to walk round for their vehicles, heading home. Sewell came out at six, gabbing into his phone. He was still gabbing as he steered his black 911 out and round the potholes towards the city centre.

Still no sight of anyone hanging around for a sight of Sarah Locke. John Reed was busy somewhere else.

Twenty minutes later Sarah came out with Gary at her side and they walked round to the yard. I jogged to the corner and retrieved the Frogeye and followed her red Audi TT out. Gary was in the passenger seat. Seemed security was twenty-four hours, which must be costing Locke. I held back as they cleared the top of the street, watching for anyone I'd missed, someone hurrying towards a vehicle.

Nothing.

I put my foot down and got the TT back into sight and followed it

34

out of the centre and across the suspension bridge towards her house. When the TT pulled into her driveway I rolled past and parked back in my earlier spot, back-tracked again under cover of the trees, looking for anyone lurking. I took an hour, worked slowly round the whole area. Spotted no-one. No cars parked in the nearby lanes. I ended up back at the gateway. Checked the house. Sarah's TT was parked alongside the black Jeep Cherokee I'd seen earlier. So the Cherokee was Gary's.

I eased back into the vegetation and waited. The sun was still high and the evening was warm and alive with birdsong. Not an arduous surveillance as these things go. Relaxing, almost. A purposeful idleness with the promise of imminent revelation, new insights, direction.

In the event I had to make do with the pleasure of the evening as the sun dropped below the trees. Revelations and insights stayed scarce. John Reed – or anyone else taking an interest in Sarah Locke – wasn't showing. I pondered whether to grab a quick bite and return for a night shift. Decided against. I'd lay eyes on Reed when he showed up for work tomorrow.

I was about to head off when a Hyundai Coupe pulled into Sarah's driveway. It parked beside the other cars and a single male got out, rolled his wide shoulders and walked across to ring the doorbell. The door opened and he went in past bodyguard Gary who came out and jumped into the Jeep. Rolled down the drive and turned towards the bridge.

Change of shift.

Twenty-four hour security. Locke wasn't taking chances.

You could see the incentive for finding his daughter's stalker.

I called it a night and drove back across the Gorge into the city. Showered and shaved, donned fresh clothes and went out to rack up a few itemised charges for Locke's bill. Found a Greek restaurant on the Harbourside and ate at an outside table overlooking the water.

The sun had dropped from sight. The street lamps shone bright round the docks. Voices and music floated across the water.

CHAPTER SIX
It wasn't a social call

I got my first sight of the guy menacing Sarah Locke when he showed up for work next morning.

I was standing back in my doorway just up from ValuAd, nerves tangoing to the quad-espresso I'd imbibed at my breakfast cafe. The buzz helped counter the chill breeze that penetrated my light cotton jacket. In an hour the sun would do the same job.

The first of the ValuAd people had gone in around eight-thirty, then just on nine a white van loaded with ladders pulled onto the pavement outside their door and I spotted John Reed's face behind the windscreen. That unmistakable goatee, the intense eyes and dark hair. He skipped down from the cab and scanned the street briefly then went in. Ten minutes later he came out carrying rolls of posters. Loaded them into the van.

I walked to the car and rolled up to the main road to wait.

Reed finished loading then drove out past me round the one-way system. I eased into the rush hour traffic and followed. He took his time, signalled lane changes, stopped at lights, and we worked out towards the Easton area where he manoeuvred across the pavement and onto an empty piece of land under a billboard on the end of a residential terrace. I pulled over and watched him work. He unloaded his kit: ladder, squeegee, backpack. Slotted poster segments into the backpack and climbed up. Ripped down expired sheets. Reached over his shoulder and pulled sheets from the pack and pasted them. Climbed down. Climbed up. Pasted. Squeegeed. Worked steadily and efficiently, oblivious to the traffic speeding below his ladder. When he was done he filled a waste bag and threw it into the van and we went on our way.

We did a tour of the city, ten sites, with a lunch stop at a canteen trailer on an industrial park. Reed ate. I went without. When he was through we drove out to a couple of larger boards that ValuAd maintained by the M32. I was getting the hang of the job by now. The trick is getting the six-by-three segments out of your backpack in the right order. Top-bottom, left-right. Align the sheets, drop them straight, work the squeegee. Don't fall off. Reed's extension pointers put him fifteen feet up. There were probably regulations about safety lines but Reed had his own way.

He was through by mid-afternoon. He slammed his van doors one last time and headed back towards the centre. We came in from the north on a road I recognised: it was the route that curved past the Pig and Poke. At which location Reed indicated and moved sedately into the Redland area. We drove up leafy streets lined by massive Victorians and reached a cul-de-sac of early twentieth century semi-detached town houses. Stone-clad, three storeys, *faux* top balconies over bay windows, front gardens tiled over for parking. Reed pulled onto the forecourt of an end house and went in through the building's side door which was the main entrance.

I tucked into a spot and walked up to stand under a tree fifty yards from the building. Unwrapped a sandwich I'd grabbed at Reed's last stop. The shade was welcome. A couple of trees nearer would have been just as shady and would have put me right outside his building but as I walked up I spotted a parked car with someone inside waiting opposite Reed's house. I stayed clear. Didn't need anyone watching me as I watched Reed.

I ate my sandwich and swigged fizzy water and waited.

Workers started to drift in from their offices and shops. Disappeared into the buildings. I pictured Reed in his, scoffing tea in front of the Six O'clock News. Or maybe he was busy on his computer, exercising his creative skills.

My distance from the building showed what looked like separate bell-pushes, flagging the house as a commercial conversion. When the waiting car drove out I moved closer and counted six bell-pushes. Two tenants on each floor.

More cars trickled in. Forecourts filled. Front doors opened and closed. Kids screamed from back gardens. An ordinary street. An ordinary house in front of me. The kind of place P.I.s spend their days and nights, waiting for the not-ordinary to show its face.

The street quietened as the sun's warmth dissipated. Seven p.m. came, then eight. Seemed Reed was in for the night. I shuffled and transferred weight, one leg then the other, tensing muscles, keeping circulation going.

The sky clouded out to the west and finally brought dusk. It hit nine. My water and sandwich were long gone and my feet were sore, and finding somewhere to eat seemed like a good idea. I'd pick up Reed tomorrow. I'd just made up my mind when he appeared and climbed into his van.

I grinned.

Dinner deferred.

I turned and walked smartish back to the Frogeye and was just firing up the engine when the van passed.

I followed.

~~~~~

Ten thirty. Almost pitch black. I sat in the car squinting through my low-light binoculars, wondering what the hell John Reed was up to.

I'd tailed him ten miles out of the city through an endless straggle of suburbs. The landscape switched continuously between lines of old cottages and hedgerows, fields, the promise of open country, then a reversal, a switch back to more housing clusters, business units, filling stations. Reed flicked on his lights. Drove steadily on through suburbs that felt like they'd never end. But then the buildings dropped away and we were in open countryside dotted with farms and houses. A mile on, Reed slowed to turn off the main road onto a lane running north and pulled up on the verge beyond a solitary copse. Alongside him was a five-foot stone wall. The wall was broken by a double wooden gate with spikes on top and a hint of a house roof beyond, maybe a three-storey structure, top dormers. The deepening dusk made it hard to see detail.

I coasted to a bend a hundred yards on and killed the lights, turned and rolled slowly back, invisible to the van. Pulled onto the verge and grabbed my binocs.

Reed was sitting behind the wheel. Didn't move for fifteen minutes. Then another vehicle pulled in behind him and its driver got out. The van and car were shadows now. The newcomer not discernible. Reed's cab light flared briefly as he climbed out to meet the guy. After that my low-light lenses picked up only shadows as they walked across and shinned the wall into the property.

I hopped out and walked nearer. Pulled myself up onto the wall. Saw the shape of a dark house and vegetation. No sign of Reed or his pal. No lights in any windows. I watched for a while then jumped down and went back to the Frogeye.

Waited ninety minutes.

Nothing moved except the occasional passing car which lit up the van to show me it was still there.

Reed and his pal were busy.

Maybe Locke's Knife-Photo guy had other hobbies. I hadn't spotted a swag-bag on his back when he went over the wall but he wasn't at the house on a social call.

Two hours.

I walked up again to stretch my legs. Climbed back onto the wall. Tried my low-light binocs. They gave me nothing. The house and gardens were just a dark mass with nothing moving. Then I caught the hint of illumination in one of the house windows. Someone with a torch moving inside. I watched for a while longer. Saw another flicker then nothing. I gave up. Hopped down and retreated to sit the thing out in the car.

No more passing traffic.

The hint of white up the lane might have been imagination.

Twelve-thirty. One a.m.

We hit three hours and I was wondering just who this guy was when headlights snapped on and dazzled me. Shadows danced as the two vehicles turned and drove away. I fired up the Frogeye and followed, lights off, until we hit the A road. Then I flicked on my sidelights and followed them back towards Bristol. When Reed's pal diverged in the outskirts I stayed with the white van.

Which led me back across the city and up to Redland.

I parked short of the cul-de-sac and jogged up towards Reed's building as the van pulled onto its forecourt. He climbed out and went in the side door and a few seconds later a middle floor rear window lit up.

Interesting.

Though what Reed's nocturnal jaunt had been about I wasn't destined to know since I'd got what I'd been paid to get: the guy's ID and his address. My job was almost done. What Reed had been up to out at that house was none of my business. He hadn't been near Sarah Locke, which was the point.

All I needed before I reported back to Locke was confirmation of the guy's ID and some evidence to confirm his fixation with Sarah along with any connection to third parties who might have an interest in her. Once I'd given that to Locke I'd be through.

On my way back to London.

CHAPTER SEVEN
Lady Smog

First thing next morning I picked up a takeaway coffee at my breakfast cafe and drove out to Reed's house. Confirmed that his van was parked outside his building and retreated down the cul-de-sac to wait in the car. Sat with the hood down. Swigged the coffee and listened to local news and feelgood forecasts. Fine weather continuing.

At eight thirty I called Lucy. She'd just arrived at her desk. Shaughnessy and Harry were in a strategy meeting in the front room. They'd taken on a search for a job-lot of cameras and electronic gear nicked from a shop in Cricklewood. A rival firm was suspected and private investigation the preferred route to locate the stuff. A one week base contract with fifty percent bonus if we delivered the goods. Which we were within an inch of doing because the trail had been as easy to follow as a marching band. Today was wrap-up, with the only complication being that the client's wife was one of the thieves and we didn't know who – she or her partner in crime and romance – had possession of the goods. More specifically, Sean and Harry didn't know where the possessor had stashed them. So the plan was to move in on one of the two and turn up the heat with a little bluff about the extent of their knowledge then follow whichever one got spooked and ran to shift the stash. The plan was simple. All Sean and Harry had to decide was which of the two was likely to be more susceptible to storytelling.

They'd figure it out.

I heard a sound like asthmatic gunfire. Lucy had the coffee on. I could almost smell it. I pulled my takeaway cup back out and popped the lid. Still empty. When I looked up Reed was backing his van out.

I told Lucy I'd be back in tomorrow and cut the call. Reed passed me and turned onto the main road and I fired up and followed. Fifteen minutes of rush hour got us to a council building on the outskirts of the city where Reed parked and went in through a side entrance and came out with posters and bags. Council notices going up, flyers flying.

He finished loading. Slammed the rear doors. Headed off for his round. I left him to it and drove back to his flat.

The main door was unlocked. I walked in through a tiny vestibule and up the stairs. The top hallway was clean but shabby – lino underfoot. A sixties jobbing conversion, mid-price rentals for blue-collar workers. Ahead of me was the frosted glass door of the rear flat.

I rapped on the glass. Just loud enough if anyone was home.

No-one was.

The building was silent bar a radio squawking downstairs.

I pulled out a couple of tools and opened the lock. The operation took eight seconds. Then I eased open the door and knocked again, quietly.

Silence.

I went in and shut the door behind me.

A tiny flat. Bedroom, bathroom, lounge and kitchenette. High ceilings. The lounge had narrow full-height windows framed by worn drapes and tired wallpaper, jaded carpeting. Furnishings had come with the lease apart from the multi gym in the tiny hallway. The flat was functional and liveable but refurbishment was a decade overdue.

A bachelor pad. No photo frames or knick-knacks or house plants. Just three framed movie posters decorating the lounge walls. Freddie Krueger glaring down, blades flashing on Elm Street. Alongside him another fearsome countenance staring out from hell, this one from the Terminator stable. The third was an oldie from the sixties. Vintage look. Vintage theme of woman tied and bound, but you needed to watch this female because Hammer had created A Beautiful Woman With The Soul Of The Devil. Susan Denberg, the Beautiful Woman in question, didn't look too devilish alongside Krueger and company but if you saw the film you'd understand.

Reed's interest in sci-fi and horror was confirmed by a bookstand jammed with dog-eared paperbacks, and a DVD rack with a hundred movies slotted in. Mostly horror. I struggled to find titles I recognised. The hard core bloodfest stuff had never attracted me after a decade shovelling through it in the Met.

A CD stack displayed Reed's fondness for metal, and a desktop PC sat on its own table in the back of the lounge. I fired it up. A gaming model. Zombie apocalypses and space shoot-em-ups and maybe some other stuff. But all protected by a password that I wasn't going to beat.

Pity.

It would have been nice to take a look at Reed's Photoshop files.

In the old days doctoring photos would have meant a darkroom, a colour enlarger and precision masks, prints hanging to dry. No password to lock you out.

Progress.

But my priority was getting proof of Reed's ID and some background. Maybe something that pointed to his fixation with Sarah Locke.

I started looking. Searched fast and thoroughly.

Got nothing.

It wasn't just that Reed didn't leave evidence of his dubious activities lying about. Maybe he was just mindful of nosey landlords, kept everything in the computer.

But he'd almost nothing in the ID department either. All I found was the flat lease taken out twelve months ago and a couple of guarantee cards for stuff he'd bought – the Samsung and a high def. TV, plus council tax and electricity bills. The guy had no paperwork associated with a bank account, no chequebook, no birth or marriage certificates. No passport. No photo ID. Nothing to tell me who he was or where he came from. The guy travelled light.

Conclusion: Reed carried his driving licence and payment cards with him and junked their associated paperwork. His vehicle registration book and insurance docs must be in the van, though that wasn't the smartest place to keep them.

I persisted. Checked every drawer and cupboard, every crack and cranny for clues to the guy's life.

Sum total of findings: a few sci-fi mags, assortment of manga horror comics and one copy of Card Player, a poker magazine. The last was buried beneath the council and rental paperwork in the computer table's tiny drawer.

I spotted a scrap of paper in the back of the same drawer and took out what looked like an old dry cleaning ticket. A place called Best Press. Maybe a nearby shop. The first connection between Reed and the streets outside.

The top drawer in a bedroom dresser yielded the only other clue to

Reed's life, another hint of his interest in card games: a pair of cufflinks buried under Reed's tee-shirts. Decorated with two dancing aces, gold on black. Maybe his lucky charms when he dressed for his poker evenings. Maybe just trinkets that had caught his eye or complementary gifts with a club membership. It was easy to see Reed as a player. His piercing eyes fitted perfectly. Good for searching his opponent's face, giving nothing in return. The advertising guy advertising nothing.

I went back for a final check through Reed's sci-fi and horror mags. They were stacked in a newspaper stand which I lifted. Nothing underneath. But when I pulled the mags out of the rack I found a stamped, addressed envelope pushed down the side. A woman's name. Address up in the Midlands.

I went through to the kitchenette and steamed the envelope open and found a bereavement card. Plain, simple, cheap. The shortest of handwritten messages: *So sorry to hear. Will call. X.*

The first item I'd found that linked Reed to any other person. I snapped a photo of the message and address and resealed the envelope Dropped the mags back on top of it.

And that was it.

Reed's life: nothing but bare bones.

And nothing that connected to Reed's late night house call yesterday. If Reed had been burglarising the place there should have been evidence. Some handy tools or a swag bag of silverware, a stash of valuables, ready for fencing or pawning or auctioning on eBay.

But nothing I'd seen tied in with Reed's night-time activities. The guy kept his nest sanitised.

And nothing to point to his fixation with TV personalities. Whatever he had was locked behind his computer password.

But I had enough.

Locke had pulled me in with the face of a stranger. Now he had a name and address, a little background. My job was through.

I checked that everything was back in place and let myself out.

Hit a problem downstairs.

A woman in her late seventies was standing in the vestibule. She had the grizzled look of the work-worn and smoked a cigarette through a six inch holder. Her stance told me she wasn't just passing the time of day. She watched me come down.

'Can I help?' she said.

I shook my head, threw a grin: 'Just calling. John's not in.'

'I know. How long have you been up there?'

More than a minute or two. Which she clearly knew. She'd heard me despite the fact that I'd moved quietly. These old places: there's always floorboards to creak.

'I thought he might have just popped out,' I said. 'Hung on a while. No luck. I'll try again.'

Her face stayed suspicious. But we're all entitled to be suspicious. I gestured for the door.

She stood her ground.

'We've had people in,' she said, 'thieving stuff. Breaking into the flats. So we're careful. Who should I say called?'

'Alec. His brother. But don't bother. I'll catch him later.'

She put the holder to her lips and took a suck. The vestibule was fogging fast.

'I'll tell John we chatted,' I promised. Reached for the door. 'I guess you're the nice lady he mentions. From downstairs.'

'If he's mentioned me he'll have told you I'm his landlady. And that I watch people coming in.'

'Very sensible. The types you get.'

Maybe the same type as Reed. I pictured him prowling that house last night. Filling a bag. Wondered whether his landlady saw a few dodgy types up and down her stairs. I grinned again and she glared straight back, clocking every detail of my face. When her memory was secure she reached and pulled open the door and let me flow out with the smoke down her steps.

I was still grinning as I walked back to the car.

Not the best choice of rental for a guy in the habit of making quiet late night entries and exits. But the building's fatigued decor pointed to a good rent deal, maybe fifty percent below market price for the street. Worth the price of a few stories for Lady Smog. And one plus: he'd always know if his landlady had been snooping in his flat.

I reached the Frogeye and unclipped the hood. Folded it back. Jumped in and sat to breathe clear air. Then I pulled out my phone and called Bernard Locke.

CHAPTER EIGHT
He was just a delivery boy

I drove across the river towards the Severn Estuary and followed directions to a supermarket on the outskirts of Portishead. Pulled up behind a red Jaguar in the car park and killed the engine but let the music play for a moment whilst I watched Bernard Locke's eyes watching me in his wing mirror. The location was two minutes from the Avon and Somerset HQ. A convenient spot to skip out of a busy schedule for a discreet meeting with your private investigator. The music ended and I muted the player and climbed out. Walked round under a hot sky and dropped into the Jaguar's passenger seat.

Locke was decked out in regalia fit for passing-out day. Full police uniform. One of the perks of the grade. I'd researched his name a couple of evenings back to give myself a little background. He'd climbed the ranks through CID in Bristol Central. Switched back into uniform to step up to ACC fourteen years ago. Then Chief Constable three years back. A nice job with a nice salary, but anonymity was now a thing of the past. You aren't going to invite your P.I. into an interview room unnoticed.

'That was quick work,' Locke said. 'You saved yourself the weekend.'

'And related expenses,' I said. The contract was fixed fee, seven days of my time. Expenses billed on top. No refund for finishing early but at least Locke wouldn't be paying for my subsistence for the next three days.

'He's the guy?'

'Name John Reed. Address as typed.'

I'd emailed a snap of the flat rental contract. The single piece of paper gave Locke everything he needed.

'I'll send the full report Monday,' I said. 'Relevant movements, a few pics.'

The report would be sanitised. Nothing to leave Locke holding evidence of an illegal entry to obtain his information. But the detail would give him a little colour: Reed working around town; his flat up in Redland; his nocturnal wanderings. Times and places. A basic sketch of the guy's movements. None of which had taken him near Locke's daughter.

'I was on him two days,' I reported. 'He didn't go near her. And there was nothing at his flat. He's not got her picture on his wall and he doesn't have a scrap book.'

Locke thought about it.

'That's a surprise,' he said. 'I was sure there'd be something.'

'Me too. So either he's smart and keeps everything protected behind his computer password or he was just a delivery boy and the doctored photo was someone else's message. In which case your problem is still open.'

Locke nodded, watching the distance.

'Understood. But I've got what I need.'

Which was the identity of the guy who'd delivered the message to his daughter. It was up to him which way to take that, though I gave him my opinion *gratis:*

'If the knife photo was primarily a threat it might be work-related. In which case you'll need to keep an eye on what's happening at TownGate. I assume you heard about Sarah's partner?'

'The threats, yes. If Sarah's photo was part of that then Reed would be just the delivery boy as you suggest.'

He gripped the wheel. Squeezed and sighed.

'I'm not exactly easy with that scenario but it's a step down from the unpredictability of a lone nutcase. And the people Sarah goes up against know that hurting her would bring the spotlight onto them. So if this is work-related then it's the lesser threat.'

'How are you going to play it?'

'I'll have to think. But I'm happier now that I know who Reed is and where to find him. If Sarah gets any more trouble from this guy then I'll pay him a call.'

'Then... I'm through.'

'Yes. Thank you for your help.'

I nodded. 'Anything further, just let us know.'

'I'll do that.'

The sun was fierce. The car was heating. We were both starting to sweat. I opened the door and climbed out. As soon as my feet touched the ground Locke fired up the engine and rolled away. Lucky I was quick with the door.

I walked to the Frogeye and sat against the wing. Took a moment to call Sarah. The call went to voicemail. I left a brief message. Summarised what I'd given her father. Suggested she talk to him. The main thing was that Locke had the guy in his sights if he tried any more tricks. Up to the two of them to stay alert.

I killed the line and pushed the ignition. Rolled back out to the road and turned towards the motorway where the evening rush beckoned.

Job over.

Ahead of schedule.

I cruised sedately back to Town.

CHAPTER NINE
Meeting over

Other people's business. The P.I.'s stock in trade. The river you swim.

Sometimes you tiptoe in and tiptoe out and the business seems undisturbed – though there'll be a report and photographs and recordings, regret on its way. Sometimes you kick things apart until all the nasty characters have scuttled out from the smashed facades of their rotten worlds.

But always: you swim and dig and kick precisely as far as your client's money directs. Send out the invoice. Forget.

Except for the cases that stick with you, the ones that leave a sense of unfinished business. The picture of John Reed came back to me a few times in the slack periods of the next ten days. The guy on the periphery of Sarah Locke's life had become more mysterious not less when I applied the magnifying glass. In part because I hadn't found a single piece of evidence tying him to Sarah beyond what her father had given me: the knife photo and the image of him delivering it to her door. But a guy sneaking around at midnight, climbing walls and disappearing into people's houses, a guy with a loner lifestyle and little to show of himself was hard to forget.

I'd done my job. Found him. The client would take it from there. And despite his words about ethical usage of police resources, if the threat to his daughter escalated then the Chief Constable of Avon and Somerset wouldn't lack the means to shut Reed down.

So I had everything covered except my curiosity. A sense of unfinished business. The job grated on a professional vanity that said I'd know more about an affair when I closed an investigation than when I started.

And this time I didn't.

Closure: high on the list of a P.I.'s needs, right after an account in the black and occasional medical assistance.

This affair didn't feel closed. In the quiet periods after my trip to Bristol the thing came back like persistent indigestion.

Then it came back in a more tangible way.

Ten days on. Normal routine restored: morning exercise on Battersea Park; rush hour drive up to Paddington; renegade coffee machine firing salvoes in the agency reception; Herbie snoring in my visitors' chair.

Monday's paperwork on my desk.

Which might be considered remiss for a Wednesday morning but I'd been chasing down a lady client for two days after her inclination to settle our final invoice dissipated on delivery of evidence that she didn't want: namely that her husband wasn't cheating on her. I guess the evidence had been a crucial presumption in her route map to a high-dividend divorce. When she didn't get it she reconsidered her obligation to settle her outstanding fees. The chase after her had lost me two days' work but it's the principle that counts. I added twelve chargeable hours to an up-sized invoice and caught up with her. Asked whether I should send the invoice to her husband's business address. She confirmed that her own name and address would be satisfactory and wrote out a cheque. We'd know by Friday whether the cheque was good. That's when Lucy would select the address for the posting.

I took a moment. Settled into my Herman Miller nineties-vintage chair behind my thirties-vintage desk. Set rotation to facilitate skyline observation. Gazed at blue sky that was bright and cheerful even with the greying effect of our cloudy glass.

I extended the reverie. Racked the Miller back to comfort-plus and got my feet onto the sill.

Dust motes floated in the warm air. Boycott and Trueman stood in my peripheral vision ready to take summer wickets, and behind me Herbie continued to snore. The sound I was waiting for was that of Lucy coming in to sort out the coffee.

Harry came in first. I heard his dry cough at the outer door, and a couple of seconds later he stuck his head in and declared that we were in for another good'un. He continued through to the front office. I heard him whistling in there. Herbie's snoring halted for five seconds to lift an eye and take in the news. Resumed just as quickly.

Then my phone rang.

I stretched. Picked it up, still gazing at grey-blue sky.

'Eagle Eye. You've got the problem, we've got the solution.'

'Mr Flynn?'

A woman's voice. Kind of rough sounding. And businesslike. When my pause extended, the voice continued.

'I'm ringing to ask about your brother.'

I didn't have a brother, unless another facet of my unusual childhood was about to gate-crash. For the moment I maintained my contemplation of the clouds, white drifting across blue, waited for something more.

'Are you there?'

I sighed. 'I believe so. What about my brother?'

'I'd like to know where he is?'

'I'm afraid I haven't a clue.'

'You're not in touch? Not spoken to him?'

'Not recently.'

'Can I believe that?'

She believed I had a brother. Who knew what else was swirling through her head.

'May I ask whom I'm talking to?'

'Elsie Flowers. John's landlady.'

Cogs rotated, tumblers tumbled. My feet came off the sill.

John Reed.

That brother!

'Okay,' I said. 'Got it. John! What's up, Elsie?'

'Well first thing, how come your name is Flynn? I thought it was Reed.'

'How did you find me, Elsie?'

'I spoke to John's work and they said somebody who sounded just like you had been there asking about him around the time you came here. The name they had was Flynn but I decided to call on the off-chance.'

A cough rattled the line.

Her explanation made sense. But a landlady calling a name she didn't recognise seemed a little strong without a very great need to connect. Something was up.

I racked up the Miller. Stood and went to lean against the roll-top shelf. Herbie lifted his head.

'I apologise if I confused you,' I said. 'My name's not Reed. I should have said *stepbrother*. You're looking for John?'

'Do you know where he is?'

'He's not home?'

'I've not seen him since right after you were here. I don't know what's happened to him.'

'You've not seen him for two weeks?'

'More or less.'

'That's odd. Is he just away, perhaps?'

'He wouldn't go away without mentioning it. And his rent was due last week. He would never leave that unpaid. He's too organised. So I'm wondering what on earth has happened to him.'

The unease I'd been feeling for the last ten days trickled back in. Not because the idea of the guy doing a runner on his rent was so far fetched but because when I'd searched his flat and watched him at work I hadn't picked up any hint of a guy getting ready to skedaddle.

'Let me understand: you've not seen or heard from him since I was there?'

'I saw him come home from work next day then go out for the evening and that was it.'

'Have you checked his flat?'

'Yes. There's nothing.'

'Nothing in there?'

'Everything's there. It's all normal apart from the fact that he's not here.'

'What did ValuAd say?'

'He hasn't been back to work since that Friday and he didn't give them any notification.'

'Got it.'

'I don't know what to do. He should have told me he was going away and paid his rent.'

I thought about it.

John Reed. Mystery character. Ups and vanishes as soon as I locate him for my client. Which was an interesting coincidence. And the more I considered it, the more it changed to a worrying one.

'Had he done or said anything unusual recently?'

'Nothing. The only odd thing was you turning up to look for him when he'd never mentioned that he had a brother. And then the other fellow.'

'What other fellow?'

'I had a man here the day after you. He was asking about John too.'

'Did he call specifically to ask about him?'

'No. I bumped into him in the hallway. He'd been upstairs. Same as you.'

I pushed myself off the roll-top and went back to the window. Watched slow-moving trains.

So someone was at Reed's flat the day after I reported to Locke. Was it Locke, calling for a chat? I described him but Elsie said no, gave me a hazy picture of a large, balding guy in his forties with an unpleasant look about him.

Not Locke, though it could have been one of his people. But was the guy related to Reed's disappearance? What the hell had happened after I headed back to London?

Ten days.

Only one way to find out.

'I'll drive over,' I said. 'Take a look.'

'Can't you just call him?'

'Have *you* tried?'

'Yes. His phone's been off.'

'There you are. Same here. I'll have to pop over.'

'Well... I'd appreciate it. I need to know where my tenants are when they stop paying their rent.'

I told her we'd sort it out and killed the line. Planted the phone back onto the desk, rotated the Miller windowards and sat back down.

People up and disappear all the time, most of it innocent, routine comings and goings even if they don't tell their landladies. And a guy dropping out of sight in Bristol didn't become the agency's affair simply because we'd tracked him down. But if Reed really had disappeared what was the implication? That the Chief Constable of Avon & Somerset had run the guy out of town or arranged a hit? All because the guy was a weirdo who'd supposedly threatened his daughter?

I didn't buy it. You get bent cops at all levels but Chief Constables aren't Wild West sheriffs. The Photoshopped picture of Reed holding the knife at Sarah Locke's neck would be unpalatable for any father but even the most unstable isn't going to race after the culprit and put him permanently out of action. Nor, if he's a Chief Constable, is he going to turn the heat so far up that the guy flees town without even packing his bags. Quiet pressure I could buy. The chat Locke had hinted at. Drastic action I couldn't. Chief Constables don't take career-threatening risks.

And yet...

My only option was to get up and do what I'd told Elsie. Take a drive.

Because ten days absence didn't sound like routine.

So I needed to know that nothing had happened to Reed because of my actions.

Lucy came in. I heard her two seconds after Herbie, who'd dropped from his seat before the outer door opened. I vacated my own chair. Locked the desk. Planted the key safely on top of it and grabbed my phone and car keys. Tapped the barometer and walked out. Pressure was steady at thirty-two. A nice day for a drive.

Out in reception I found Lucy commiserating Herbie as she reached for the biscuit tin. Herbie was on his back, motionless apart from the tell-tale flicker of his eyes. Harry came out too and planted his cup by the machine. Shook his head.

'You never feed the mutt, Eddie? He can never stand up.'

'I had him microchipped. I thought that covered everything.'

'Poor baby,' Lucy said. She was wearing a tee-shirt that matched her hair which had turned violet since yesterday. I heard dogs have lousy colour vision, don't see violet, which explained why Herbie wasn't running for his life. And when she pulled out a digestive and squatted the patient recovered his strength and came upright. Crumbs sprayed like shrapnel.

Lucy headed over to work the coffee machine and I decided that two minutes wouldn't change things either way in Bristol. I planted my mug. Harry made himself a black tea and stood sipping as the coffee started dripping through.

I gave them the news. The Reed job had closed ahead of schedule and on a fixed price and I should have known it was too good to be true.

Harry smiled. Lucy frowned.

'Wow, Eddie,' she said, 'it doesn't sound good – the guy disappearing the moment you fingered him.'

I grinned at her. Felt the load lifting from my shoulders.

'We looking at dirty cops?' Harry said.

'Not yet. Locke had a good reason to find the guy. Most fathers would chase after a guy acting out his weird fantasies near their daughter.'

'I love Sarah,' Lucy said. She pulled out the pot and topped up my mug. Pushed sugar and milk over. 'She's smart. Kicks backsides. I've just never pictured her looking over her shoulder when she goes home.'

'It's the price of celebrity. She seemed comfortable with it.'

'You heading back there?' Harry said.

'Soon as I've finished this.' I held up my coffee. 'Quick out and back. One day.'

'You'll find the guy in a day?'

'I doubt it. But I'll know how things stand. Whether I'm looking at some unpaid footwork.'

Lucy sipped her coffee.

'The up-side,' she said, 'is no fee, no invoices to chase.'

Which I hadn't considered. That's Lucy: find the positives.

Me, I was going to leave it until tomorrow morning. That's when I'd either be back here at my paperwork or extending my stay in Bristol. I'd decide then what the positives were.

~~~~~

The trip started badly, jammed in Orbital traffic north of Heathrow. The hood was down and though my headphones muted the din of idling engines they did nothing against the fumes. I stayed with the positive. Told myself I'd soon be back in the same jam, opposite direction, heading in through the evening rush, the John Reed puzzle sorted behind me. Then the lanes started moving. A little at first then spaces opened up. I went with the flow and hit the M4 slip, accelerated west below heavy jets.

The road stayed clear after that and I made good time on the hundred miles west and hit Bristol just before noon. Drove across the city and parked on a side street just up from the ValuAd door. I let Herbie out to stretch his legs then we crossed the street and went in. Reception was still unmanned so we went straight up. Same office, same pens, same crew. Same blue streaks in Sue's hair though her Snow Bunny tee-shirt had switched to an unbranded top. But her

55

face stretched into the same smile when she saw my face: the exotic fragrances guy, back to talk business. She'd begun to doubt me. Then she spotted my sidekick and her smile widened. She threw a chorus of oohs and heys and came out from her desk. Heads turned.

'Aren't *you* a cutie!'

I gave her a bright smile but she squatted.

Cutie sat and lifted a paw and grinned wide-screen. When Sue reached out to shake it he collapsed with a sufficiently dramatic flourish to raise dust. I grinned round at the audience whilst Sue fussed my assistant. When she'd finished she stood. Realised she had a reason to talk to me.

'Hey, do you know where John is? You said you knew him.'

I hadn't said that but that's the hazard of misdirection: it often comes back on you.

'More a social acquaintance. But that's why I'm here. I heard he'd gone missing, thought I should check on him.'

'He's not been in since right after you were here. Do you think something's happened to him?'

I didn't venture an opinion.

'He's always so reliable,' Sue said.

'He's worked for you for a while?'

'About a year. He took over the round from a previous contractor who'd retired.'

'Has he ever taken time off? Been away?'

Sue shook her head. 'Just the odd day. He's never needed a stand-in.'

Office business had come to a halt. Everyone listening in. I guess the world of flyers and posters wasn't so riveting. Distraction always welcome.

But if they were hoping to hear what was going on with Reed they were disappointed. I had nothing. Made do with a few platitudes and a declaration that I'd ask around. Then worked up a concerned frown as a lead-in to an exit. Sue caught the vibe and switched topics.

'If we can still be of help in the meantime...'

I looked at her.

'Exotic fragrances...?'

I grinned. Tugged at the lead to rouse Herbie.

'We're keeping ValuAd very much in mind,' I said. 'John may have brought you some business yet.'

'That's good to hear. Call us anytime.'

'Soonest,' I confirmed. I tugged again. Herbie double-checked the place for signs of handouts then turned to follow. We headed down.

The street was hot and the traffic was the same as London minus the dust. I walked round and Herbie jumped into the car whilst I sat on the wing and called Bernard Locke. His phone rang for a few seconds and went to voicemail. Either he'd set the divert to short or he'd checked incoming ID and hit reject. In a meeting, I guess.

I re-dialled. This time the line went straight to voicemail. Still in that meeting.

I changed tactics. Sent a text. I'm not the hot-finger type: texts are too easy to ignore – unless you choose your words.

I chose the words.

Sixty seconds later the phone rang and Locke's ID was on the screen.

Meeting over.

I winked at Herbie. He was up on the seat grinning through the windscreen, focused on the concept of movement.

'In a moment, pal,' I said. I picked up.

My text had said "I know you did it."

Locke said: 'What is this? Did what?'

'Sorry to disturb you, Bernard.'

'Did *what?*'

I grinned. Turned to watch a van unloading on the main street. Boxes and plastic-wrapped bundles going into ValuAd. Ink and paper. Coffee supplies.

'Rejected my calls,' I said. 'It's less obvious if you just silence the tone and let it ring through, as if you're not nearby, or maybe driving, can't pick up.'

'Come to the point, Flynn. You've pulled me out of a damned meeting. Did the payment not clear?'

I held the grin. The guy unloading caught my eye and saluted across the traffic. It was that kind of day.

Payments that don't clear. We get them. But if you post us a duff cheque it will be Lucy on the other end of the line and she's there to tell you her life story until you capitulate and stump up. Locke's payment had cleared fine. The job was a good one from that point of view, spoiled only by the unpleasant whiff of something bad having happened as a consequence. Whether Locke was part of it I didn't know. But he hadn't jumped out of a meeting over bill payments. So he suspected something.

'I've had some follow-up,' I told him.

'On John Reed?'

'I've been told he's missing.'

That silenced Locke as if he'd been switched off. I checked the screen to make sure we were still connected. We were but the silence went on for a couple more seconds.

'Where did you hear that?'

'Reed's landlady contacted me. She hasn't seen him since a week last Friday.'

Another silence. Then:

'That's odd. Has anyone else seen him?'

'Not his works contacts.'

'That is odd. But there'll be a simple explanation.'

'I'm confident of it. But I was just wondering whether it's an explanation you're familiar with.'

A shorter pause. Intake of breath.

'Of course not. What are you saying?'

I waited.

'You're suggesting I've done something? Don't be ridiculous. I haven't seen the guy. And I'm the head of a damned police force for Chrissake.'

'You intended to have words with the guy.'

'If he came near Sarah again. The next time he stepped out of line he was going to hear the hard truth.'

'But he didn't go near her? You didn't talk to him?'

'I didn't even see him. I watched his flat for two evenings to get a sight of him and see where he went but he never appeared. So I just warned Sarah to be vigilant and stepped back.'

'That's it?'

'Dammit, Flynn! I paid you to do a job. Not to come harassing me over the guy just because he takes a trip.'

'It did,' I said.

'What?'

'Clear. The payment. And I'm not in the habit of extending interest in a job beyond the last cheque. But this one might be coming back. And if anything has happened to Reed I'd be part of it. You see my point?'

'Not unless the something that happened was related to me,' Locke said. 'Which it isn't. And dropping out of sight for a week or two doesn't mean anything. You're jumping the gun, Flynn, unless you know more than you're telling me.'

'Right now you know everything I know,' I said. 'The guy's been reported missing and maybe there's nothing behind it. But the timing is a little unfortunate. You understand how I might put two and two together?'

'And get the wrong sum. You need to be careful with your insinuations.'

'Did you pass Reed's details to anyone else?'

'What the hell are you saying?'

'That should be clear.'

'Clear as hell. Well keep your insinuations to yourself. I gave Sarah the basics – Reed's name and the area of the city he lived in – and that's it. And don't start working up nonsensical ideas about my daughter. The job's finished. Leave it at that.'

'Has Sarah caught any further sightings of the guy?'

'I spoke to her two days ago. She hadn't seen him then.'

'Her bodyguard still with her?'

'No. But not because I've chased Reed off.'

'Then why? You must still be concerned about Sarah.'

'I am. But twenty-four hour security is not sustainable. I've got the guy identified and located and I'm ready to move in fast if he troubles Sarah again. I'm happy with that.'

'But if he's disappeared you no longer have his location – in the event that you needed to reach him.'

'I know that now. But if he's out of town then he won't be bothering her. And when he's back I know which door to knock on.'

He paused. Took a breath.

'Okay,' he said. 'I can understand your concern, Flynn. I'd be puzzled too in your position. Let me talk to the landlady. If I think she needs to put in a missing person's report then we'll take it from there. But unless there's any sign of foul play this isn't going to be a police affair. And I'll call you if I learn anything.'

'Fine,' I said.

'But if insinuations get back to my ears I'll be unhappy. Are we clear on that?'

'Clear. Let me know when you've got something.'

I disconnected. Left Locke to return to his meeting. More likely, to skip the rest of it and head back to his desk where he could sit down and worry about how his pulling a P.I. into this affair was coming back on him.

The question was, did he have any deeper reason to be concerned? The guy sounded genuine but so do most bad guys.

If he called back with any useful information I'd be interested.

But I wasn't waiting for him.

CHAPTER TEN

I sensed something odd about the guy

I drove over the river to TownGate Productions and parked on their yard next to Sarah Locke's car. According to her father she'd had no further contact with Reed but I've a preference for first-hand accounts.

We went upstairs into the same bright reception and checked in. A few seconds later Sarah came out with a puzzled look that dissolved into a smile. The London detective was back in town with a sidekick. I didn't know whether dogs were allowed in the building but Sarah had the grace not to comment, nor remind me that she was a busy person. She just took us through to the same meeting room we'd used last time and sat me down before squatting to fuss Herbie.

'My,' she said. 'What's your name, handsome?'

The room shook. Sarah stood up, startled. Herbie was on his back, legs up. She looked at me.

'He gets these fits,' I explained. 'Mostly with the ladies. My guess is there's some trickery involved.'

She grinned. Squatted again and tickled.

'You taught him that?'

'No.'

'Are *you* going to faint on me?'

'Only if you're too nice.'

'I can be nice sometimes.' She looked up, meaning in her grin. Then she stood again and leaned back against the table.

'I didn't expect to see you back in town,' she said, 'after that sudden departure.'

'When a job ends I'm back to my desk. I didn't expect to be here either.'

'But...?'

'But we've had a complication. Related to Reed. He seems to be missing. Since the day after I dug him out. So I've popped across to see that nothing's wrong. Loose ends, and so on.'

'That's dedication. But that's odd about the guy. Do you think something's happened to him?'

'I don't know. But I was here in the centre, thought I'd check in with you. See if he'd given you any further problems. The guy could have dropped below the radar as part of something he's up to.'

'I see. But no, he's not bothered me again. You really think something's happened to him?'

'Since I was the one who located him I need to be sure that it hasn't.'

'I understand. Basically you're worried that my father has caught up with him.'

'I'm still neutral. Leaning towards believing his story – which is that he knows nothing. But I still need to know why Reed has vanished.'

'Of course,' she said. Though there was not much concern in her voice.

'I hear your security's been pulled back. You okay with that?'

'Yes. I'm just happy that my father's no longer footing the bill.'

'Okay. Well if I catch up with Reed we'll know whether there's still any threat. Maybe put everyone's mind at ease. And *I'll* know that I'm not complicit in something underhand.'

'Maybe his vanishing means nothing. Just gives us what we wanted.'

Her face didn't signal any specific meaning behind the words. All we'd wanted, if I recalled, was to block any danger to her. What Reed did with the rest of his life was up to him.

I smiled. Let it go.

'Okay.' I stood and whistled for Herbie. 'Well, stay alert. Call me if there's anything further. Meanwhile, my enquiries will shift elsewhere.'

'Actually,' she said, 'Reed dropping out has not been the end of our problems.'

Oops a daisy...

I waited. Herbie stayed belly-up.

Sarah pushed herself off the table and looked at her watch.

'Have you eaten?' she said.

I hadn't.

'Let's have lunch,' she said, 'and I'll tell you about it.'

Lunch. The word initiated a rumbling in the back of Herbie's throat. Another piece of vocabulary he'd picked up since joining us. As far as I knew he'd learned the word from Lucy. Left to me there'd have been no clear concept. Something that might or might not happen. Like Pavlov's bell with the clapper missing. The bell rang now, loud and clear. Herbie stood up fast, tail signalling his vote, and I figured a quick break and watering wouldn't go amiss.

And I wanted to hear Sarah's problem.

I signalled affirmation with a grin that matched Herbie's and Sarah took us down to grab the cars and we followed her Audi TT back into the centre.

~~~~~

Sarah selected a waterside Italian and we ate pasta and shellfish under an umbrella. I quenched my thirst with fizzy water. Sarah sipped white wine and described the trouble she'd mentioned.

'It's not related to John Reed. But you recall that my partner Mark had received a threat letter telling him to drop an investigation?'

'The Bardi Stradivarius affair.'

She nodded. She'd mentioned the letter when we first spoke. I'd not had a sight of it since things had wrapped up rapidly and I was gone.

'You've had something else?'

'The same message but delivered more forcefully. Mark's house and car were vandalised last week. Someone coated his window frames and car with paint-stripper. They also sprayed his lawns with weed killer – wrecked them. And pushed another letter through his door. Mark was pretty shaken. Was in two minds whether to ditch the investigation.'

'Are you sure the threats were about the Stradivariuses?'

'The letter wasn't specific but there's nothing else fits. And for an attack on that scale the only candidate is Pauline Granger's operation – or the client who commissioned the theft.'

'You're confident that Granger was behind the robbery?'

'Everything Mark has seen has pointed the same way. We're sure.'

'And you're continuing the investigation.'

'Mark took some convincing but this is what we do. If we pull back every time we're threatened we'll deliver nothing.'

'Sounds good to me. But you say the threats are not related to John Reed. That's probably true but his knife photo was a clear threat, maybe a warning-off, so I'm keeping an open mind. Though the guy vanishing doesn't tie in with him being in the pay of someone attacking TownGate.'

'I agree. I think he's unrelated. That was just some kind of private fixation, even if the timing of his threat was unfortunate.'

I forked pasta and took a swig of fizzy.

'You should know,' I said: 'there was something odd about the guy beyond his fixation with you.'

I gave her the picture I'd picked up. The guy with limited interests – sci-fi and horror, mainly the latter – a guy with no evidence of a wider life lying around his flat, no evidence of any relationships, a loner who crept out at night to break into houses. The guy I'd uncovered was way off centre.

'And his going missing,' I concluded, 'puts everything on hold. We won't know if he's still a threat to you until I get back on his heels.'

Sarah nodded. Sipped her drink then planted her glass. Looked at me.

'I'm sorry you're stuck with a mess because of this,' she said. 'This is a long way from home for you. But if you do find Reed I'd be grateful to know about it.'

'You're top of my contact list,' I promised.

That brought back a smile. It looked like she was about to say something else but then caught herself. Looked at her watch.

'Wow. Gotta get back. Two-thirty meeting.'

We stood. I looked round for the waiter but she touched my arm.

'My treat. I appreciate what you've done. Even more so if you can tell me that Reed is no longer a threat. The least I can do is buy lunch.'

The world-wise P.I. is nothing if not an opportunist. I grinned and acquiesced as the waiter clocked his celeb guest signalling and came hurrying over.

We parted and I walked Herbie along the harbour, thinking about Sarah's problem for a while. Then pushed it aside and came back to my main business. Forced or voluntary? That was the key question about Reed's disappearance, though his failure to show up at work and his abandoning of his flat along with his belongings and rent arrears didn't point to anything planned.

I needed to start digging. Get my first pointer.

Because I needed to find out fast whether I'd been complicit in something bad – or whether something bad was still happening.

CHAPTER ELEVEN
It's gonna be harder this time round

I went back out to Bishopston and revisited the streets where I'd first searched for Reed. Started at the same place.

The Pig and Poke proprietor remembered me. Gave me the same brush-off. He still didn't recognise the face on my screen.

'You've got persistence,' he said. 'More than sense, you ask me.'

He moved on to a more pertinent point. 'We don't allow dogs.'

I looked at the extravagantly framed painting at the end of the bar. An Old English tavern interior. Roaring fire. Rosy cheeks. Fleshy serving wenches. And dogs snoozing on the benches. Good cheer all round.

I nodded at the painting. 'I guess that lot wouldn't make it in nowadays.'

'None o' them. We go with the times. Demand.'

I checked the line of taps. Heineken, Fosters, Diet Coke. The shelves behind were stacked with Bud Light and prawn-flavoured crisps, pork-flavoured scratchings. I got the guys' point. Thanked him. Tugged at the lead and left via a tour round his three occupied tables. Held out my phone. Got nothing. We went out.

We covered the main road retail again in both directions, barging into the same places plus a few I'd avoided the first time round: a hair salon; a pet shop; mortgage advisor's. Reed's photo didn't jog memories anywhere. I stuck with it, telling myself the search wasn't hopeless. I knew something I hadn't known first time: that Reed lived in the area. These were his streets.

But he was as much a ghost as before and my optimism was balanced by the logic that if his landlady and his work contacts hadn't seen him for ten days then he wasn't likely to be drifting casually round the streets. My footslog was due diligence only. Avoidance of later regret.

I took a break. Pulled up an internet search for the name on the dry-cleaning ticket I'd spotted in Reed's flat. Found only a single business with the name Best Press Laundry. The business was listed in Lewisham, London. If there was a local business with the same name they weren't advertising. I continued walking. Pushed open doors, showed my photo, asked questions, got nothing. Face and name unknown. Laundry unknown.

The afternoon grew late and my plan for a drive back to London with the Reed affair sorted was shredded. Just before seven I hit the end of my trail: The Mason's Arms where I'd scored my original hit with the guy who'd known "Reedy". But Reedy's pal wasn't there and no-one else knew anything. I went back out with a strengthening sense that this was turning into a quag.

'Logically,' I told Herbie, 'it's got to be harder this time round, since we know the guy has disappeared.'

A neat reversal of my earlier optimism.

Herbie grinned up, turning over his own priorities which related to food.

'Good point,' I said. 'Things always look better on a full stomach.'

We drove back into the centre and checked into the same Travelodge. One night. Option to extend. Ten quid supplement for Herbie.

We went up and I fed Herbie and showered away the dust from a long day. Hit the streets at nine to search for a canine-friendly eatery. Polite head-shakes at three pubs so we wandered onto the Harbourside and opted for al fresco at the Greek. The guy came out and asked if we needed a water bowl. Herbie recognised the accent. Our favourite eatery back at Chase Street was run by a Greek guy. Herbie grinned. Draped his tongue low. Greek accents were associated with plentiful handouts. Herbie's smart but it had never occurred to him that the handouts back at Chase Street weren't handouts, and that Connie didn't give floor-service discounts. Or maybe he was smarter than I reckoned, knew who was paying the tab.

I ordered a Fix Hellas and a slab of moussaka. If the place was any good they'd serve it up as a solid block, tray-baked. Good for an empty stomach with a decent hand-down left over.

Whilst I waited I pulled out my phone, thinking about the Pig and Poke. The pub had thrown up a blank again but Reed had been snapped in their doorway, and when I'd re-checked the notice board on my way out I'd seen the same classes and meets listed for the room upstairs. The same Livingstone Club flyer. Same information:

Tuesday meets, 7 p.m.

I called the number and left a message to supplement the one they'd ignored two weeks ago. I guess recruitment wasn't their priority but I repeated my message and threw in Reed's name. Whether he was a member of the club I'd find out if they ever called me back.

My beer turned up in a frosted glass and twenty minutes later a slab of moussaka was heaved across, steaming and crisp-topped on a plate of garden salad. I pushed aside the fact that I shouldn't be in this city and told myself that tomorrow would deliver my ticket home. Tucked in on that comfortable reassurance. The meal was off-expenses but tasted fine.

Finer than it should have.

CHAPTER TWELVE
Lobotomies and all that

First stop next morning was Reed's flat over in Redland.

To his landlady's untrained eye the flat was undisturbed but if her tenant had taken a trip there'd be signs. I parked on the spot Reed's van had once occupied and jumped out, pulled off my shades. Reed might have dropped out of sight but his van was out there somewhere driving the roads or abandoned where no-one would notice. If this thing didn't resolve itself I'd need to start looking for it. I walked down the side of the building and rang the bell for the downstairs flat, and Reed's landlady appeared and scrutinised me with the cigarette holder still clamped between her lips. She offered an unenthusiastic good morning and asked if I'd found Reed.

I hadn't. Couldn't even get through to him. Wondered out loud if I'd got an out of date number. Elsie pulled an ancient phone from her waistcoat pocket and read one out and I confirmed that it was the one as I memorised it.

She pushed her phone away and switched her attention back to me.

'John never mentioned a stepbrother.' The same suspicions as two weeks ago. 'Do you not keep in touch?'

'Rarely,' I admitted. 'And truth be told: I'd no idea he was going away.'

'Me neither. But in my case there's the matter of rent. I'd say it's just good manners to inform your landlady if you're going to be away for a while, and make sure the rent's paid.'

'I don't recall John being away like this before,' I said.

'He's never away. And he's organised. Reliable. I'm quite disappointed.'

I nodded my sympathy.

'I apologise for him,' I said. 'I'm just hoping he's okay.'

'I hope so too. But this is very irregular.'

'The guy you mentioned – the one who came asking about him – did you see his car?'

'No. I don't know if he drove or walked. Is that a pittie?'

69

She was watching Herbie who was checking the vestibule's scents. Something interesting going on down there.

'Staffie.'

'He can smell my cats.'

He was lucky to smell anything in the growing fug. Elsie's cigarette holder put her fag nearer to me than her but she was still at risk from secondary smoking. The fire people say down near the floor is the best place to be which maybe explained why Herbie hadn't noticed.

'Mind if I take a look?' I said.

'If you must.' Elsie was still watching Herbie as she pulled a key ring from another waistcoat pocket. Then she went up the stairs ahead of me and unlocked the door. Herbie and I followed her into John Reed's flat.

The place was dead.

The musty stillness of abandoned rooms.

Maybe just my imagination. Psychology aside, first impressions were that everything was the same but I knew it wouldn't be. There'd be small differences, subtle tells. In most empty homes the fridge is a reliable pointer, right behind uncollected mail. There was no mail but I went through and opened the fridge and saw that Reed had put nothing in and taken nothing out since I was here two weeks ago. A rotting pack of tomatoes, out of date milk and eggs.

Okay.

I did the rounds. Elsie followed, trailing smoke.

Small differences. Subtle tells.

Elsie hadn't noticed it but lots of things had changed.

Reed's clothes, his bathroom toiletries, the books and mags and CDs, all the stuff of his bachelor lifestyle, were still there.

But someone had been through it all.

The place wasn't ransacked but magazines and books were pushed all ways into place. Clothes were bunched and crumpled inside drawers. And the little paperwork Reed possessed had been taken from the computer table and pushed back in a messed-up order. It was the same everywhere. Stuff had been pulled out and checked then pushed back, superficially not obvious but if you were looking you couldn't miss it.

And John Reed hadn't made those rearrangements.

Someone had been here after me, someone with a lazy search

technique or maybe in a rush.

I moved fast myself, stayed ahead of Elsie's smoke trail and was through in twenty minutes. Everything I recalled was still there except for one thing: the dancing aces cufflinks had gone.

That was it. If Reed had taken a trip he'd packed light.

But my guess was that his trip wasn't planned. The day after I'd given his details to Bernard Locke someone had been in here. Then later that day Reed's landlady had seen him for the last time. He'd walked out and simply not returned.

Not a trip. Not planned.

On the off-chance it might give me a connection I took the dry cleaning ticket then thanked Elsie and said I'd be in touch the moment I heard from John. Went out, thinking over my next move.

As I walked across the forecourt my phone rang.

~~~~~

A voice I didn't know asked for my name.

I confirmed I was me. Waited.

'Andy Lightfoot,' the voice said. 'Livingstone Club.'

The club with the notice in the Pig and Poke doorway. Which might be relevant to John Reed or not, dependent on whether he was a member. I opened the car door and Herbie jumped onto the seat.

'Thanks for ringing,' I said.

'No prob.'

Clearly.

'John put me on to you,' I said.

'John?'

'Reedy.'

'Okaaay! You're in the business?'

'No. I'm looking for John.'

'Friend of his?'

'Stepbrother. I'm struggling to contact him.'

'Gotcha. That's funny – I've not seen him either. He didn't show the last two weeks.'

'Show?'

'Club night. Last two Tuesdays.'

'John never mentioned what the club does.'

'Explores. Obviously.'

Obviously. Enlightenment stayed stubbornly distant, like the donkey's carrot.

'Explores?'

'Yeah.'

'Where do you explore?'

'Mostly local. Odd trips out. Bath and Taunton.'

Bristol, Bath and Taunton. If the Livingstone Club was opening up the frontiers of the West Country they were a couple of millennia late. I still didn't get it.

'What do you explore?'

'Anything. Properties. Industrial heritage. The usual. Urbex.'

Urbex.

Understanding clicked into place. The dial hit frequency. The signal came through.

Urban exploration. Exploring old buildings and abandoned places. A recent vogue, fuelled by internet video postings. I pictured oddballs in anoraks treading on rubble and glass. Taking photos. That was pretty much the limit of my knowledge.

And it was Reed's hobby.

'John mentioned an explore two weeks ago,' I said. 'Was that the club?'

'No. Just me and him. Grantham House. The place has been on the market for ten years. Half derelict. We did a night explore.'

The tuning centred. Frequency strengthened. Understanding solidified.

Reed wasn't a burglar, just a guy with a weird hobby.

'Have you seen John since that night?'

'No. Like I said, he hasn't shown at the meets.'

'That's awkward,' I said. 'Because I really need to talk to him. Thought one of his friends might help.'

'Sorry, pal. The guy's gone AWOL. Complete radio silence. I dunno what he's up to.'

'Do you know any of his other friends? Places he visits?'

'Not really. Reedy keeps himself to himself. We're mates, like, but I don't know who he hangs with. Just see him at club nights and the meets.'

'Is he hitched? Girlfriend? Relationship?'

72

'He's never mentioned it.'

'Is he into TV? Anyone in the media he talks about?'

'We talk urbex. That's it.'

'Gotcha. So he hadn't mentioned any upcoming trips away?'

'No.'

I sensed a dead end. Background is good to have but solid leads are better.

'The only thing,' Lightfoot said: 'he said he was gonna do the Perseverance. A week last Friday. I've been intending to go in there myself but I was stuck with the wife's birthday and Reedy didn't want to wait.'

'Perseverance?'

'The hospital. Old sanatorium out Portishead way. Closed ten years ago. Spooky as hell. The main facility shut down years ago but some of buildings were used as convalescent accommodation until the early 2000s.'

'What's spooky about it?'

'Stories. People have seen things. The Perseverance was originally a mental hospital. Early 1900s. Padded cells. Lobotomies and all that. All the ingredients. There's old cells under the main building and an operating theatre and morgue, and a chapel that's meant to be haunted. A photographer's dream.'

'Is it derelict now?'

'Pretty much. Developers bought it in '01 or '02 but then went bust. Left the place to rot.'

'And John was planning to visit the place a week last Friday?'

'Yeah.'

'You always visit these places at night?'

'Mostly. Helps on prohibited sites, thought the Perseverance is out of the way. He was planning to go after work.'

'And you've not heard from him since two weeks back?'

'I saw him at the club evening on the Tuesday then we did Grantham House on the Weds. That was it. Nothing since.'

I thought about it. Lightfoot's info. filled in most of Reed's last four days before he disappeared. He'd been in the upstairs room at the Pig and Whistle on the Tuesday evening while I was watching Sarah's house, then I'd had him in my sights at work all the following day and later as he indulged in his night-time hobby. Then I saw him off on his rounds the next day before I searched his flat. And Elsie Flowers had spotted him the day after that, heading out on the Friday evening. Which might have been Reed's trip to the derelict hospital.

And that was the end of the line.

I sensed a picture coming together. The only problem was that it was two weeks out of date.

I thanked Lightfoot and ended the call. Checked my phone and located the hospital a few miles out of the city, half way to Portishead.

It was a long shot that I'd find anything there but if I didn't catch sight of Reed in the next twenty-four I'd check the place out.

Then my phone rang and Sarah gave me a more urgent destination.

CHAPTER THIRTEEN
Bond would have had a quip

The TownGate receptionist was expecting me. She jumped up and took us through to Sarah's office at the far end of the open-plan space. The office had a glass wall, giving me a view of her working at her keyboard and phone. The adjoining office was dark, backlit by its window. Sewell was out.

Sarah cut her phone conversation short when we came in, and came round her desk to offer me a seat in a cluster of executive easy chairs. Took the seat opposite. The chairs were padded leather, comfy as hell. Had me wondering if I'd ever climb back out. Herbie rolled over for some introductory fussing then eyed the chair next to me. I warned him off. The chairs were a different class from our guest seats back at Chase Street. Different class of client. Herbie sighed. Flopped onto the carpet. Closed one eye.

Sarah opened with an embarrassed half-laugh.

'I'm really sorry,' she said. 'I'm sure you're busy.'

I smiled. It was hard not to, sitting across from her. There was something about her face that the TV couldn't capture. A suffused warmth that made you want to reach out and touch. An elegance that could overpower. My memories from the screen had her dressed in jeans and jacket, businesslike for the camera. Today was softer stuff, a light cotton dress, rouched so it seemed to flow round her figure. A pastel summer colour. And an expensive perfume I couldn't quite place.

'How did it happen?' I said.

'I'm sorry.' She was still on the apology thing. 'I shouldn't have called. It was just impulse. Threats against TownGate aren't related to your search here. I feel I'm just taking advantage.'

I held the smile.

'I'm an easy guy to take advantage of,' I said.

They should have awards for quips. I'd be up there. Gold medal material. Sarah smiled resignedly, probably thinking the same thing.

'He was attacked last night. Two guys were waiting after he left a club in the early hours. They grabbed him as he was getting into his car and dragged him into an alley. Beat him rather badly. '

Mark Sewell. The explanation for his dark office.

'How serious?'

'Serious enough. He ended up in A&E. Mostly just cuts and bruises but they'd broken a finger. He's still pretty shaken.'

'Did either of his attackers look like Reed?'

'It was dark. He only got generalities: white guys, big. He didn't say anything about a goatee though so it was probably not John Reed.'

'Did they take anything?'

'It wasn't a robbery. It was a message for TownGate. They instructed him to shut down his investigation or pay the price. A final warning.'

'Did they mention *which* investigation?'

'Yes. They told him to leave the violins alone. They couldn't have been clearer.'

'So what are you going to do?'

'Mark's already decided: he's pulled the plug. Says the project is not worth it.'

'You go along with that?'

'No, but Mark hasn't given me a choice.' Her face had dropped its cheer. This was a woman under attack, her professional work, her business, threatened. 'He wasn't in the mood for discussion. He was scared. Angry. And *he's* holding most of the research material. I tried to argue that continuing or not was a joint decision but he told me bluntly to forget it. *He* was the one with the broken bones. So unless I start from scratch I've nothing.'

'Not quite nothing. You've an idea who the key players are.'

'I know about the art-theft operation and the dealer Pauline Granger. But I've nothing else. Mark had picked up a lead pointing to Granger's client for the theft but he hadn't given me the name. So I'd be way back, wouldn't know where to start looking.'

I thought about it. Herbie's second eye had shut. He snored quietly between us. Shop talk.

'And this doesn't concern you, Eddie. You've got your hands full trying to clear up your John Reed problem. I'm sure this is not connected. I shouldn't have called you.'

'Maybe Reed is not involved in this but I never ignore even remote possibilities. Your father brought me to Bristol two weeks ago on the basis that there was a threat against you. And I never found out what that threat was. So I'm not dismissing this one. Your partner may have taken the beating but last night's attack was a message to the company, including you. Which is a connection.'

'You're too generous.'

'Have you told your father about the attack?'

'First thing this morning, right after Mark phoned me.'

'Did he suggest bringing your bodyguard back in?'

'He said that if we've stopped the Stradivarius investigation then there should be no risk. And if John Reed comes back into the picture he'll be straight onto him.'

Which was interesting.

Because ex bodyguard Gary's Cherokee had been behind me on my way here. Was parked down the street as I came in. I let it go for the moment. Turned things over.

'Okay: your Stradivarius investigation is over for the moment. I guess your father's right: everything should quieten down.'

'Probably. I don't see Mark changing his mind.'

I made up my mind.

'I'll take a quick look,' I said. 'If I don't catch up with Reed in the next day or so then I'll need every line of attack. So I'm not going to ignore the fact that his photo was part of a threat against TownGate. Same as the attack on your partner. If it turns out he *is* involved with whoever is pressuring you over the Stradivarius investigation then that might be my only link to him.'

Sarah smiled. 'Thank you,' she said, 'for not saying I'm wasting your time.'

'No thanks needed,' I said.

I saw her eyes flicker. Sensed a deeper message.

'The Granger woman,' I said. 'She's your suspect for the theft. Take me through it again.'

~~~~~

My impression of Mark Sewell as the trendy up-and-coming *media artiste* was bolstered by the first sight of his trendy and expensive home. I turned off a lane ten miles south west of Bristol onto a short driveway that dropped steeply to an ugly concept house hanging over land sloping away to views of the Mendips. If you ignored the house the view was fine. This side of the building all you could see was a Lloyd Wright throwback without the pretty roofs. Seemed architectural college hadn't moved its designer on from his kindergarten building block phase. But the whole blocky mess shouted *arrived!* or at least *on my damn way!* and I realised that Mark Sewell couldn't have lived anywhere else.

What I also saw was that the lawn beside the driveway was wrecked. Streaks and patches of dead grass where the earlier vandal had spread the weed killer. And blighted woodwork where the windows and front door had been attacked with paint stripper.

The four-by-four parked on the concrete nearby was pristine but that was probably a stand-by vehicle. Sewell's Porsche, which had taken the stripper, was still away in the body shop.

The sloping land had inspired the house designer to support the far side on stilts so that the shoe box seemed to float. The ground floor was on the high side of the slope at driveway level but set out a deliberate three feet from the slope so you had to cross a short wooden bridge to get in, like a ship's boarding ramp.

I left Herbie snoozing in the car and walked across the bridge and rang the bell.

Nothing. I tried again. The delay stretched. Sewell, holding back on the socialising right now. But I wasn't here to socialise. I gave up with the nice stuff and held my thumb on the button. Thirty seconds later the door opened and a sleepy looking girl stood there. Early twenties, dark straggly hair, flimsy beach wrap over what looked like swimming gear. Seemed I'd pulled her from a lounger by the pool. The house bell must have had a repeater out back. Nothing that Sewell had heard, though.

I asked if the guy was in. Smiled to show I was harmless.

The smile had no effect. The girl was used to smiles – from guys in bigger cars than mine. Her eyes flicked briefly to the Frogeye but there was no spark of interest. She logged only the fact that it was small. I could have pointed out that some very rich people drive small cars but she didn't look the type for detail.

'Sorry, he's not home,' she said.

'Of course he is. That's his car back there.' I leaned to look past her into the house. Took her silence as an affirmative and stepped smartly past her into an entrance space with open wood stairs climbing up to a gallery. Beyond the space the house opened out at this level. Open-plan.

'Hey, Mister!'

'I just need a quick chat. You have a name?'

'I'm not sure...'

'Well, Ms Sure, I'm Eddie Flynn. Mark knows me. Is he this way?'

I walked towards the light and came into a vast open-plan area that was nicely furnished but architecturally sterile. But what mattered was the sixty feet of floor to ceiling glass, the view of the hills. Ms Sure slammed the door and padded after me. The sleepy look had gone.

'Okay. Mister! Stop. I'll go and get Mark. But you don't just come walking into people's houses...'

We'd already crossed most of the main room, which meant that technically we were walking out of the house but I got her point. A twelve foot stretch of the glass wall was slid open right ahead of us. I aimed for the gap and five seconds later we actually were out. Not in anyone's house at all. I was walking into people's gardens now, or at least onto a massive wood-decked platform overlooking them.

Down below was a pool levelled out from the slope to give an infinity edge against the Mendips. Alongside the pool was a row of loungers and sunshades. Next to one of the loungers was a towel, a drinks tray and a paperback book. Ms Sure's roost before I rang the bell. Mark Sewell was nowhere in sight. I turned and smiled at my guide. She glowed golden in the sun. She was nice looking.

'Do you have a first name?' I asked.

'What?'

I grinned.

What Sure.

Made me think of the Bond movies. With her movie star looks and a name like that she'd fit right in. I turned again and scanned the garden for snipers and guys with metal teeth. Nix. This was Bristol after all. Scene of no Bond adventure.

'Tell Mark I need ten minutes,' I said.

'I could have told him that whilst you waited at the front door.'

'But it would have been a long wait, since you said he's not in. Your story's better back here. And it's sunnier.'

She shook her head. Indignant. Angry. My obtuseness, I guess. Something What Sure didn't come across much. What she usually came across was instant agreement with her views and wishes. I didn't know if the word was "spoilt" but it would fit. Were the Bond girls spoilt? Some were certainly nasty.

'Mark is indisposed, is what I was trying to tell you.'

'Well let's see if we can get him re-disposed. Then you can go back to the pool.'

I gave her an encouraging smile. Waited for her to see the way forward, though I couldn't help wondering:

'Do you live here?'

She turned away.

'That's none of your business. Stay there.'

She disappeared back into the house in search of the guy who wasn't home. There were six or eight bedrooms upstairs, three or four rooms on this level and maybe another four in the built-up part downstairs. Fifteen rooms, say. If she worked methodically and took thirty seconds for each room she'd get to Mark in an average of four minutes. If she knew exactly where he was and was able to cut to the chase we'd be down to thirty seconds plus griping and persuasion time. I counted on her persuasion being enthusiastic. Time away from the pool and all that...

It took her two minutes.

Then Sewell came out onto the platform with What Sure a step behind. She was about to point out the culprit but Sewell figured it out and came across.

His face explained why he was holding back from the social scene, why he wasn't in work. His attackers had smacked him around pretty heavily, though without the intention of serious damage. No bandages or plaster-casts or wires. Just lots of puffy yellow-blue bruises and closed up eyes. And his hand, bound up in a sling. Both arms had angry weals and his left shoulder looked like it had scraped concrete. There was probably a mess of bruising under his tee-shirt and slacks.

So he wasn't a happy guy.

He stopped just near enough to be in my face, far enough to give me a view of the damage. Then compressed his lips and lifted his good hand to wag a non-broken finger.

'When I say I'm not at home I mean I'm not at home. I'm not looking for visitors or for sales reps or for private investigators. You're still after Sarah's stalker? Good for you. But I can't help. And it's nothing to do with this.'

He held his bad arm out as best he could.

'Heard about that,' I said. 'And you may be right: it's perhaps unrelated but if you give me two minutes of your time it might help me get the picture.'

'Who is he?' What Sure asked.

Sewell closed his eyes. Spoke without looking back.

'A private investigator, Baby. The guy who was looking into threats against Sarah.'

'He doesn't look like a private investigator.'

What Sure's look delivered her words on a silver platter. If I'd known she was big on appearances I'd have brought my trench coat and hat.

'The threat against Sarah,' I told Sewell, 'might reasonably be seen as a threat against TownGate. As might the attacks on you. That's why I'm here.'

'Well you're damn sharp, Flynn. I'd say the attacks on me are indeed an attack on TownGate. But Sarah gets weirdos on her tail all the time. Nothing to do with the work we do. That's what your guy Reed and his idiot photo was about. Weirdo land. You're wasting your time talking to me.'

'Could be. But I'm always hopeful until something pops up to say I'm on the wrong tack. Which it rarely does. Usually, the more something looks like a waste of time the closer I look.'

'Well, good for you. So why are you still around? You've found your guy. I thought you'd gone home.'

'Me too. But there were complications. The case re-opened.'

Sewell cocked his head, becoming interested in spite of himself. What Sure was listening too, keen to absorb the messy details of others' futile lives. Boost the feelgood factor of her own sun-kissed existence. Existence as partner to an up-and-coming producer. Or was it just a casual girlfriend? How solid was her ground? Maybe there was symbolism in Sewell's choice of a house on stilts.

Sewell turned to her.

'We'll sort this out, Jan.'

What Sure threw a scowl, either at Sewell or me. Unused to being dismissed. But her interest had been shallow. She headed without protest down the steps and back out to her book.

Sewell turned back to me. Despite his injuries his nerves were hopping with impatience, which was mostly focused on getting me back out of the door.

'The guy I identified, John Reed, has vanished,' I explained.

Sewell thought it through for a second then switched to a short laugh before pain brought the scowl back.

'What are you saying? You're looking out for the bad guy now?'

'Not exactly. But if something's happened to him I'd be concerned that I played a part.'

Sewell tried the laugh-frown thing again. It still hurt.

'Who gives a shit about the guy? Who told him to harass Sarah?'

'I don't know.'

'I do: no-one. The guy's just a weirdo freak. He and all his type can go to hell.'

I understood his anger. Because the people threatening *him* weren't weirdo freaks. They were people with a purpose. And unlike John Reed's approach to Sarah, which had been a little unclear, the intention behind the house and car vandalism and damage to Sewell's face were not. Even in normal circumstances I doubted that Sewell lost sleep about the weird freaks pestering his business partner. Given the present events he couldn't care less.

'You may be right,' I said. 'Maybe no-one put Reed up to harassing Sarah. But I don't like coincidences. And simultaneous threats against your partner and you are quite a coincidence. So if the two are connected then I'm interested in your side of things. There might be something there that gives me a lead.'

'Well good luck, Sam. You're looking for something that's not there.'

'Maybe. I'll have a better idea when you tell me about whoever attacked you.'

'Nothing to tell. I wasn't taking notes.'

'But you've a good idea who they were?'

'I've speculated.'

'It's more than speculation. You had to be pretty sure it was the Stradivarius people to justify binning all those hours, all the work, a hell of a juicy story.'

'Of course it's them! But I've no proof. And if anything else happens I'll know I was wrong.'

'But they're your only suspects?'

'Chrissakes yes! Which is why I won't be helping Sarah to continue investigating, in case she sent you out to persuade me.'

'She hasn't sent me out. But I'm in the same business as you. Just a different approach. Different market. Fact is, if I got to these Stradivarius people it would help you as well as me. I could tie them to the attacks on you and make it unattractive for them to take further action.'

'Or you could provoke them into getting really nasty. I'm not putting my neck on the block for a sixty minute documentary. I'm out, Flynn.'

'We don't need to leave evidence that you're helping me. If I can grab a few pointers I'll work independently. These people will have no reason to come back to you until it's too late.'

'The second they find out that someone's still poking their nose in will be reason enough. They won't need proof. You're not listening, Flynn: I'm out. I'm staying out. Discussion over.'

I grinned. Looked out over the pool and garden. Turned and looked at the house.

'Nice place,' I said. 'Must have cost a bob or two.'

'It did. Are we through?'

I looked at Sewell. His face shone bright and yellow in the sun. All except his eyes which were darkening into a badger mask, reacting to their mistreatment. I thought about things then decided.

'Yeah. We're through,' I said.

'Thank god.'

Sewell went to the rail and called down to the girl. When she looked up he gestured and disappeared into the house. What Sure pushed out a sigh deep enough to carry up to the platform. Divested herself once again of her drink and book. Didn't bother with the wrap. Came up to pad through the house beside me in a string bikini. The minimalist type. Bond would have had a farewell quip ready when she opened the door, but by the time I'd got mine figured out she was gone.

~~~~~

The house call hadn't delivered much illumination but it had given me one pointer, which was that if I was going to follow the line from Sewell back to the Stradivarius theft then a good place to start was Mark himself. Behind the fancy house and media-mogul ostentation, behind the wall he threw up against outside intrusions, I saw a guy whose abrasive attitude looked more like facade, a guy who was throwing away a prime investigation project a little too readily. The damage to his face might be a credible incentive for the backing off but to do so without even a token fight didn't gel. If Sewell had felt vulnerable he could have protected himself and the company with a tax write-off security operation. Even if it wiped out their profit for the investigation there was still the reputational value of bringing down a big player. TownGate shouldn't have pulled back.

Which made me think there was more to Sewell than met the eye.

I put in a call. Lucy would have left the office at lunch time, which is why I used her personal number. Caught her at her uncle's music shop which she tended afternoons. The sound of jazz piano came down the line like a customer-hold track but the music continued after she started to talk. Live. Someone test-driving one of their Yamahas.

Lucy had friends in the media business, one in particular who worked in TV production. I gave Sewell's name and asked her to squeeze. Lucy wilco'd me and promised soonest information. Asked about John Reed. I told her he was firmly out of sight.

'You'll find him,' she said. 'It must be easier the second time.'

I grinned at her logic. Her logic was often spot on but when it wasn't it flew way wide.

'Call me back,' I said. I killed the line and drove out and back towards Bristol, noting the black Cherokee that followed me up the narrow lanes. Sarah's ex bodyguard. Still with me.

I hit Bristol and drove out for a final check round Reed's stamping ground. I started up in Redland. Parked and covered the busiest streets back down to Bishopston, talking to people out walking dogs and pushing strollers. Nothing. I hit the Pig and Poke. Trudged up and down the main street, mingling with the afternoon shoppers, poked my nose in doorways. Most retailers knew me by now. Waved me off. Herbie kept pace and picked up the occasional fussing and one sausage. By five p.m. the afternoon was still hot and my feet were sore.

I hadn't held out much hope. Just due diligence before I dived in at the deep end.

And I wasn't the only one with sore feet.

Sarah's former bodyguard was still with me. He'd followed me back in and stuck with me all the way round Redland. The guy was lacking basic skills but I couldn't fault him for stamina. Three hours and he was still there.

But my blank meant it was time to move into high gear. Ditch Herbie back in London, grab a few things then check back into my Travelodge room.

I called in at the Pig and Poke as I passed. Walked the tables and poked my head into the pool room. Nothing, bar the landlord shaking his head and pushing out religious expletives under his breath.

Second time is never as easy.

We got back to the car and I fed and watered Herbie. Put the hood up and slotted in an early Sonny Rollins and set off back to London. As I pulled onto the motorway I saw the Cherokee peel off as Gary, bodyguard and covert operative, figured out where I was heading and called it quits.

Good decision.

CHAPTER FOURTEEN
Walking Picasso

Seven a.m. Same motorway. Opposite direction. Outbound traffic moving sedately west past the inbound stasis. I accelerated west as it thinned, was slowed only briefly by the valley mist as the road dropped towards Chippenham. By nine I was back in Bristol. I parked in the centre and finalised my plans over an omelette and quad espresso at my breakfast cafe. The plans comprised attacks from both ends of the Reed trail.

At the near end: look for any indication that the guy was still on the planet; fish for a hint of his whereabouts the last couple of weeks.

Far end: backtrack from the assaults on TownGate, based on the faint possibility that Reed might have been involved. If he hadn't then I'd be tugging two different lines.

Neither of them guaranteed to deliver.

And if I worried about it I'd never shift from my cafe table and their lunch menu didn't come online until eleven.

The TownGate end of the line actually comprised two threads. One was the campaign against Sarah and Sewell, which apparently centred on art dealer Pauline Granger, the organiser of the Stradivarius theft. The other thread was Sewell himself. Bad guys messing up your property and face might have considerable intimidation value but I couldn't shake the impression that Sewell was as much angry as scared, and his anger didn't gel with his decision to ditch a promising investigation that was almost in the bag.

The omelette and coffee did their job. Calories and caffeine cancelled doubt and motorway fatigue. The sun was bright outside. I left another fiver under my plate and saluted the counter girl and went out to drive across the river.

I was almost at the TownGate building when a group came out of their front entrance and headed round to the parking yard. A gang of eight. Sarah and Sewell plus six staff, moving as a troupe, hefting boxes and bags. Off to a shoot.

I reversed into a gateway. Waited.

Sewell was a surprise.

I'd pictured him recuperating beside his pool for a couple of days to patch up his confidence and image and maybe work up a justification for ditching the Strad investigation so he could work with Sarah without a long sit down.

But there he was, leading the charge in his wrap round shades, a draped jacket hiding the sling on his left arm. Seemed the guy's energy was not just nervous.

Thirty seconds later three vehicles rolled out of TownGate and passed me in convoy. Out front was Sewell's four-by-four, Sewell its sole occupant driving single-handedly if not quite legally. Sarah's red TT followed it, a passenger with her. Then a people carrier with the remaining crew.

I flicked the Frogeye into gear and was about to swing out after them when a black Subaru hatch decked out in heavy glass tints and a bonnet turbo intake pulled out from down the street and accelerated after the convoy. I waited until its lights flared at the turning then followed, holding well back on a hunch that the vehicle was following the TownGate cars. When the convoy turned south and then west, away from the river the Subaru stayed with them and my hunch solidified.

Three miles out my hunch was still good. I checked my mirror. Maybe Bodyguard Gary's Cherokee would show up. We could form a parade. But the rear-view was clear. Seemed Gary didn't know I was back in town. Leaving me to focus on the question of who the Subaru was and whether they were the people who were giving TownGate a hard time.

Twenty minutes west we passed under the M5 and skirted Clevedon to reach an industrial park on the south side of the town. The convoy turned into the development and the TownGate vehicles pulled onto a grass verge. The Subaru rolled past and disappeared between the neighbouring warehouses. I found my own spot and jumped out just as the Subaru nudged back into sight with a view of the action. I walked up under cover of parked vehicles and found my own spot behind a recycling skip.

We were opposite a warehouse displaying the name of a national consumer products company, and I watched for an hour as the

TownGate crew milled around and huddled, smoked, checked clipboards and best shots. Then Sewell was waving his good arm and people were moving. Sarah ditched a clipboard she'd been rehearsing from and walked onto the grass beneath the company name. Sewell gave the go and she walked and talked, preceded by two guys with a camera and boom. She gestured at the warehouse as she said her piece. I was too far away to hear but I didn't sense good publicity as the camera swung away from her and panned the length of the name. The company had been caught out at something. I made a note to steer clear of their shops.

I took a moment and walked away from the action and round the adjacent buildings. Found a route up to where the Subaru was parked. Checked the vehicle out.

Two silhouettes were visible through the rear windows. Nothing significant about the driver but his passenger was big. Head touching the roof. I crossed the road and walked up for a gander at the guys' faces but the screen tint and the fact they were turned towards the TownGate action thwarted me. All I got was the fact that the regular sized guy was not sporting a goatee. He was either shaved or bald. And the big guy seemed to have some kind of spiked hairdo. It had been fanciful to imagine that I'd spot John Reed working a surveillance two weeks after he'd vanished but I'm not in the habit of dismissing the fanciful or insane until I've checked them out.

I left Spike and Baldy to their surveillance and retraced my steps. Got back to my original spot just as the TownGate group moved round the corner of their building to the adjoining office block. I spotted blinds moving on the upper floor, sensed excitement inside. A quick huddle then Sewell gave the go and Sarah walked over and pushed in through the plate glass doors with her camera guy filming, ready for a shot of her being thrown out. The company's HQ was in Manchester so she wasn't here to catch the top execs with their pants down. TownGate probably had a trip up the M6 scheduled but today was just a regional big shot's career going down in flames.

Sarah was inside less than thirty seconds before her camera guy backed out filming her being escorted through the door by a guy who didn't look like a big shot. The cut of the guy's suit said security. Sarah was asking questions but once they were out the guy just stared into the distance, let her complete her questions to deaf ears routine.

When the camera guy had what he needed Sarah quit and Sewell strode forward to check the screen replay. The security guy stood his ground like he wasn't interested, though if they'd waved him over he'd have sprinted. But the footage was fine. Sarah waved to him and he raised his hand and went back inside. Sewell flapped his arms carwards and we had a wrap.

I pictured a similar jamboree back at Chase Street after we'd screwed up on something big. The difference was that we didn't have our name on the building, lessening the visual impact. Maybe we could finance a sign for Rook and Lye, get the lawyers' name over the door, just in case. We'd also need a security guy. Maybe Shaughnessy could handle that. He was good at looking mean. And if anyone got past him we had Lucy waiting upstairs. Two minutes with her and the media people would be trampling each other to get back down the stairs.

The TownGate crew packed themselves back into their vehicles and we moved out. The Subaru followed the media people and I followed the Subaru. We made our way to another spot on the far side of town and I parked out of sight and moved closer again, puzzling over this location's connection with the previous shoot. We were outside a secondary school, kids milling on a playground at the end of lunch hour. Sarah stayed outside the railings to deliver her piece to camera, and the fact that she'd not changed clothes suggested we were on the same topic. Whatever the warehouse company was up to they respected no age limits. I'd keep out of their shops for sure.

In other circumstances spending a day watching a media crew might have been educational. But my mind was distracted by my impatience to talk to Sarah and get an idea moving. And by the question of who'd sent the Subaru.

Another hour dragged as the crew milled around and discussed scripts and shots, messed with equipment and smoked some more. Sewell sent Sarah back out for two more pieces. By the time he had what he wanted the school kids had long since disappeared. Then the party broke up. The convoy too. Sarah and the people carrier drove off but Sewell hung back to make a call and the Subaru hung back with him.

Interesting.

The surveillance was for him.

Sewell's call was a long one. Hands free, good arm gesticulating. I walked back to the Frogeye to wait. Ten minutes later he moved, turned and accelerated past me with the Subaru right behind. I gave them a start then followed. We made fast progress. Sewell's one-armed driving wasn't impeding him but I guess he'd not notice his limitations until something unexpected happened. He called by at his house, killed another hour then led us back into Bristol and the Friday rush hour. Traffic lights and pushy vehicles, bicycles and emerging buses. Hard work when you're tailing someone. I was forced closer to the Subaru than I'd have liked but the driver's attention was on Sewell not his rear-view.

Down by the docks Sewell pulled into a metered slot. I wrenched the wheel to get out of sight as the Subaru's reversing lights came on and it backed into its own spot. I hopped out on a side street and went back round. Sewell was gone but the Subaru's big guy, Spike, had climbed out and was disappearing into a narrow cobbled side street that cut towards the river bend. I followed. Half way up the street the guy stopped opposite a trendy bistro bar featuring upper and lower bow windows. Seemed Sewell had gone to earth.

Spike found a spot to wait. I took the proactive approach, angled across the street and followed Sewell into the bistro. If Spike saw me it would mean nothing.

The building interior was a contrast with the olde worlde exterior. Bright lights, pale varnished wood, mirrors, pastel leather. Trendy.

It was just after five. Late afternoon and early evening crowds were mixing. Shoppers and after-work drinkers. Early diners and latte-and-cake groups. No sign of Sewell on the ground floor so I took the stairs up and spotted him. He'd grabbed a table at the bow window. The window tables were tiny, two-seaters, to get the maximum head count in view. Sewell was alone but expecting company. I grabbed a table at the back and looked busy with a menu.

Then I caught movement on the stairs and saw that Spike had gone proactive too.

The guy was over six feet, pushing maybe twenty stone, muscled but not agile. Not built for speed. His face was a gritty kind of handsome, sharp rather than smart, into funny hairdos. He was wearing a grey hooded sweater and white slacks, black and white trainers. He stood for a moment, jittery at having let Sewell out of his sight. If he'd stayed cool he'd have reasoned that Sewell would come back out of the front door sooner or later. But I guess reasoning wasn't one of his strong points. He clocked Sewell and stepped forward and grabbed a table in front of me. Sat facing the window.

I grinned. Keeping tabs on Sewell was going to strain my neck but I couldn't have asked for better cover.

I leaned and watched a waiter take Sewell's drink order. Another waiter came to hover by my table. I'd eaten nothing since the breakfast omelette. A little refreshment appealed but I needed to stay flexible. Ordered a beef and pickle sourdough and bottled water. If I was here for a while they'd see me through. If things ended suddenly I'd cram half the sandwich into my mouth before I left. The waiter moved on to Spike's table. Spike looked at him like he was crazy. Hadn't thought that far ahead. Shook his head. But when the waiter stood his ground he changed his mind and ordered without looking at the menu. During the distraction a smartly dressed fortyish woman came up the stairs and walked past me and across to Sewell's table.

She stood whilst she greeted him. Sewell stayed seated. Said something back to her that must have related to his recent misfortune because he concluded by snatching the shades from his face and glaring up at her. The woman stood back startled for a second then reached to touch his cheek and finally sat down. Sewell pulled the shades back on with the same furious energy.

I was leaning on an elbow to get a view round Spike's back. Spike was watching too. When his beer came he barely acknowledged it. When it registered he lifted it and took a sip. I sipped my own drink and watched.

Sewell and the woman were deep in a conversation that wasn't about the weather or the menu. The woman had a wide, attractive face, the faintest olive tone to her skin, a frame of lush dark hair. A curvy rather than slim figure. I pictured an athlete in a strength sport – javelin, hockey, swimming – someone used to burning energy. She wore an over knee linen skirt, sharp blouse and embroidered jacket that all looked expensive.

Maybe a media contact. Upper management. But the meeting didn't look like business. Sewell's angry display of his damaged face hadn't looked like negotiation. And there was something else between them. As the initial agitation died a hint of warmth came through, a more comfortable conversation. The woman twice reached out to touch Sewell's arm, gave him understanding smiles, and Sewell gradually relaxed. When the woman's drink came she sipped and leaned forward in an intimate posture and Sewell finally sat back, the cool producer guy again.

Spike sipped and slurped in front of me and his pint went down steadily. My sandwich turned up and I paid the bill. The trick is never to get snagged by formalities if you need to leave fast. Throwing down twenties and rushing out might work in the movies but in real life you're going to take the double hit that you get collared as you make your run, which loses you your target, and then when you point out the cash on the table and everyone is friends again you find you've dropped three times what you owed.

Up-front is easier.

Then my phone rang and brought me back.

'No-fee detection agency,' I said.

'Hey Eddie, you still AWOL-ing?'

Lucy. Checking up.

'The case is yet to resolve itself,' I said.

'That sounds bad. Are you taking the weekend?'

'Well, it's Friday evening and I've already got the Monday morning blues. The signs are not good.'

'You should bill the client additional hours.'

'If this is his doing I will. But if he's been involved in something dirty he may end up beyond our bank manager's reach. Unless I can bill him before turning him in.'

'Anything on the Reed guy?'

'Nothing. The guy's a ghost.'

'Bad choice of words, Eddie.'

'Let's hope so. I'm still hoping he'll tell me what this is all about without the help of a ouija board.'

'Are you still looking at Mark Sewell?'

I leaned to maintain my view round Spike.

'I am,' I said.

'Okay. Well my contact got back. Here's the story.'

'Listening.'

'Sewell's going places. Got noticed for his work with Thames – their *Open Cases* show – and now for *Exposed*. He's already signed TownGate up for two follow-on seasons with rumours of up-front retainers in seven figures. He's got a reputation for shaking things up, producing stuff that audiences like. You should watch his shows, Eddie.'

'Next time I mislay my life.'

'You're thinking of breakfast TV. Oprah. Sewell's programmes pack a little more punch.'

'Funny you should say that. The guy got packed a punch himself two days back. Apparently one of his investigation subjects hit back. The guy looks like a walking Picasso. The big question is whether our rising star has got any shady side.'

'Rumours say yes.'

Attagirl!

The detective tugs. The grapevine flexes. Fruit fall.

'What's the word?'

'For a start Sewell's hard to work with. He's got a reputation as a bully and a tantrum kid. Happy to tear up contracts if he falls out with you, whether you're an employee or a client. His approach is to hit the shredder and letting the lawyers glue things back together. And he likes to play hard – playboy lifestyle, manic work habit – all that stuff. Maybe too hard. He's been in both drug and alcohol rehab. Nominally on the wagon but my source says he's up and down. He parties hard, likes the girls and nose candy and can be unpredictable.'

I'd not spotted the partying or drugs but it wasn't hard to picture a particular crowd round that infinity pool. And nothing I'd seen of Sewell conflicted with Lucy's information. Maybe I was watching a guy who was just beginning to show the damage of easy success. The beauty who'd opened Sewell's front door attested too his taste for the girls but was she the only one? That was harder to picture. And did "girls" mean necessarily younger? Could there be something between Sewell and the woman leaning towards him in the bay window?

'Apparently TownGate is solid financially,' Lucy continued, 'but my contact says that Sewell has a reputation for getting through cash. Lives the over-extended lifestyle. Living five years in the future is how she puts it.'

The house and Porsche tied in with that. Sewell's mortgage had to be lifting ten grand a month from his wallet even before he made up the gardener's and pool guy's wage packets. Sarah hadn't mentioned any concerns over her partner but maybe that was discretion. Maybe they just kept things on a professional footing. As long as Sewell was delivering for TownGate they got on.

In summary: Sewell was the arrogant upstart I'd put him down for. Living too near the edge.

The question was whether that lifestyle had opened up a weakness that had been exploited to shut down the Stradivarius investigation. Though simple fear for his life, an aversion to broken bones, might adequately explain that.

And if fear and intimidation had paid a recent call the big guy in front of me fitted right in. Maybe whoever was pushing Sewell back was staying close.

'Okay, Luce. Your info. ties in with what I'm seeing. I'm going to dig a little deeper. Problem is this may be unrelated to Reed and I need know fast whether I'm chasing wild geese.'

'So you're definitely there for the weekend.'

'My plans, what few they were, have been shredded,' I confirmed. 'I'm here until I find what happened to John Reed.'

'Wow, Eddie. All I've got this weekend is a day at Uncle Umberto's and a concert. A do-nothing day Sunday.'

And all I had was the Travelodge and footslog. But that's a P.I.'s life. I thanked Lucy. Killed the line and ate my sourdough, still leaning to keep Sewell and the woman in sight.

Then I leaned back in sharpish. Spike had lifted his menu to cover his face in a nice parody of professional espionage and beyond the menu the two of them were standing. A quick kiss then a parting. I ducked my own head as they crossed the room towards us. Was that a friendly goodbye kiss? Or something deeper?

When they hit the stairs Spike dropped his menu and jumped up to follow them but wasted five seconds in flustered decision-making before throwing a couple of fivers onto the table and following them down.

As I said: up-front is easier.

I quit my table and followed Spike down. Strode fast up the street behind him to where Sewell was climbing into his car alone. The woman had split. As Sewell drove off Spike held back, stood watching until the Subaru rolled alongside him. He climbed in leisurely. No race to catch up.

Shift over.

I was already jogging for the car. Pulled out into the road just in time to see the Subaru turn out of sight. I put my foot down to recover the distance and turned after them. Spotted them a hundred yards ahead. Followed.

Time to watch the watchers.

CHAPTER FIFTEEN
Square one with complications

The trip was short. The Subaru took a few more turns and pulled into a car park on the water where the two guys got out and fed the machine. I chose a slot ten cars away and bypassed the ticket formalities to stay on the guys' heels as they headed off along the street. I walked a parallel route on the car park where trees and vehicles gave me cover. The street was mixed residential and business. No retail till we hit the end, where the two crossed the road and entered an art shop called South West Galleries.

Which was interesting.

Because I knew the name. From Sarah.

I was looking at the auction business run by Pauline Granger, the supposed brains behind the art-theft operation TownGate had been investigating.

So Spike and Baldy were Granger's people.

Suggesting that Granger was staying close to Sewell after the warning-off. It looked like Spike and Baldy were reporting back to her on Sewell's activities, on anyone he was meeting. Making sure he'd stopped talking to parties who might have further secrets to spill.

It was a little after six. The gallery was closed but the street doors were unlocked and the lower and upper floors were lit. I pictured Pauline Granger in there, listening to the duo's report on their day in media production.

The threads were beginning to connect from the TownGate end. All I needed was John Reed to show up and I'd have a wrap.

It's nice to dream.

I spotted a cafe-bar across from the gallery with glass walls that were purpose-made for surveillance. Went in and grabbed a spot. The bar was quarter-full with early-evening socialisers. End of day coffees and wine. Most of the drinkers were clustered on the river side. I settled in by the street and watched the gallery with a double lungo in front of me, cream on the side, a shortbread and ginger biscuit. Paid up-front.

The shortbread was too big for the cup. I snapped it in half and it fitted. I settled in, dunked and sipped, waiting for Spike and Baldy to reappear.

Twenty minutes later they did.

The two came trotting out of the entrance and crossed back to the car park.

I let them go. Waited. Dunked my biscuit.

A while later the gallery's upstairs lights were extinguished. Then the ground floor went dark and ten seconds later a woman came out and locked the doors behind her.

And I sat up sharp.

Because we suddenly had a new turn of events.

The woman locking up was the woman I'd watched an hour ago, socialising with Sewell.

I lifted my camera and zoomed. Took snaps as she turned from the door and walked away. I stayed put. Sipped cold coffee and thought about it.

Then grabbed my phone and searched the web for an image. Checked it out and sat back, grinning out through the window. A waitress turned from the next table and smiled back, misunderstanding. My grin was for the image I'd pulled up. Which was the face of Pauline Granger. A face that matched the one I'd just seen. So that had been Granger hobnobbing with Mark Sewell in the bistro.

The guy who was supposed to be investigating her.

Which gave us a funny little triangle.

Because if Pauline Granger was threatened by TownGate's Stradivarius investigation she was being mighty nice about it, if you discounted the beating Sewell had taken from a party presumed to be close to her – and I couldn't help thinking of Spike and Baldy in that role, delivering a message on her behalf.

Kisses and fists.

Which made no sense.

One or the other might do the job of deterring Sewell but what could both achieve?

When you tug lines they don't always come straight. More often than not the first thing you fish out is a tangle. But you can always smell the pull of a live one and you know that the line will take you where you need to go if you can just get past the knot.

Everything makes sense sooner or later. It's just a matter of viewing things from the right angle. All I had to do was find the angle.

I pictured that brief kiss again and wondered what was going on between Sewell and Pauline Granger. Wondered if it had already been going on when TownGate's Stradivarius investigation pulled Granger's name out of the hat. Had that been a surprise to both of them? Or was their liaison new? Whichever it was, if Sewell and Granger were close then his backing off from the Stradivarius investigation made sense – but it would have made sense without the damage to Sewell's face.

I tussled with the contradiction for a while, worked it and squeezed, prodded and kicked, looked at it from all angles until I finally got the first inkling that I was beginning to see it. That maybe the line was straightening. Maybe I was moving forwards.

Leaving only the question of whether any of this was related to John Reed. This afternoon's entertainment changed nothing related to my main business.

Reed was still missing and I still didn't know why or where.

Square one with complications.

The place most investigations lead.

CHAPTER SIXTEEN

Cold blood and tentacles of fear – that kind of stuff

I freshened up at the Travelodge then walked round and grabbed a pizza and beer at an Italian a few doors up from my breakfast cafe.

I ate slowly, toyed with the idea of an early night then decided that a run out of town would give time for the food to settle. At least it would be dark when I turned in. I checked directions on my phone, paid the bill and went out.

Friday night in a strange city, walking the streets on unpromising business. Couples and groups passing the other way in the early dusk. Oblivious of me. The P.I.'s life can be a lonely one.

But less lonely than you'd like, sometimes.

I was being tailed.

By Sarah's ex bodyguard Gary.

He'd picked me up a little late in the day but maybe he had a nine-to-five job. I hadn't spotted him when I walked up from the hotel but he was there in a discreet spot thirty yards from the restaurant when I came out. I walked back along City Hall with him thirty yards behind, dodging behind arches and statues each time I turned to check.

He was pretty good.

I retrieved the car from the Travelodge and crossed the river with Gary's Cherokee holding fifty yards behind. I stayed below the limit and we rolled along sedately as I worked through the question of who might have put him onto me.

At some point I'd ask him but I didn't need him with me tonight.

As we got to the messy interchange by the football ground I slammed my foot down and jumped a light that was just turning red then flicked the Frogeye onto a side street that ran up between business units. Spotted an opening and pulled into a yard and moved well away from the road. Ten seconds later the Cherokee screamed past. Gary had hesitated at the red, which had been a bad tactic. You either go or you don't. And now that he'd closed the distance his arithmetic was off. A simple calc. should have told him I'd not had time to reach the end of the road up ahead. That I should have been in sight. I rolled back out of the gates and saw his brake lights flare three hundred yards away as reality caught up and he looked for a chance to turn. Five seconds later I was back through the interchange, heading out towards Portishead and Gary was history.

It took me thirty minutes to find the place. I followed old signs and turned down winding lanes through fields and woods and reached a chained gate in high walls. According to John Reed's urbexing pal the derelict complex beyond the gate was the last known stop on Reed's trip to the Twilight Zone.

The Perseverance Hospital.

The place had been built as a psychiatric hospital back in 1904, thirty acres of grounds within a ten foot brick wall, housing the main hospital and a scatter of outbuildings along the driveway. I hopped out and squinted through the gate at the decay illuminated by the dying sun. The gate's chain and locks were intact and a warning sign up top threatened prosecutions for intruders but a pedestrian access gate alongside the main ironwork was patched with plywood sheets that yielded to a push. I shouldered my way through and walked up the driveway.

First impression of the urbexers' haunted hospital was a let-down. The weed-strangled avenue was lined with leaning street lamps and knee-high grass surrounding boarded-up brick cottages that looked about as haunted as a council estate. According to my information the cottages had been respite residents' accommodation in the facility's final days as an R&R hospice. When they shut their doors for good they left everything to rot: refuse sacks and traffic cones, an old window frame, a rusted bicycle propped against a door, tipped-over wheelie bins everywhere. Abandoned but never cleared.

The driveway curved round the cottages and gave me a sight of the hospital itself. I walked up and stood on a derelict parking area dotted with weeds and shrubs, refuse and rubble, and looked at main building.

Which was the real thing.

The urbexer's dream.

If you wanted haunted this was it.

The core of the old hospital was a two hundred foot brick building, three storeys high. Ground- and first floor boarded-up. Up above them a line of rotting dormers jutting from a mould-blackened mansard roof. The upper brickwork gleamed red in the setting sun. Half of the dormer sashes were open, most of the glass panes smashed.

Like a row of rotting teeth.

The building was the size of a country mansion but its low entrance porch and mean-proportioned regimented windows had a utilitarian starkness that must have scared new arrivals to death. The nineties developer that Reed's pal had mentioned must have had quite a vision when he saw his luxury apartments. But then he'd gone bust, which probably meant something.

The entrance porch was barred by institutional double doors in solid wood that blocked the way in but didn't stop a dank chill seeping out when I stood close. I walked along the building, dodging rubble and litter, and found a ramp into an annex at the far end. The entrance was blocked by another institutional door but this one moved when I pushed. Its lower hinges had gone and by grabbing and lifting I could ease it back, dragging on the concrete, until I had a gap.

I pushed through and stepped inside.

My tac. light illuminated a shattered hallway littered with fallen plaster. I walked in. Graffiti danced around me. Doors hung open onto dark rooms. Shadows jumped. I went deeper and turned through a short connecting link into the main building. Walked a corridor back to the central reception area behind the main doors. Swept the walls with my tac. More shadows darted. Dank mould permeated my nostrils as chill fingers slid under my tee-shirt. And so on. All that spooky stuff. There if you looked for it. All it really added up to was the grim carcass of an abandoned building, devoid of any sense of its previous life.

Though if Reed had reached here two weeks ago the spooky stuff would work.

I climbed the main stairs towards the top floor and a reflected light. The air improved with altitude but the red illumination up top brought the sordid wreckage into a dismal focus. I was on a corridor running the length of the building, littered with debris and illuminated from the open doorways either side. A row of tiny rooms ran out under the dormers. Maybe patients' individual bedrooms. I went into one and crossed to the window, watching for bad spots in the floor. Stood on a tiled area to look out. Early summer greenery proliferated, hued by the reddening sun. The hiss of a faint breeze. Birdsong. Life continuing.

I watched a while, kicked at a couple of metal fittings on the tiles and decided I'd had enough exploring. Perhaps this was the end of John Reed's trail or perhaps he'd never been here. Perhaps I was trespassing. I headed back down and exited through the same annex. The warmth outside was welcome.

A final spark of interest took me on a tour round the back of the complex. The main building looked pretty much the same from this side, just more depressing with the mess of annexes and cast-out junk. I walked paved pathways through a wrecked garden and came to another driveway. This one ran out to a rotting double gate hanging askew under a brick archway in the rear walls. The old tradesman's entrance. I squeezed between the gate and brickwork and came out into an old access lane.

And found John Reed's van.

I stopped dead. Looked at it.

The van was parked close to the wall behind a burst of shrubs and weed. The perfect discrete spot if you were here for a little illegal wandering about. The vehicle had no side markings but the ladders up top and the registration both confirmed it was Reed's.

The vehicle sat there, silent and dark. It might have been newly parked or might have been here two weeks.

I walked over. The rear doors were locked. I tried the driver's door. Unlocked. I hefted myself up into the seat and flicked on the courtesy light. Fished in the glove compartment and all the hidey holes for keys but found none. I dropped back out and checked the wheel arches. Felt the ground behind the tyres. Nothing. Reed had taken the keys with him.

I'd come here for a quick reconnoitre, a sense of the place Reed might have visited before he disappeared two weeks ago. And now the van confirmed that he'd been here, probably that night.

And hadn't driven away.

I pushed back into the hospital grounds and strode across the complex and down the drive to the main gate. Retrieved the Frogeye and navigated a tiny lane round the walls to park behind Reed's van. Pulled a tool from the boot and got the van's rear doors open. Lit the interior with my tac.

Empty.

I closed the van back up and stood a moment, thinking about it.

Only one conclusion.

I went back through the rotting gate.

When I walked into the annex this time something new tingled along my spine. Cold blood. Tentacles of fear. The spooky stuff was flowing nicely now that I knew Reed had been here and might not have left.

P.I.s are familiar with unsavoury places and in my old job in the Met I could always sense when the most mundane house or apartment or church hall was hiding something. Sometimes you could smell it, even before the doors were opened. I'd sensed nothing on my quick walk through the Perseverance Hospital beyond its own natural miasma but there was no way John Reed's van should have been out there.

It took me an hour this time. I started at the top, using the last light from the upper windows. Walked endless rooms and spaces. Missing roof tiles had dropped water and bird shit onto the floorboards, and the woodwork felt ready to give. I trod carefully. Found nothing. Went down. The floor below was a little more weatherproof but the boarded-over windows wrapped a cloying black atmosphere around me. My torch cast shadows across room after room, wards, living spaces, sordid bathrooms with smashed sinks and lavatories, torn pipework. A myriad of tiny rooms in the back annexes with remnants of furniture, smashed lamps, metal desks, one computer keyboard lying on the floor. I walked a corridor of cells with iron beds and hefty doors, maybe confinement rooms. Others with nothing, just bare spaces. I guess the padding had been torn out.

But no sign that Reed had ever been there.

If something had happened to him in this place the signs should have been easy to spot. The wrecked empty rooms had no hiding places. My problem was the size of the hospital: a hundred rooms scattered through a maze of annexes takes time in the pitch black with each step threatening to drop you through the floor.

The basement was impressive when I got there. A real torchlight tour. I trod rubble, walked in and out of rooms that were beyond grim: wrecked equipment lying around, tables with obscure apparatus that had your imagination working overtime. I found the old boiler room. Pulled open the boiler's rusty door and illuminated decades-old ashes and dust motes inside. Closed it up. Walked on through mean corridors of blighted plasterwork. Storage rooms and a couple of offices with fallen cabinets and smashed light fittings, pools of water where damaged half-windows had leaked in. Old crates, mounds of sacking.

The room that topped it all looked like some kind of operating theatre or morgue. A stainless table, smashed lights and fittings, a few surviving implements to keep the imagination fired. Shadows jumped and raced. I was keeping my eyes on the floor by now: I'd spotted needles in two of the upstairs rooms. But the basement turned out to be clear. I guess you wouldn't come down here no matter what you were on.

And no sign of Reed.

I climbed back to the main floor, resisting the urge to look over my shoulder. Stood a moment.

I couldn't be sure that I'd seen every room. The place was too large. But I'd toured ninety-nine percent and there hadn't been a hint.

The building was empty.

But Reed hadn't driven away from here. Which left the grounds and the cottages and a heavy weekend up ahead.

One last check: the annex on the far end of the main building. If I could find an open door there I'd be closer to the rear gates. I went through, walked a corridor of sloping tiles and caught the reflection of my light on the boarded glass of an exit door. I was in a little reception area which I guessed was the tradesman's entrance. If the door opened I'd be out.

I stepped forward and my feet caught something.

I squatted and lifted a smartphone.

Its screen had been stamped through with sufficient violence to destroy it, bend and break the circuit boards inside.

It could have been anyone's but who drops a phone and smashes it to pieces? If you drop your phone you check it for life, maybe take it for repair. I stood and angled my tac., looking for anything else. Saw that the plaster and rubble by the door had been disturbed, raked by some kind of scuffle. Some darker patches spotting it. I went over and squatted again. The close-up view confirmed I was looking at the dried residue of blood. Then I saw something else. Reached to retrieve a ring of vehicle keys half hidden behind a length of metal ducting dropped against the wall. The ring had a fob and the fob had a Toyota logo.

I was holding Reed's van keys.

I went to check back along the corridor but found no signs of disturbance. The scuffle had happened right there by the exit door. I walked back and checked the tiny office behind the reception window. Empty. Just a mess of fallen plaster and a boarded window. Graffiti on the wall. Then I caught a glint of light in the far corner and went across and found a camera, resting where it had been kicked. I picked it up. Scuffed from the kick but not destroyed. If this was Reed's, and if he'd been ambushed here, which was my guess, then his assailants had got sloppy. Cameras hold evidence.

The camera still had power. I lit the screen and scanned the images. Fifty or so snaps taken in here, views I'd just seen for myself but better lit and more depressing. Documenting John Reed's trip through the blighted hospital. None of the pics showed bad guys coming for him. The last one was of the sloping corridor down to this exit, a parting shot back into the bowels of the hospital, bright graffitied walls fading to distant shadow.

Reed had taken the snap, turned to walk out, and been jumped.

His assailants probably checked the camera and saw what I saw: nothing of interest. So they'd just tossed it. But you never know. I pocketed it.

I went across to the exit door and pulled the handle. The door dragged but was movable. The way out.

Easy to see how it happened. Probably two guys, surprising Reed as he appeared from the corridor. Stepping in before he could react, knocking him down with a rapid violence that drew blood. Phone, camera and keys grabbed and checked. Smashed and scattered. Then Reed hustled out.

I exited. Walked back to the Frogeye and stood in the darkness behind Reed's van, looking back through the broken gate.

I had an answer to my first question about Reed: his disappearance hadn't been voluntary.

And I had the where and when: here, on the Friday night, the day after I'd handed his details to Bernard Locke.

Which meant that whatever happened in that annex was a consequence of me finding him.

The question was why did it happen?

Reed's threats to Sarah might still link him to TownGate and even the Stradivarius theft but in that case why would he disappear? And if he wasn't part of the Stradivarius affair why was he menacing Sarah? Just a personal thing? Whatever explanation, Reed was still coming up on radar as one of the bad guys. So what happened here? Did he meet some badder ones?

The only certainty was that I was stuck with this thing until I dug out the answers.

CHAPTER SEVENTEEN
Bad party

I started the weekend at seven a.m. with circuits of the hilly park behind the hotel. Pain as therapy: helped shake off the effects of a night's sleep disturbed by a subconscious sense of losing control. Investigations frequently lead to diversions that have little to do with the original job. It's what you expect. And as long as the client keeps paying you keep hacking through the jungle until the view becomes clear. The difference this time was that I no longer had a client and didn't know what I was looking for. What I had was the sweepings-up after a bad party. No advantage to be gained beyond the hope of clearing my conscience over whatever had happened to John Reed.

Sometimes the only way to fight stress is with the physical. Give the psyche something real to worry about.

The park circuits were barely half a mile round but the climb to the tower on each lap gave my calves and cardio a much needed seeing-to. I set myself a target of thirty laps, lost count around twenty-eight as the sweat soaked my headband, and ran a final two circuits on empty before slogging back to the top to call it quits.

I cooled down for ten minutes then jogged down to the street

Traffic was building. Shop blinds going up. Refuse collectors jogged behind their wagons and threw smirks. Buses roared up the hill and threw diesel fumes.

I escaped asphyxiation by diving into my breakfast cafe.

The girl was all smiles. I was a regular. Recognisable even in the Rambo gear. No need to talk up the coffee order. It came thick and black with cream on the side. I sat and sipped whilst my scrambled eggs cooked in the back. Pulled off my headband to stop the funny looks. Resisted the urge to wring it out onto the floor. I hadn't the strength.

I made a call.

Sarah Locke picked up.

'Eddie. Still in town?'

'Yeah. We need to talk.'

I had a plan and I needed Sarah to kick-start it. A drive across the

Gorge, a chinwag in the sun on her garden terrace and all would be explained. Sarah gave me an alternative picture: told me she was on her way to the office. We could meet at TownGate. Which was more convenient if less picturesque. We agreed to meet in an hour.

I ate my breakfast and jogged back for a shower, then drove across the river to the TownGate building. My rear-view stayed clear. No Cherokee following. I guess bodyguard Gary got weekends off.

I pulled into the TownGate yard and walked round and Sarah came down to open the outer door. She looked good in blue jeans and white shirt. The jeans matched the blue of her eyes and her eyes made you smile. She took me up and offered coffee. I said I was fine.

She sat us both down. 'You must be pissed off as hell,' she said.

I raised my eyebrows.

'Stuck over here. Cleaning up whatever it is.'

I relaxed. Grinned.

'I didn't have much on,' I told her.

'Really? I don't see a London P.I. spending his weekends watching TV.'

I didn't disagree.

'I bet you know all the places. All the characters. See a different London from the rest of us.'

I shrugged.

'I see strata,' I said. 'What lies beneath. People exist on their own level and think the ground's solid under their feet. I see reality. The characters down below, mining for gold. Undercutting. Destroying. And sometimes a P.I.'s line of work brings him up against those characters. So yeah, we see things differently. But mostly we serve notices and watch straying spouses and post out invoices.'

'You were a Met detective. I bet you lost a few weekends there.'

Most of them. One of the perks of shifting to the private sector was that I was down to thirty percent. Of which the current weekend was the worst kind: unpaid and not likely to end well.

'The P.I.'s life will always seem glamorous to most people,' Sarah said. 'The danger. The intrigue. Everything that no-one wants but everything that fascinates them.'

I didn't disagree. Held the grin. Everything that no-one wants. I'd talk to Harry. Get that onto our cards. A business needs a slogan.

'Mostly,' I said, 'it's just boredom, which you get used to, and futility, which you don't. If I want the glamorous side I go to the movies.'

Sarah laughed.

'I'm not buying the boredom. I followed what happened last year. It's not boring stuff that gets you into the news.'

Which is why investigators value peace and quiet. The tranquillity of a midnight street, falling rain. No-one interested in who you are or why you're there. The person who should be interested blissfully unaware.

'And,' Sarah said, back to her point, 'I really don't picture you taking quiet weekends.'

'I walk my dog. Paint a little. In summer I play cricket. Which is where I should have been today.'

She gave me surprised.

'Painting and cricket? You're spoiling my fantasy of the action hero, Eddie. My image of a P.I. never included artists' palettes and cricket flannels.'

I laughed and she settled back in her chair, pleased that she'd pushed me back.

She was smart but she wasn't familiar with league cricket. Had never faced a googly coming in with nearly half the energy of a 9mm bullet and with the drawback that you're expected to face fifty of them and still walk off smiling.

'And the P.I. gets the ladies,' she said. 'Good girls and bad girls. I bet they all chase you. On those "quiet" weekends.'

'Most ladies I meet are chasing someone else's husband. And they're not usually too pleased to see me.'

She laughed. 'I'll bet. Personally, I love London. If I'd not set up roots here that's where I'd be.'

'I you ever relocate you can come and watch me chase the bad guys. You'll see it's not as exciting as you think.'

'So what's your plan for this weekend? Since you're here to tell me.'

'My plan is to find John Reed.'

'You're really determined to get to him?'

'I've no choice. If something's happened as a consequence of me finding him then I'm not happy with that.'

I didn't mention the evidence I'd collected last night which said that something *had* happened. And that the something wasn't good.

'I spoke to my father. He's as puzzled as you are but he assured me he's done nothing. He hasn't approached Reed. His only plan was to keep an eye on him.'

'Do you believe him?'

Delicacy. Another skill P.I.s value.

The question brought a flicker to her face. Her smile became less natural. She sat forward again.

'Of course. Dad's over-protective of me but he doesn't take the law into his own hands. It's not his way. And he's not about to wreck his career by doing something stupid.'

'It's just that funny coincidence of timing,' I said. 'Hard to ignore.'

'So you said. And I agree. But maybe that's all it is: coincidence. Maybe Reed will just turn up again.'

I changed subjects.

'I've got news about your Stradivarius problem,' I told her.

'Related to John Reed?'

'My guess is no, but I'm checking all avenues. It would be good to understand the Stradivarius theft so I can put it aside. And maybe help you in the process.'

'What have you found out?'

'It's not good news,' I said.

I told her about Sewell. His connection to Pauline Granger. How the connection was maybe a part of his reason for shutting down the Stradivarius investigation, alongside the damage to his property and face. And how that damage itself might have come from Granger, which left a nice puzzle.

As she heard the news the good mood dropped from Sarah's face. Nice puzzle or not, what I'd just told her was that her partner was conspiring against her and TownGate. That news wasn't just bad, it was catastrophic. What it said was that her business partnership, the production company she was nurturing with Sewell, was headed for the rocks. Her face dropped further as she took it in. No more chit-chat about London and cricket and the ladies. Sarah Locke's weekend was now as wrecked as mine.

She was quiet for a moment, unsure how to proceed. Realised that the news I'd brought meant that getting to the bottom of the Stradivarius thing was as urgent for her as it was for me.

And that co-operation was in order.

'We need to stir the nest,' I said. 'Get people diving for cover, talking when they should be keeping quiet. I want to watch and see where things lead. My guess is that whoever commissioned Pauline Granger to steal the Stradivariuses is the main party trying to shut down the TownGate investigation. It's someone bigger than her. Someone with more to lose. Someone who's not prepared to lose. If I can get to them we'll maybe see the whole thing, including how your partner fits in. And whether it has anything to do with John Reed.'

Sarah nodded.

'What do you want me to do?' she said.

I told her.

CHAPTER EIGHTEEN
I think he swallowed it

I drove back to the cafe-bar opposite Pauline Granger's business and grabbed table by the plate glass window. The bar was busy with weekend customers but they'd opted for the view of the water, same as yesterday. I sat alone with my coffee and shortbread. The biscuit was still too big for the cup but the previous technique still worked. I snapped it, dunked it, swigged coffee. Across the road people were in and out of Granger's gallery.

I pulled out John Reed's camera and checked the Perseverance Hospital pics again, keeping half an eye on the gallery. But the screen zoom didn't support forensic inspection and the images told me nothing new. Just Reed's grim record of the hospital. No chance snaps of kidnappers faces through a window or assassins lurking in the shadows. I flicked back to earlier dates but none of Reed's photographs featured people. No faces or figures or vehicles. Just wrecked interiors, the record of Reed's weird hobby. Right before the Perseverance was the set of snaps from the house whose wall I'd watched Reed and his pal climb over. No shots of said pal. And no shots of a Frogeye parked down the lane, a shadowy guy watching. Then the battery died and Reed's photographs were extinguished.

Photography.

One of the facets of the urbex hobby.

And a guy who snapped old interiors probably spent time at his computer, selecting and enhancing, polishing his Photoshop skills. Which were handy when you wanted to send a TV celeb. a scary composite: her, you, the blade.

Prowling round derelict properties honed other skills too that might help you get close to your target, see how they lived.

But if Reed had been harassing Sarah on behalf of Granger or one of her clients then his services had for some reason been terminated.

It was hard to see a scenario that fitted the facts but the one near-certainty was that Reed was out of the picture. Permanently. Whether he'd been taken out by someone he was working for – maybe related to TownGate or Granger – or by pals of Locke or by someone else wasn't guessable. And if his disappearance was nothing to do with Pauline Granger or the Stradivarius affair then my weekend was progressing down a road to nowhere.

My phone rang. I slipped the camera back into my pocket. Picked up.

'I think he swallowed it.'

Sarah. Reporting on the opening broadside of my scheme.

'He tried to sound cool at first,' she said. 'Sceptical. But he kept asking questions and got damn angry when I led him on.'

Sewell. Hearing our concocted story, which was that Sarah was continuing the Stradivarius investigation without him and had made progress, had a contact who was about to give her the name of the buyer.

Sewell had said no way, they were out, demanded explanations and answers, but she'd refused to discuss the affair until he agreed to come back into the investigation, which they both knew was not on the cards. Then she applied pressure: by Monday she'd be talking to her contact. She'd know who the Stradivarius buyer was. And the investigation would be moving ahead with or without him.

That was the point where Sewell lost his cool. She'd hung up on the sound of panic.

Maybe panic sufficient to sent him running to whoever had pushed him off the TownGate investigation, which my bet said was Pauline Granger.

'Are you watching him?' Sarah asked.

'I'm outside the gallery. He'll either show up or call. But it's Granger's reaction I want to see.'

A pause. Then:

'Okay. Good luck. Let me know what happens.'

I said I would. Went back to watching the gallery.

For twenty minutes.

Which was the time it took for my crystal ball work to come good.

My peripheral vision clocked a figure crossing the street from the parking area with the stiff gait of someone whose muscles are aching and the sour look of someone whose face was giving him hell under his wrap round shades.

Mark Sewell.

He reached the gallery and stopped at the door. Looked round to make sure no-one was watching. Then went in.

I sat back. Lifted my coffee cup.

Sewell had decided that his news warranted a face-to-face confab.

Which meant I was on the right track.

I'd known it.

Sewell was in the building for half an hour. Plenty of time for a heated discussion and for temperatures to rise. When he came out the visible part of his face was even more colourful than when he'd gone in, though he checked the street just as carefully before scarpering.

I waited.

It took eight minutes.

Then Pauline Granger was out and hurrying across the street.

Go!

I abandoned my table and jogged round to the car park to fire up the car. Was rolling as Granger backed an E-Class coupe from her spot and pulled out onto the street. I followed. Stayed two cars back in the morning traffic as we drove out of the city towards the M5. Free of traffic she accelerated onto the motorway and drove north at a steady eighty-five. Seemed Granger was heading for her own face-to-face. I turned my phones up and matched her pace, two hundred yards behind.

We drove for thirty minutes. Passed all the legal traffic. Put Gloucester behind us then Cheltenham. Finally came off the motorway at the Worcester junction. Granger slowed and stayed just on the limit as we drove towards the centre. Then she turned with the one-way system away from the river bridge and swung into a car park. I pulled into a separate area across the road and walked out after her, back towards the bridge. I was on familiar territory: right across the river was the cricket ground where I'd watched Yorkshire open last season with a one-sided thrashing of Worcestershire. It was the only match I'd got to see last year and I'd drawn lucky: tickets for the rest of the season bought you a ringside view of the Titanic going down as Yorkshire plunged for the bottom. I was probably the only Yorkshireman with a good memory of the summer. And sixth sense said I was about to get lucky again as Granger dodged traffic and walked out onto the bridge to talk to a guy in a suit who was leaning on the parapet, mid span. Late fifties, angular face, short dark hair. I pulled up my telephoto and brought him closer, grabbed snaps as they chatted. Pauline was six inches shorter so she spoke with her head tilted back whilst the guy watched the river, arms on the stonework. He spoke calmly. Asked questions. But didn't look happy. Finally he stood up and turned to Granger to emphasise instructions. Emphasised a warning with a finger and walked away across the river.

Pauline turned and came back my way. I didn't wait. Sprinted for the car and cut round the one-way system at speed. By the time I hit the bridge the guy had vanished. Which wasn't a problem since the only place he could have gone was the cricket club. I swung into the half-empty car park in time to see him climb into a Bentley Continental.

I turned and waited near the exit, let him get out onto the main road then followed, two cars back.

We drove west out of the city towards the Welsh border. I eyed the Frogeye's fuel. If the Bentley continued for more than thirty miles I'd lose him. And bodyguard Gary's Cherokee still hadn't appeared in my rear-view, so no chance of a lift.

The Bentley continued sedately, ate up twenty of my budget, putting my gauge on fumes. Then it slowed and turned down a country lane and pulled in between the imposing brick gateposts of a country estate. I rolled past and found a parking spot then walked back. The property's wrought iron gates were latched open and there was no obvious sign of cameras or security. I accepted the invitation and walked in. Hiked up through a copse onto open parkland and stopped to whistle. The Bentley should have told me: the house across the park was up there in billionaire territory.

Pauline Granger's contact was either a loaded guy or a loaded guy's butler.

But you don't send your butler out for urgent face-to-faces concerning high-stakes thievery.

I raised my camera and grabbed a few pictures of the house. Then brought the bridge pictures back up.

Wondered if the guy who'd scuttled out from this house was at the centre of the Bardi Stradivariuses theft. Because whoever was in the market for high-value art was going to live some place like this. Someone accustomed to paying millions to sate his collector's bent.

And maybe when what he wanted was not for sale he called Pauline Granger.

Was this her Stradivarius client? Was the TownGate pushback coming from here? Did the order to slap Mark Sewell around come from the suited guy? I didn't see Spike and Baldy polishing the silverware in the house across the park but maybe when the suited guy needed things done they were his people.

I switched off the camera and walked back. Sat in the car to transfer a couple of pics to my phone and fire off an email. Then drove back to the main road in search of a filling station.

CHAPTER NINETEEN
I wasn't expecting guests

Back at the Travelodge I regained my tail. Bodyguard Gary, covert operative, was standing out of sight behind a glass bus shelter across from the hotel. He'd probably been there all day. I shook my head. Went in. Showered and lay on the bed to contemplate options. Italian or Thai? After ten minutes I came to the conclusion that either would suit and planted my feet back on the floor to check my phone. Found I'd missed a call. Hit call-back.

'Eddie, you should pay me overtime.'

'No can do, Luce. You handle the wages. It wouldn't get authorised.'

'You're lucky I'm trustworthy.'

'And tight fisted.'

'I try to be responsible. You know how things are.'

How things were was that things were ticking nicely. Costs were covered. Wages paid. Christmas bonuses accruing. But in the investigation business ticking along is just one bad cheque away from going short. But Lucy wasn't the only one working pro bono today. More importantly, she wasn't the one sitting in a Travelodge.

'Your contacts came through?' I asked.

'You should pay me double.'

'Twice zero we can afford. What have you got?'

'Well first of all that's no two-up-two-down in your snap. The picture you sent me is Wallingbury Park at Ludlow. I spoke to Philippa and she put me on to a friend, Tabitha, who's the editor or a social rag over in Shrewsbury. And *she* told me that the guy in the suit is Marcus Richmond. Lord Richmond. Inherited Wallingbury in the eighties along with family business interests that trace back to the East India Company and later to cotton and slaves. The guy is currently active in the stock markets and commercial banking. Current worth around two billion. You're weekending with the jet set, Eddie.'

I grinned. Glanced round my Travelodge room. Sterile and spatially challenged. I didn't see Richmond turning up for canapés.

The nearest I'd get to weekending with Richmond's class would be if I bought a copy of the society mag.

'Any hint of dodgy stuff? Scandals? Suspicions?'

'None that Tabitha knows of. She comes across all kinds of funny stuff on her social rounds but her access is always limited. What goes on in the stratosphere stays in the stratosphere. Richmond's world is out of reach beyond any crumbs he scatters. But Tabitha had one interesting crumb.'

'Let me guess: he's a virtuoso violinist. Plays Stradivariuses.'

'Way off. Tabitha has never had a whisper of any family talent except for making money from money. But Richmond does have an interest in the arts, music in particular. When he entertains he's in the habit of splashing out on a chamber orchestra to play in his grand gallery. Local DJs don't get a look in. And he's enough artwork on his walls to refurbish the Tate.'

'A collector. Doesn't mean he's pinching violins, of course. I love Ellington but I don't nick pianos.'

'Sure, Eddie. But you said it yourself: there are things money can't buy. And it's gonna be the billionaire class who hit that ceiling. The Bardi Stradivariuses would fit.'

'And we've got Richmond hobnobbing with a known art thief. So maybe he is a frustrated collector. Are musical artefacts part of his thing?'

'That's where it gets interesting. Tabitha described a music room at Wallingbury House that she says is jaw-dropping. She's been in there a few times – Richmond wants his face in her magazine the same as most of the upper class. Tabitha has never picked up any hint of impropriety when she's been there but she did tell me one interesting thing...'

I walked to the window. Checked the street. Gary was doing some kind of callisthenics across the way. Limbering up. The sight of me had energised him. Lucy told me her interesting thing:

'Richmond has a castle near Innsbruck.'

'An actual castle?'

'The real thing, Eddie. Decked with enough towers and battlements to have Ludwig yelling for extensions. Rumour says the property set Richmond back a couple of hundred mill.'

'Sounds like an impressive holiday home. But that's a nice area.'

'Must be. He spends three to four months of the year there. And according to Tabitha the castle is reputed to be a treasure palace. Richmond's grandfather built up an art collection at the family's Swiss chateau that was rumoured to have drawn on stolen artworks never recovered after the war. Apparently the old guy raced round Europe in forty-six and -seven with a sackful of cash. When Richmond inherited the chateau he sold it and moved the artworks to Innsbruck to form the basis of his main collection. And Tabitha says the story is credible: the castle has never featured in any society mags out there. No access permitted. Family and trusted friends only. And even if there was only the wartime loot in there it would mean that Richmond was sitting on a hoard of dubious provenance.'

'Got it. I wonder if there's a music room over there?'

'Bet on it, Eddie.'

I was.

'Problem is,' I said, 'I'd be pushed to get to Austria this weekend even if I had my grappling hooks. And I doubt whether Mark Sewell's contacts who tipped him off about the Strad theft were phoning from abroad. My guess is that Sewell was talking to someone closer to home. Maybe the Wallingbury estate. People who know Granger.'

'You think the Stradivariuses might be stashed there?'

'If Richmond is the client Wallingbury could be a staging post.' I thought about it some more. 'What's Harry doing this weekend?'

'Same old, I guess.'

'Okay. That's him in. So all I need now is someone who's good at distraction...'

'I'm stocktaking tomorrow, Eddie. Promised my uncle.'

'*You?* Okaaaay! Great idea.'

'Stocktaking, Eddie.'

'Luce, how interesting can that be? Don't you ever yearn to see how the other half lives?'

'I read the mags. I see how they live.'

'It's not the same. You have to walk the walk. Sink into those carpets.'

'If I know anything it's more likely we'll be running the run.'

'Probably. But it would be worth it. Don't tell me you wouldn't like to see the inside of a country house that's not roped off by the

National Trust.'

'Course I would. You know me, Eddie.'

I did.

'So let's stocktake next weekend. It can't take you long. It's all big expensive stuff. Easy count.'

Lucy hesitated.

'Attagirl! Call Harry! He'll be glad of the trip.'

Lucy started to say something but the line cut out.

I watched the street. Thought how we'd work it. If Richmond was the end of the Stradivarius trail we needed to confirm it. And if the affair was unrelated to John Reed I needed to move in a new direction.

Maybe food would bring ideas.

There was a knock at the door.

I wasn't expecting guests. And Gary was still across the street.

Okay.

I turned away from the window and walked across. Recognised the perfume even before I got the door open. Then the flash of blonde hair and a wide smile in the corridor gloom.

Sarah Locke.

'Surprise!' she said. 'I thought I'd probably missed you. Have you eaten?'

I told her I hadn't.

Her smile brightened.

'Neither have I. Funny old world.'

She was wearing a short denim dress and jacket, brown leather ankle boots. The outfit made her look younger and taller and all kinds of other things. You could see why Sarah Locke had a fan base.

I realised I was staring. Stepped back.

She came in and I grabbed my stuff whilst she looked round and took in the life of the private investigator. Tiny hotel room. Travel bag open on the chair. Dent in the bed. Her smile was steady when she'd checked the place out, unfazed but probably not impressed. But if she'd seen some of the places we crashed, some of the spots in which we holed up to catch a sight of funny goings on, she'd say the room was the Ritz.

Getting ready took five seconds. Lift jacket, check keys and wallet.

Escort lady out.

I asked the lady about her taste in food and we headed back to the Greek on the docks. Too late to get a view: all they had was a table in the back. But the view didn't matter. We ordered. Gyros for me, king prawns on a green salad for her. Tzatziki and beer to start.

'I hope I'm not intruding,' Sarah said. 'I thought you'd appreciate company. Having sacrificed your weekend.'

'No intrusion noted,' I said. 'And company appreciated. Even if it's beyond the call of duty.'

'Not entirely. I appreciate the fact that you were looking out for me when my father hired you, even if I didn't share his concerns. And I appreciate that you've got yourself stuck with a situation because of it.'

I sipped beer. Scooped tzatziki with a chunk of bread.

'The problem is,' I said, 'that I might have helped create the situation.'

I still didn't mention my discovery at the old hospital, which pushed the odds to near certainty that *something* had happened to the guy. Opted for discretion. If Reed had been snatched as a consequence of me finding him then that put Sarah's father in the spotlight as the guy who'd set things up, and that meant that I might need to be careful. I wasn't ready to turn the spotlight on Sarah yet but I'd been watching her face since I opened the hotel room door. So far I'd seen nothing except friendliness, happiness to be here, appreciation of tzatziki. But it didn't take her long to switch to the main subject.

'Did our ruse work?'

'Yeah.'

I described her partner's flying visit to South West Galleries and Pauline Granger's consequent sprint up the M5 to talk to Richmond. Sarah's eyebrows lifted, poised for the conclusion.

'We may have your Stradivarius buyer,' I said.

She gripped her bread. Stared open-mouthed.

'Marcus Richmond! My god, this is getting big.'

'Big as it gets. We still need to confirm that Richmond *is* the client but the signs point that way. I think you're looking at a juicy catch for your show. A firecracker.'

'And Mark knows it but he's thrown it away to play some kind of game. What's going on between him and Granger? And why would her people be attacking him?'

'Beats me. But your partner is putting something or somebody before you and TownGate. So you'll need to watch him if you take this forward. But you've got Pauline Granger and her steal-to-order operation and now Marcus Richmond is looking good as her client for the Strad theft. You'll just need the fine detail.'

Sarah scooped Tzatziki. Took a bite.

'We'll get the detail,' she said. 'But if Mark has thrown this away then TownGate is over as a joint enterprise. I don't need a dirty partner no matter how good he is.'

'Hard to see an innocent side to his activities. Though something's off. That was real damage to his property and face. Points towards coercion. But then why is he so cosy with Granger? Worst case: her involvement says he's been bought out. And with big cash to make the damage to TownGate worthwhile, but these people have big cash. If Granger was exposed we'd be talking about damage to her business maybe in the tens of millions. A million or so payoff wouldn't be a bad investment to get the door slammed shut.'

Sarah shook her head. Her eyes closed briefly. When she looked up she'd lost any trace of cheerfulness.

'Mark's betraying me whatever the motivation,' she said.

'No other way to see it.'

Things glummed down for a while then Sarah tried to pull herself out of it. Changed subject. Dug for snippets on how private investigators operated.

Most of the snippets related to investigation work are as interesting as an accountant's diary. Half the action involves moving paper from one side of the desk to the other, and half the danger – for our own firm at least – comes from our landlord and utilities companies chasing their pounds of flesh. But Sarah kept prodding and when our mains arrived I entertained her with a few embellished stories. They seemed to interest her.

'Moving into private investigation was a risky step,' Sarah concluded, 'after the security and formality of the Metropolitan Police.'

'There never was security. Though there was plenty of formality. Losing the red tape was a major plus.'

'I guess you lost the rules too.'

'I'd say we bend them, sometimes, so we can go where the policeman fears to tread.'

'But you lose that protection when you're up against the bad guys. There's no organisation to back you up, no team looking out for you on the street.'

I grinned. Swigged beer. Planted my glass.

'The only protection I ever needed was against the organisation. The street was the safe place. And I've got the best team in the world behind me.'

'You needed protection against the Met?'

'I'd a tendency towards the unconventional, which didn't sit well with the Kremlin. Nor with me, sometimes: I always had to watch that I wasn't putting my own people at risk, career wise. I never asked them to do anything I wouldn't but that was hardly a recommendation.'

'I remember the media tagging you last year as an ex high-flyer. Your approach couldn't have been too objectionable.'

'My solve rate got me promotions, got my name on the sheet as SIO in a few cases even though I was a mere inspector, but my methods were always going to catch up with me. Maybe I could have made one more step but that would have been it. Any higher and I'd be hands-off, directing teams, and you can't direct teams to break the rules. You can't take "do-as-I-do" up the ladder. I was always going to hit the ceiling. In the end I didn't get the chance. The thing fell on me.'

'I heard politics pushed you out.'

'You heard right.'

Not that it mattered after eight years. I'd found a good place and I was fine. And nowadays the only time I worried about ceilings was when the damp patches leaked over my office.

'Out of the Met but still chasing the bad guys. Must be in your blood.'

'Most of the people I chase aren't bad. Just loan defaulters and wandering spouses. Bad-guy investigations don't pay our rent.'

'But you don't hesitate when the bad guys show up.'

I grinned at her. For the moment she was lost in the conversation. The storm clouds over TownGate were holding back for a few seconds. She'd quit eating again.

'I remember the Barbers,' she said. 'And that serial killer. You got results where the police failed.'

I quit eating too. Reached for my drink again.

'Don't believe all you hear,' I said. 'You've got the standard stories. If there were bad people in the Barber case I never found out who they were. And our serial killer got away.'

'The Diceman? That's not what my father says. Every police force in the country believes you got your man.'

'Coppers love fairy tales.'

'Including the one about you and your partner taking that trip to the Bahamas? Coming back with nothing to say about some trouble that happened whilst you were there?'

I sipped. Planted.

'A vacation. Nothing more.'

'At incredibly short notice. Just overnight bags and open tickets. Some holiday.'

'I travel light and whenever. A perk of being self-employed.'

'And your Diceman hasn't shown up anywhere else. No more sprees.'

'The guy is known for going to ground. It means nothing.'

She shook her head. Leaned forwards. Smiled sweetly as if that would change the story.

'C'mon, Eddie: give a little. I've never met a real-life tough guy. At least give me a hint. Your guy hasn't gone to ground has he?'

I smiled back. Went back to the lamb.

'He never was my guy,' I said. 'But if I ever hear from him I'll let you know.'

We ate for a while. Then:

'Okay. Tell me this: is John Reed a good guy or a bad one?'

'Interesting question. Though it's hard to see the good side of a guy sending you doctored photographs. But there's a no-man's-land between stupid and bad. I'm wondering if Reed was wandering about in the middle of that and got hit by a shell.'

'You mean he was just being stupid? Got caught up in something? Is he dead?'

It was the first time she'd asked the direct question. I told her the truth.

'More than fifty-fifty.'

'And who fired the shell?'

'I don't know. My only concern is that I might have helped load the gun.'

'The reason I'm asking is that if you're thinking what I'm thinking then please believe that my father wouldn't get involved in something like that.'

'I hear you. But I'm looking at all possibilities. That's why I'm checking your Stradivarius thing. I'm looking at everything that might link to Reed.'

'My father too? Will you look there?'

I sighed. Shook my head.

'Right now,' I said, 'I don't know where I'll look.'

'Damn.' Her face had clouded again, maybe with the realisation that the only reason she was eating with her supposed tough guy was because he'd been pulled into town by her father. And if something was off in her father's motivation then nothing good was going to come out of my digging round. Even a score on her Stradivarius investigation didn't change that.

We finished out meal on lighter stuff – media stories and scandals, the Bristol jazz scene – then went out.

It was dark. We stood a moment, watching the lights dance on the water.

'How about a nightcap?' Sarah said. 'I know a good place. Open all night.'

'That's tempting,' I said. 'But I've an early start tomorrow.'

'Some other time then. Unless your hotel mini bar is stocked.'

She was standing close. Perfume and pale skin. Eyes reflecting harbour lights. I grinned.

'Travelodges don't have mini bars,' I said.

She waited. Smiled back. Then leaned in to peck a kiss.

'Got it, Eddie. The old police ethics. Don't get involved with the parties you're investigating. I thought you were free of those rules.'

I smiled back.

'I guess some things never leave you,' I said.

Though the old detective inspector would have lied about the mini bar. Sarah wasn't the enemy. Just in her own no-man's-land. But in the rules-free world of the private investigator you define your own ethics. And stick to them.

~~~~~

I walked back to the hotel.

My friendly student receptionist, a guy called Hazeem, was on the night shift. I went over to see what he was studying behind the desk and he held up a copy of a Nietzsche tome.

'Any good?'

The boy grinned and planted the book, ready to talk. I guess the night shift could be slow.

'The guy was a genius,' he informed me. 'He's the philosopher who said that what doesn't kill us makes us stronger.'

One of my favourite maxims, though the investigation business uses a variant: "What doesn't kill you will probably try again." But the murder detective's affinity for Nietzsche comes from the one warning of his that we don't alter: "When you chase monsters watch out you don't become one." Like Hazeem said: a damn visionary.

'You a philosophy student?'

'Medicine. Night off.'

I grinned. When I did my PhD at Hendon nights off were usually spent in the pub. But then I wasn't sitting behind a Travelodge check-in to help pay for my lodgings. I liked this guy.

I left him to it but didn't head for the stairs. Instead, I walked through the building and out of the rear parking entrance. Followed the narrow street round the block and got back to the main road three hundred yards down. Crossed and walked back to the bus shelter from which the silhouette of a big guy was watching the hotel entrance.

'Give me your number,' I said, 'and I'll send you my schedule. Save the waiting about.'

The guy spun round into a defensive crouch. He was still close on six foot even in the crouch. His muscles strained the leather jacket.

'Fuck!' he said.

I grinned.

'Hello Gary. I never caught your last name.'

'Fuck! Where...?'

...did I come from? That was a kind of weak query to throw at the guy you're supposed to be watching. Which Gary sensed. He cancelled the enquiry. Reverted to safer ground, which mostly involved expletives.

'Take it easy,' I said. 'I'm just here for a chat.'

'Like hell. You sneak up like that again and you'll be chatting in hospital.'

He was still tense, waiting for a move. Presumably the kind of move I couldn't have made whilst he was oblivious to me.

'Relax,' I said. 'I'm doing you a favour. You want to stand out here all night? That's up to you. I'm just letting you know that I won't be going out again.'

'What makes you think I'm waiting for you?'

I shook my head. Where do they get these people?

'Call it a hunch,' I said. 'But what I don't know is who sent you.'

'And you think I'm gonna tell you?'

'I doubt it. And since you don't know *why* they've sent you there's no point me asking that either.'

'Ask whatever you want. But thanks for the tip. I'm outta here.'

He turned and started walking away. I walked after him and we headed down the street, shoulder to shoulder.

'My guess for the first answer,' I said: 'Bernard Locke hired you to watch Sarah's back so I'm guessing it's him who's handed you another little assignment.'

Gary kept moving. Turned a corner. His Cherokee was parked on the pavement. He moved towards it without speaking.

'If it's Locke,' I said, 'that's cool. The guy might have a reason to keep an eye on me. But if it's someone else then that could create difficulties. Ones you might get caught in.'

'I'm scared, pal.' He reached the Cherokee.

'You should be. Locke brought you in to fend off a lone nutcase. But I think there's something bigger going on. Involving people who are not nutcases. Who may be ruthless and capable. Caught in the middle could be a bad place to be.'

Gary pushed his key into the lock. Turned to sneer.

'What are you? My friggin' babysitter? Piss off, Flynn.'

'Piss off? It's you who've been following me, remember? I should be the one getting shirty.'

Gary climbed in behind the wheel.

'Catch you later,' he said.

'If you're not working for Locke,' I said, 'if it's other people, then that could be dangerous. Either directly, because some people don't tolerate screw-ups, or indirectly when you're caught in the fall-out which I assure you is on the way.'

Gary slammed the door and fired up the engine. Pushed the Jeep into gear but waited: wound the window down.

'The hard-nut investigator,' he sneered. 'Thinks he's in control. But *you* be careful, Flynn. Because you haven't a clue what you're up against. This isn't about John Reed. It's bigger than that. And your best option is to piss off back to London before *you* get into something you can't handle.'

'You know about Reed?'

But Gary stamped on the pedal and the Cherokee jumped forward and pulled off the pavement. I watched it go. Stood gazing at the empty junction. Listened to sirens closing fast. A police van raced by on the main road. Screaming blue lights. Then a patrol car, hot on its tail. Saturday night medley. The sirens echoed and faded and I walked back round to the hotel.

CHAPTER TWENTY
Charade

I hit the M5 northbound as the sun was coming up. Too early for Gary to come on shift and too early for a stopover at my breakfast cafe. I picked up a coffee in lieu at a motorway stop then put my foot down and was parked on a farm track three hundred yards from the Wallingbury Park gates by five-thirty. I walked down to take a look. The gates were closed and locked. I re-checked for cameras. Confirmed there were none there or along the walls, though the house itself would have solid protection unless Richmond had an adventurous insurer.

I walked back and found a spot a couple of hundred yards from the gate where there was tree cover inside the wall. I hopped over and dropped down into the property and jogged out towards the house.

I circled the building on a two hundred yard radius, partly cloaked by the mist that sat on the parkland and gardens. The house came slowly clear as the sky brightened and I cut in across damp lawns to take a closer look. The house was a three storey red-brick Georgian. Well maintained. The twelve-foot ground floor windows were all double glazed replacements of the originals. I pictured a local window company owner munching his cornflakes on his yacht somewhere in the Med. this morning on the back of the contract. I reached the building and stood under one of the windows. The house was raised on a three-foot plinth which put the sill at chin height so I had to stretch to get a look inside. Checked out the room then continued round and checked a few others. Confirmed my assumption: Richmond had solid security. Hints of wireless contact sensors. The flicker of area sensors under the ceilings. Richmond's butler would disable the system during the day but you'd still struggle to get into the building unless you found an open door.

By six-thirty I was through.

I went back to the car, grabbed my cold coffee and walked back to watch the gates.

At seven o'clock a nondescript Nissan pulled into the gateway and a sixtyish woman hopped out and tapped in a key code. The gates swung open and she drove in. Thirty seconds later the gates closed silently behind her. The cook, heading in to fire up the Aga.

Nothing else moved until eight thirty when a second woman let herself in. Same procedure. The housekeeper, perhaps. The gates closed behind her too but five minutes after she'd gone in they swung silently back open. Ready for visitors and service people.

But unless Richmond had guests there'd be just him and his wife in there with their cook and housekeeper. I'd seen no sign of live-in staff or security, no parked vehicles, no occupied estate cottages. Staff would drive in as needed, which left a small entourage in residence right now by billionaire standards, though if I factored in two or three staff over in the Austrian castle and maybe four or five tending the superyacht moored at Monaco we'd have eight or ten employees drawing paycheques dedicated to Richmond's comforts this morning.

Things stayed quiet for the next hour. No-one else in or out. Which was good. And passing traffic averaged ten cars an hour. Also good.

Then thirty minutes later a Mondeo in rust-blighted seaweed green rumbled by and disappeared down the lane. I quit my spot and jogged down to where it had parked beside the Frogeye.

Harry and Lucy were just getting out.

Harry stretched and groaned like they'd been on the road for a week. He was wearing dark slacks and a navy cotton jacket. Dress-down. His herringbones were reserved for business days. The other dress-down was Lucy. She'd dyed her hair black and was wearing denim jeans and jacket over a red top. Her appearance threw me.

'Quit the act, Eddie,' she said. 'You wanted discreet.'

'I'm cool,' I said. 'But I might need to ask for ID.'

'Harry can vouch for me. He was asking about my new place. And who'd know those details except me?'

Harry looked at her in astonishment. Lucy was confusing asking with listening. When you're stuck on the M4 for a couple of hours you might not ask but you'll listen unless you can get the door unjammed. Lucy had moved home a month back and the saga of her redecoration project was growing more Wagnerian at each telling. We'd taken to keeping our doors closed at Chase Street. And if we understood Lucy correctly her decorator was going through his third nervous breakdown. The place was going to be a treat to see.

But right now we had a house with a whole different level of decoration waiting.

I gave Harry a summary of the park layout and security system. He shook his head.

'A billion quid in the bank and Mona Lisa up on the wall and the guy's not secured the walls. If it was me I'd have watchtowers and machine guns. Maybe the guy thinks he's the only one stealing artwork.'

'Prospectively stealing. We've no evidence yet.'

'We'll get it. What about those guys? They showed up?'

'No. I'm seeing them as Granger's people. Maybe the ones who smacked Sewell around. I don't think we're going to see them.'

'That's good,' Harry said. 'I'm not as fast as I used to be.'

'Stealth will work fine,' I confirmed.

'Got it.'

Harry locked the Mondeo – he's a funny guy sometimes – and trudged off down the lane. I got Lucy to help me stow the hood and we hopped into the Frogeye to wait. I pushed in a Gillespie and we listened to some quiet improvisations as the sun finally broke through the mist and started to heat up. I pushed my shades on and relaxed back in the seat.

'Just like old times,' I said.

Lucy grinned. 'Those were the days, Eddie. We covered a few miles in the old Sprite.'

'A few out of it too.'

'Not as many as you remember. Most nights you were out watching someone else have the fun. A girl could get lonely.'

'But you always kept the bathroom window unlocked. Knew I'd show up eventually.'

'That was so romantic: being burgled twice a week.'

I was grinning too. Burglary wasn't the half of it.

Lucy laid her head back to get the sun on her face.

'That routine wouldn't work any more,' she said. 'I'm two floors up. Though there's a drainpipe, so I guess there'd be the excitement angle, wondering when it was going to give way. I'd have to get a camera installed.'

'You'd need to keep your drainpipes maintained,' I said. 'I'll take reasonable risks, but expecting to die each time I called wouldn't build ardour.'

'If we get back together I'll talk to my maintenance guy.'

'You've got a maintenance guy?'

'Figuratively. I pick up the phone when something needs fixing. And my budget's tight. I'm still paying off my makeover consultant.'

'You need a consultant for a spot of painting?'

'This is a paint job you need to see, Eddie. And did I tell you he's put all new woodwork in? Have you heard about Costa Rican teak?'

'Let's go,' I said.

I fired up the engine and backed past the Mondeo, careful not to damage Harry's rust. Drove down to the estate gates and turned in.

Lucy's "Ooohs" and "Woooooows" as we rolled up the driveway tickled a sense of pride. I still knew how to show a girl a good time.

Voila! The humble abode of my latest suspect.

The places P.I.s hang out.

We arrived in front of the house and Lucy toned down her gasps as we hopped out and climbed the portico steps. Let her popping eyes speak for her.

The bell was answered by the woman who'd driven in earlier. Elegant, slender, greying. Pristine skirted suit. Head of Richmond's house staff, was my guess, maintained the household roster, ran admin, maybe looked after Richmond's social diary.

We weren't in the diary, and the unannounced visit seemed to throw her. I explained that we were from TownGate and she still looked blank then apologised, politely and unfussily, and suggested we make an arrangement during the week or at Richmond's office. His lordship wasn't available at weekends.

I nodded, understanding. Didn't usually do the rounds myself at the weekend but this was something I really needed to clear up, and I was passing right by so...

'If you just let Marcus know we're here,' I said. 'I think he'll make an exception to his weekend policy.'

She looked at us for a few seconds then invited us in to an impressive marble and tile hallway where she told us to wait while she went to look for Richmond. Thirty seconds later she came back and took us through to a drawing room with a fifteen foot vaulted ceiling in gold and blue, oak panelling hung with the artwork I'd heard about. The room was fussy with antique furniture around a massive carved fireplace, and two people were enjoying their Sunday morning beneath the window. Richmond was standing waiting for us and his wife was sitting with a magazine in her lap.

Richmond thanked our guide in a way that dismissed her then waited, with the hint of a frown. He didn't come over to shake hands or ask who we were so I filled him in.

'The name's Flynn,' I said. 'My assistant: Ms May. Thanks for seeing us at short notice.'

'There was no notice,' Richmond said. 'Which is a little inconvenient. Can I help you?'

'We're here on behalf of TownGate.'

'Who on earth is that?' Richmond's wife came into the conversation, silhouetted against the window.

'I know who they are, dear,' Richmond said. 'TV Production Company. Bristol.'

I liked the guy's style. No point wasting time on phoney confusion.

'Do we have an appointment?' Richmond's wife asked.

'We don't,' he said. 'Let me see some identification.'

I handed him a card. The card said:

Edward J Flynn
FBAPI, ALev
Contemporary Solutions

That's J for Joe. Or John. Or Jeremiah. Harry says middle initials give you style. Though my election to the British Association of Private Investigators was news. Assuming there was such an organisation.

Good old Harry.

'So you're not TownGate?' Richmond read the card and looked at me.

'Consultants. Assisting an investigation. I wondered whether we might have a short word with you.'

'Not at the weekend,' Richmond said. 'And I'm baffled, frankly.'

Though not as baffled as he should have been.

'You say you know TownGate Productions,' I said. 'So you'll know they specialise in documentary features. Matters of interest to the public. Insider views, all that stuff.'

'Those people!' his wife said. 'TownGate produce the *Exposed* series.'

'They're the ones, Mrs Richmond.'

'Lady,' Richmond said. 'And as I say, I know who TownGate are. How can I help?'

'TownGate are looking into some suspect transactions in the art world. The acquisition and disposal of classical works.'

'And how is that relevant to me?'

I'd walked over to check out the gilt framed landscape over the mantelpiece. It glowed with the morning light and I was telling myself that the painting had to be a skilful copy, signature and all. But the guy behind me was a billionaire. So I had to ask.

'Is this an original Constable?'

'I don't collect copies.'

I turned. Whistled.

'I've got his Salisbury Cathedral,' I said. 'The 1831. A copy, though. I've nothing like this job.' I jabbed a thumb.

Richmond took a breath.

'Are you going to tell me why you're here?' he said.

'As I mentioned: acquisitions and disposal of art works.'

'Are you looking for commentary? If so, we'd need to make an appointment. Today is out.'

'Gee: Mrs Richmond...' Lucy diverted from the business in hand. She'd something of her own on her mind. 'Would you happen to have a bathroom? We've been on the road for three hours.'

Richmond's wife studied Lucy for a moment then planted her magazine and stood.

'There's one at the back of the house. Let me show you.'

She escorted Lucy out and sent her on her way. Returned to stand beside Richmond. The pair were silhouetted against the window but even in the tricky light you could see Richmond was about to blow a fuse. He opened his mouth but his wife cut in.

'As my husband says: this is not convenient. Our secretary will give you her number. She'll sort out something.'

'Or we could get it over with right now,' I proposed. 'We'd be five minutes max.'

'Mr Flynn, we've wasted five minutes just stumbling around the subject. You've not told us what TownGate actually want.'

'The company is researching the Bardi Stradivariuses. Have you heard of them?'

Richmond's fuse was leaking smoke. He glared and shook his head simultaneously.

'Stolen from Lenbury House,' he said. 'How do they concern me?'

'I hear you take an interest in classical music.'

'I do. So what?'

'You're known as a collector. Have some expertise in these things.'

'Yes and yes. But I've nothing for public consumption. My interests are private.'

'But you know the music world. Collectors, artefacts, original instruments and manuscripts. That kind of stuff.'

'Yes. Do you have a point?'

'We hear you've a nice collection of art and musical instruments, mostly kept over in Austria. I'm more a contemporary guy: Parker and Ellington. Coltrane. But if I had my dream collection it would include a few of the instruments the greats once played. Just a dream. But I guess one of the positives of being wealthy is that you don't need to dream. Nothing's out of reach. I guess you've some interesting stuff over in Austria.'

'My collections are private,' Richmond said. 'And privacy is another asset the wealthy appreciate. So all I can tell you about my collection in Austria...' – he turned to smile at his wife – 'is that it doesn't include any jazz memorabilia. No artefact has value beyond its base art and I've never managed to appreciate that particular branch of the musical world. If I found Charlie Parker's saxophone in the loft it would probably end up in our church fete.'

I grinned.

'I'd appreciate it if you'd call me first,' I said.

'I will. Now can we end this charade before our whole morning is wasted?'

The door opened and Lucy came back in and thanked Richmond's wife. The good Lady told her not to mention it.

'You won't disagree with me,' I said, getting back to our conversation, 'that some things *are* out of reach, no matter how fat the bank balance. That's the meaning of the word priceless.'

'With sufficient cash there's nothing that's not buyable. All things have an ultimate price.'

'Well, I'm no billionaire,' I said, 'but even I know better than that. There's a whole world of desirable goods out there that will never come to market. Not whilst institutions or families survive.'

Richmond cut back to the key point.

'Precisely why do TownGate want to talk to me?' he said.

'They'd be appreciative of a comment on the Bardi Strads,' I said. 'Anything that might help explain what happened to them.'

'And what would I know? Do TownGate think I know who nicked them?'

I waited.

Richmond's fuse was still smoking but what I was looking for was concern. Didn't see it. The guy was solid behind his Great Barrier Reef of cash. And the barriers that cash builds may be invisible but they're there. If Richmond wanted a life where he never saw my face again he could arrange it. I waited a little longer and for an instant I thought I saw it: a transient look. Was the guy sensing a breach in his barrier? Something to be repaired? I wondered and took another kick.

'The Strads didn't go missing without a buyer,' I pointed out. 'Someone with an interest in classical music and the funds to curate a private museum.'

I watched his face.

'So if you know anyone in that stratum we're open to suggestions. What are we looking at? Ten or twenty candidates globally? Oil magnates, Russian mobsters and so on. Or even someone nearer home.'

Richmond had no suggestions. Nor the good Lady, though her mouth had opened. But then Richmond moved. He stepped over and lifted a phone and ten seconds later his suited assistant trotted in.

'Gillian, Mr Flynn's leaving. And if he or TownGate get in touch again perhaps you could let them know that we won't be talking to them.'

'Certainly, Sir.'

She turned to us.

'If you please,' she said.

She raised a hand, invited us out.

I smiled at her. Grinned at Lucy.

Out.

We complied.

But I turned at the door.

'If you change your mind call me. I've got some puzzling information that links your name to the theft. Probably there's an innocent explanation but better to chat now than to TV reporters.'

For a moment no-one moved. Then Richmond spoke again, quietly.

'Thank you, Gillian,' he said.

I grinned at his assistant and turned to follow her invitation out then stopped once more for one last kick. Which was more in the nature of a grenade this time.

'I'm looking for John Reed,' I said. 'Do you happen to know where he is?'

Our hosts' mouths had closed and they stayed that way. Maybe Richmond's frown deepened but it was more puzzlement than surprise or fear.

The grenade rolled across the room, ricocheted off a table leg, bounced over the cat's tail and disappeared under the couch.

A dud.

I turned and followed Gillian out.

We walked down the steps without another word from our chaperone, and she waited at the top of them to accept a cheery wave and toot of the horn as we pulled away.

We drove back down the driveway and out to our parking spot. Nudged back in alongside the Mondeo. Then I killed the engine and we waited, listening to the birds in the trees.

'I think that ruined their Sunday,' Lucy said.

I grinned. Though I wasn't so sure.

'People like that, with money like that, can fend off problems. If Sarah wants to push the investigation Richmond's way then he'll push back.'

'Bit if they're behind Sewell clamming up then they're gonna be on red alert,' Lucy said. She sat back. Got the sun on her face again. 'They thought they'd shut TownGate's investigation down and now it's just exploded in their faces.'

'The nest has been poked,' I agreed. 'Now we'll see what we see.'

'You think this is getting you any nearer to John Reed?'

Which was my problem. Because I didn't think that. I tapped the wheel and considered things. Richmond's blank look when I threw in Reed's name didn't suggest we were moving closer to the guy. If Reed was connected to Richmond's and Granger's shenanigans the connection was buried deep.

But I kept replaying that brief expression. Marcus Richmond was uneasy about something, if only a little. Maybe we were on the right track for getting to the bottom of the Stradivarius theft. Which might help Sarah at TownGate but be irrelevant to my own interest.

Then we heard feet and heavy gasps and Lucy sat up as Harry appeared and came to plant his weight on the bonnet and mop his brow. The Frogeye sank low.

'Damn wall!' he said.

I gave him innocent.

'Looked fine to me.'

Harry grinned down. 'Try hopping them when your twenty years older and twenty pounds heavier.'

'You could probably have gone in the gate, in retrospect,' I informed him.

'Now you tell me!'

'So: we get anything?'

'We did.'

Harry pulled his camera from his jacket. Gave it a jiggle. Photos clattered around inside.

'What was Richmond's story?' he asked.

'He was offended. Knew nothing about any stolen Strads.'

Harry smiled. Pushed himself off the wing. Tossed his camera up and caught it. Held it up.

'He lied,' he said.

Lucy and I exchanged grins.

We'd known it.

CHAPTER TWENTY-ONE

He's not going to be nice to you

We grabbed a garden table at a village pub and ordered Sunday lunch. Agency tab. Harry was on the clock and normally eats out of his hourly rate but I was feeling inclusive. He'd got the dirt. Climbed over walls. Sunday roast was the least we could do.

He gave us the gen whilst we waited. Lucy and I huddled in the shade of the table's umbrella to get a view of his screen.

If Richmond had secured his grounds or kept security people round his house his secrets would have been safer. In the event all it took was Lucy releasing a rear French window and the guy had Harry and his camera wandering all over the place. Harry had shifted fast, opened doors, taken snaps.

The snaps showed high ceilinged, expensively decorated rooms. Dining, sitting, library. The dining and sitting rooms had more artwork than a national gallery would nail up and the library had shelves that needed ladders. Harry brought up a snap of the grand gallery where Richmond entertained his guests with thirty-piece orchestras. The room could have doubled as a football pitch. Then he showed us the music room, which was the one we were interested in. A smaller room, plainer decor, seats and music stands, a grand piano at its focus. I clicked and zoomed. Checked out the array of instruments hanging and standing on display. Cellos and violas and Spanish guitars. And on the rear wall, three violins. Harry had walked across for detail and I zoomed the software but didn't learn anything. No labels visible inside the instruments, and the display didn't look new. And hanging stolen goods in front of local dignitaries wouldn't be smart. You're going to get someone in, sooner or later, who recognises what he's looking at. The room signalled Richmond as a serious collector but those weren't the Bardi Stradivariuses up on his wall. And why would you put a third instrument on display with your prized pair?

Our roasts turned up and Harry tucked in whilst Lucy and I continued flicking through his snaps.

'After the hallway shots,' Harry said. He sliced at his Yorkshire.

Mopped gravy. 'The cook came out from the back and nearly caught me there. I dived clear into a service corridor and spotted a cellar door under the servants' stairs. Took a look.'

We found the cellar snaps. Not the usual low ceiling and joists, dust and cobwebs, boxes of junk. The basement had eight feet of headroom and a panelled corridor feeding storage rooms stacked with paintings and artefacts. Too much stuff to count. Maybe Richmond liked to rotate stuff through the house.

'The room at the end. Locked tight. Took me a while to get in,' Harry said.

He sliced at his beef and we flicked through the shots.

The room he was referring to was smaller than the others and mostly empty but a table at its centre held two violin cases. In the first shot the cases were shut. In next they were open to reveal two very old instruments. The violins upstairs had looked antique but there was something different about these, an ancient mellow you couldn't define. The room was no place to exhibit the jewels in your collection, which these would be if they were the stolen Strads, but maybe this was temporary storage. A transit stop on the way to Austria.

I looked closely, zoomed and tracked. Harry's close ups caught the grain and the hues of the varnish along with interior labels. Violin provenance is beyond my expertise but I'd have put money on these being the stolen Strads.

'Wow, Harry,' Lucy said.

'Yeah,' Harry said. He quit sawing to hold up his knife. 'If those fiddles aren't dodgy I'm the Queen of Sheba.'

'The labels look right,' Lucy said. Lucy actually had some qualification for the statement. Her own speciality was the clarinet but she hadn't come out of the RCM without a smattering of music history. She'd probably handled one or two Stradivariuses in her time.

I grabbed my camera and copied Harry's files across then attacked my own lunch. Came up for air after ten minutes.

'Richmond's our thief,' I said.

'The commissioner, at least,' Harry said. 'I guess Granger's people did the dirty work.'

'Sarah believes that Sewell had ID'd the buyer before he backed off. I'm thinking he has Richmond's name.'

'And now *we've* got it,' Lucy said.

That we did.

We cleaned our plates. Decided against dessert. Harry and Lucy wanted to beat the Sunday flow back into Town.

'What's next?' Lucy asked.

For which I'd no clear answer. Because interesting though Harry's pictures were my real job was to find John Reed and I wasn't sure that this had any connection to him other than the common link to Sarah and TownGate.

I stood. Pulled out my wallet.

'I'll be following you back in,' I said. 'I've got a couple of things to check back there.'

Harry smiled. Stood and stepped out into the sun.

'When you need us we're ready,' he said.

They always were.

~~~~~

Before heading back I drove into Bristol. Crossed the suspension bridge and found Sarah entertaining family and friends in her garden. The sun was hot but a breeze kept the temperature in check. Sarah had patio tables out with buffet food. Kids running round. No sign of her father. She greeted me with a warm welcome and peck on the cheek but skipped introductions. Ushered me inside to a quiet room to hear what I'd got.

What I'd got all but knocked her down. She stared at the pics of Granger and Richmond chatting, at the pair of violins secreted away in Richmond's basement. She flicked the pics back and forth, taking it in. Looked at me.

'So Richmond *is* the buyer.'

'The labels say those violins are Strads. I'm giving it ninety-five percent they're the stolen pair. I'll email you a few of the shots along with the Granger-Richmond pics. Maybe you can talk to the people at Lenbury, see if they recognise their stolen property.'

'I'll do that. Richmond isn't hiding legitimate property in his basement. And if Lenbury recognise the pair we'll go with the story. We'll have enough circumstantial evidence to ask Granger and

Richmond some pointed questions without risking lawsuits. Put the onus on them to prove that the violins aren't the Bardis.'

'You'll be working alone, though.'

'Yeah. That's a bummer. When we expose Granger and Richmond that's the end of my partnership. We've put three years of insane work into getting TownGate into the marketplace. Now Mark's just pissed it away. And I still don't know why.'

'Running round with Pauline Granger right after he's scotched the Stradivarius enquiry is part of the answer. Shows a massive conflict of interest. I hate to bring bad news but at least you know the truth. You can start planning.'

'I am. And I'm not going to be nice to Mark when we talk about it.' I smiled.

'Could be the other way around: Mark is not going to be nice to you from tomorrow.'

I told her about the tale I'd spun Richmond – about TownGate being on his tail and holding evidence to back up their assertion that he'd nicked the Strads. A tale that was now true.

'Granger and Richmond thought they'd put a lid on this. Now it's about to blow up in their faces. They know they need to act and they're going to co-opt Mark to try to cauterise your investigation from the inside.'

'I'll be ready. No doubt we'll have ourselves a little charade. He'll play innocent and I'll pretend I don't know about his ties to Granger. But I'll be informing him that our partnership is history and stick to the story that I've got all I need. Which I do, thanks to you.'

'I don't know what Sewell is up to with Granger and why he took a beating from *her* people but he's the enemy. We can't change that.'

'Damn. We've achieved so much.'

'I guess you could try to hang on to the company name. When you run the Strad story it could be the end of Sewell as a producer. He'll have more things to think about than contesting you for ownership of the company goodwill.'

She smiled but her lips were pressed tight.

'I've been thinking about it. We'll find a way through,' she said.

She offered refreshments but I said I was fine. Had a drive ahead of me. She walked me through the house to the front door.

'I'm very grateful,' she said. 'You didn't need to tell me all this or give me the pictures. This isn't the reason you're here. And if I'm right you've still a blank sheet on John Reed.'

'You're right. But that's investigation. Delivers dead ends like confetti. The trick is to retrace and take another turn. And if anything comes up that does link Reed to the Stradivarius theft I'll at least know the lay of the land.'

She opened the door. 'You P.I.s are quite the philosophical type,' she said.

'Part of the training. Philosophy is often all we have. But things usually works out. Then we ditch the philosophy and run the cheque to the bank.'

'Are you coming back?'

'Yes. I'm not going to clear this in London.'

'Then we should get together. Continue our chat from last night.'

Her smile sweetened the invitation and made getting together seem like not such a bad idea. The only fly in the ointment was that fact that I didn't know how her father – or she – fitted into all the goings-on. When I'd found John Reed I'd be in a better position to consider her invitation.

I said yes, getting together would be nice.

Some time.

I left her to it and drove back to London.

CHAPTER TWENTY-TWO
You live a dangerous life, mister

I was out at seven the next morning putting in my standard five laps of Battersea Park. The familiar routine felt good, solid ground, even if it was only a flying visit. I wasn't going to clear up the John Reed thing in London. But two of the threads that might move me towards him started here. I needed to give them a tug. If anything tugged back I'd follow them back out.

The first thing was the Best Press laundry ticket I'd picked up from Reed's flat. I'd checked again and the only business in the country with that name was here in Town. An address over in Lewisham. Maybe Reed had passed through the city, months or years back, and dropped off a jacket for dry cleaning. But maybe there was something more because his flat search had given me a second thread and that started here too.

The second of the pointers was the pair of cufflinks. Taken with the copy of Card Player magazine I'd spotted, the dancing aces logo on the links hinted at more than a passing interest in poker. When you're wearing your hobby on tie pins and cufflinks it suggests a certain closeness to the subject. So I'd called an acquaintance, a semi professional who played tournaments up and down the country. Sent him a picture and asked if the dancing aces logo meant anything in a Bristol context. He gave me a negative on Bristol but told me that the aces were the trademark of the Double Ace poker club right here in London.

Barely five miles from the Best Press laundry.

Which made me wonder whether Reed had been more than passing through, whether he had a connection to the area.

Whether someone might know him.

I ran the laps and sensed solid ground.

Herbie ran beside me as the sun came up. His diversions and catch-ups took him twice the distance and left him matching me gasp for gasp back at the gate. When our cardiac episodes subsided we headed over to pick up fresh rolls from the bakery down on the main road. Jogged back to kick start the day with a decent breakfast. At eight-thirty we went down and I got the hood stowed and we worked our way through the Monday rush towards Lewisham.

Best Press was located on a narrow cobbled street off Lee High Road, squeezed in amongst a jumble of bread and butter businesses that operate round the back of every high street: hardware and second hand furniture; life insurance and funeral plans; appliance repairs; haircuts. The facades got flakier as we walked up and finally petered out into shabby residential. I spotted the Best Press name at the end of the retail stretch above the window of a narrow two-storey building. A sign on the door said they were open at nine thirty. I eased onto the pavement to get clear of the double yellows and turned up the volume to bounce Gillespie off the surrounding brickwork. Got a few looks. Then a refuse truck trundled up and drowned the music with its hydraulics whilst the crew worked. A couple of them stopped to yell something inaudible at me but their thumbs up delivered their message. Frogeye admirers. I returned the salute and the truck took its banging and screeching down the street. I was motivated by the moment. Racked the volume further. Gillespie blew shrill. Herbie's grin widened. Brickwork resonated. The private investigator, blending in. In front of us the sign turned in the Best Press Laundry door and I killed the music and hopped out.

The counter inside the door was tended by an Asian woman in her late twenties. A mix of Chinese and something else taken from a good recipe book. The kind of face that lights a room.

'Hello, Sweetie,' she said.

I turned from closing the door and grinned at her. Shrugged my jacket straight. Tried to combine sweet and tough. Saw that her eyes were focused floorwards where Herbie was sat to attention.

I'd known it.

'Baby,' the woman said. 'What you want?'

A badge on her blouse said "Kim".

Baby widened his grin and collapsed. Rolled over. His lead got tangled. I stooped to free it.

'It's a condition,' I said. Herbie's grin held firm as the whites of his eyes clocked Kim's concerned face peering over the counter. His tail whipped the floor.

Kim babied him a little more and his condition worsened.

Sidekicks are good in the P.I. business but the key is training.

Herbie could look mean enough to snap metal bars in his jaw but I'd never figured out how to bring that side out when the ladies appeared. The compensation was the small chance that the ladies' affections would transfer: cute dog, cute owner. You see the logic.

Kim threw some last baby talk then gave me her attention as I pulled out John Reed's ticket.

Her smile held for a second after she took the ticket, then took a dive.

'You serious?' She looked at me. 'Is a year old! You never come collect?'

I switched cute to chagrin. Shrugged.

'This probably sounds dopey but I only found the ticket last week. Don't recall if I ever came back for the item. I'm sure I must have, but better safe than sorry.'

'We print out tickets now. Since year ago. So this older. We only keep uncollected for twelve month so if you no pick up,' she fluttered her fingers, 'is gone.'

'Understand. Where would it go?'

'Homeless charity. They pay fifty percent our cleaning charge then get clothes all ready to sell.'

'Damn. I guess I've lost it.'

'Let see. Maybe you collected. What was it?'

'A jacket, I think. Or trousers. Maybe a shirt. Something I'm missing.'

'You obviously not missing damn much.' She pulled out a book and flipped pages. Traced her finger, matched the number.

'Okay mister. Here is.' She turned the book. 'Jacket. You no pick up. Hope it wasn't expensive.'

'I doubt it.' I grinned at her. 'Better pay more attention next time.'

She smiled again. 'Better had. But lemme check. Is only thirteen month. You might be lucky.'

She went across to the Uncollected rail. Rummaged for a second then let out an exclamation and pulled out a hanger. Came back carrying a suede jacket under a polythene cover.

'You lucky, mister,' she said. 'Would be gone any time now.' She planted the jacket and grinned at me. 'You live dangerous life, mister. Hope your doggy got microchip.'

'He has,' I confirmed, 'and he stays close. Hard to lose.'

'Poor baby,' she said. Her eyes were on the floor again. Herbie's tail went into overdrive, sawdusted the floor.

'I guess I owe you,' I said.

'Thirty-six pound.'

Not too bad. I'd paid more, though mostly for my own clothes. I didn't need a suede jacket and this one wasn't going to tell me anything, but leaving it with the shop might look a little odd. Look unfriendly at least. No point in spoiling Kim's day. And I still needed her on my side.

'I'm sure I didn't bring it in,' I said as she worked the till. 'Am I in the book?'

Kim dropped change into my hand.

'Who else gonna be?'

'Maybe my girlfriend. I bet she dropped it in. It's gonna bug me forever if I don't find out.'

Kim pulled the book back out from under the counter. Planted it and searched again.

'What girlfriend name?'

'Tracy.'

'This you or her?' She rotated the book, finger on a name.

The name wasn't me and wasn't my girlfriend. And it wasn't Reed's. The jacket belonged to someone called Cousins. I made a show of triumph. Shook my head.

'I knew it! Tracy brought it in and forgot about it.'

'That's nice jacket,' Kim said. 'You need get more careful girlfriend.'

I grinned and said the very soonest. Picked up the jacket and tugged on the lead. Thanked Kim and went out.

Wondering who the hell Cousins was.

CHAPTER TWENTY-THREE
Magic Wishes Inc

I drove back towards the river. My poker-playing acquaintance had told me that the Double Ace Club was located in Southwark but was otherwise a little vague. His knowledge was second hand since he'd never visited the place. Had a notion that it was located past the Borough Tube station, up from St George's. I parked and walked the street looking for a name or logo. Saw neither. The street started as modern apartment blocks that ran on into four and six storey refurbished Edwardians. Permit parking and bicycle racks. Nouveau affluence, still in its shabby phase. Property prices creeping towards the million mark. A scattering of retail and restaurants operating at street level.

I collared passers-by. Most of them held their distance from Herbie whilst they shook their heads. Some waved vaguely up side streets that took me nowhere. Seemed Southwark residents weren't into card gaming. I tried a few eateries. Nothing. No dogs allowed. Forty minutes of failure got me back to the main road, wondering about the accuracy of my directions. 'Down past Borough' could in theory put me across the river.

Then I got lucky.

A guy rummaging in the back of a tradesman's van knew the name and directed me past the Tube, further up the main road. Told me to look out for the Blue Albion. The poker club was upstairs. I thanked him and headed that way. Looked for a pub. There wasn't one. I began to feel like a Kafka character. There was something here but I could never quite get to it.

Then I spotted the Blue Albion nameplate on the door of a stone-clad three-storey across the road. I went over and found that the place was a diners' club.

The diners got to sit behind impressive sash windows that added a classy touch more in keeping with Belgravia, though there was nothing they could do about the street view. But the door was solid and shiny and open for business. And a tiny plate beside the Albion brasswork had the name Double Ace etched across it. We'd passed the building on our way up from the car. Could have saved an hour if I'd been a bit sharper. But there you go. Shoe soles are solid for a reason.

I walked Herbie back to the Sprite, fed the meter and left him in charge.

'Ten minutes,' I said, 'then we eat.'

Herbie flopped onto the seat. Was asleep before I turned to head back to the club.

I got back to the Blue Albion and went in through the shared entrance, and the inner glass door was opened by a big guy in a suit. His face was impartial, straight out of bouncers' finishing school, until it lit up in surprise.

'Eddie! What the hell? How you doin' mate?'

I grinned and stuck out my hand and how-the-hell'd him back.

'I'm great, Tommy. How's things with you?'

Tommy Tavenor was one of Harry Green's old pals whom we'd helped out a year or so back when his wife tried to frame him for a post office raid in a revenge scheme after she found out about his indiscreet dalliance with his then-secretary. Tommy and his wife hadn't been hitting it off for a while and, as he told Harry, needs sometimes must. Hence the dalliance. Tommy ran a skip hire business whose admin had been run by the aforementioned secretary since start-up though his transgressions with her were recent. All the years that things had been going sour with his wife he'd never strayed, but it had taken only two nights with his secretary and the bad luck of being spotted to let the cat out of the bag. What Tommy didn't know was that his wife had been having a fling of her own for two years and that her own third party was a character who'd made a career out of cons and scams and occasional robberies. Some women with secrets might view their husband's wanderings as just tit-for-tat but apparently Tommy's wife had higher ideals. The news that Tommy was now following her example pulled out a vindictive streak in her and she and her petty-crime lover devised a scheme to make Tommy pay whilst they cashed in. Her lover took the opportunity to raid a post office and leave behind incontrovertible evidence pointing to Tommy and suddenly Tommy was facing a stretch inside whilst his wife got busy filing for divorce and splitting the seven thousand post office cash with her boyfriend.

With incontrovertible evidence and no alibi Tommy had been a cooked goose. And call Tommy naive but he hadn't cottoned on who'd set him up. Hadn't seen what was under his nose. Luckily he did see that he needed help.

So he asked Harry about HP terms. The agency doesn't do HP, for sound business reasons, but Harry said he'd take a look off the clock. And the clock hadn't ticked long before he spotted the scam and ID'd the players. But then the bad guy found out that Harry was onto him and it turned out that he knew other bad guys and things escalated, forcing Harry to pull back and call in reinforcements, and Sean and I said what the hell, things were a little quiet, and any pal of Harry's etc., and we pitched in to sort things out. Skipping the detail of the ensuing fireworks, some of which were unintentional, the upshot was that Tommy's wife and her post office Romeo took the fall for the robbery and Tommy walked free. Afterwards, he came up our stairs and shook hands all round and said he owed us. We put him right: asked what are pals for etc., until Tommy shuffled out all teary eyed and landed us with a lecture from Lucy, who'd passed him on the stairs and said we needed to treat clients more sensitively.

Now and again, when we ran out of topics at Chase Street, we asked Harry how Tommy was doing and Harry gave us the same story that the skip business was fine and that Tommy was working steady hours at his second job, which was in security, and that his secretary was still with the guy she'd run off with right after the post office affair, which turn of events had shown that life's not all rose petals.

So Tommy shook my hand fit to wrench it off and asked what I was doing at the Blue Albion since I wasn't wearing a jacket and tie which was the regulation dress. Bottom line: Tommy was here to keep people like me out. Which would have been no problem. Tommy was fifty-seven years old and looked a decade older but his muscles were steel.

Which counted for nothing when he bumped into Harry's pals. My biggest fear was that he'd burst into tears right there in the vestibule.

So I told him I was looking for the Double Ace club. Understood that they lived upstairs.

'Yeah, mate. Way in's through the dining club. But they'll want to see an invitation. You thinking of joining, Eddie?'

'Just here for a chat. What's the chance?'

'Can't say. I just look after the door. I don't get involved with what goes inside. But you're welcome to go through and ask.'

I grinned. Looked down at my gear. Cotton jacket, red tee-shirt. Navy slacks.

'They going to be happy to see me?'

'Tell 'em I sent you through.'

'I wouldn't want you to get into trouble.'

'You won't, mate. They know I'm reliable. And I've plenty of other work. I can take or leave this.'

'Thanks, Tommy. Come up for a cuppa sometime.'

'I'll do that. Tell Harry I'll see him.'

I left him to it and entered an open doorway into a lounge bar. A doorway on the far side broadcast the quiet buzz of a dozen diners in the main room beyond. The doorway was guarded by a deserted reception stand. I took a gander. The dining room was big and plush but the shaded windows subdued the light a little too much and the lit chandeliers weren't the thing for such a nice day. The place needed a terrace. I turned back and walked over to the bar.

The barman gave me a funny look and started to give me the 'sorry mate' but then logic caught up and told him that Tommy must have let me through and that executive decisions that might cross their doorman were above his pay grade. So he brought me a sparkling water and I sat on a stool and looked round. My water delivery included the charge slip. Non-members' tariff. Eight pounds twenty, which came out at about ten pence per bubble. I handed over a tenner and asked if the Double Ace was open. The guy said no.

'Anyone up there? I've some business needs talking through.'

The guy hesitated. Thought about it. Turned and walked over to pick up a phone. Spoke briefly then put the phone back down and went to the far end of the bar to polish glasses.

I sipped water. Savoured the bubbles.

Two minutes later I sensed footsteps behind me and a guy in a suit appeared at my shoulder. Late sixties. Weather-worn face. White hair. Delicate hands.

'Good afternoon, sir.' He squeezed out a smile that combined charm and disdain.

'Hi.'

'You were enquiring about the club?'

'I heard good things about you. New in town. Thought I might call in for the odd evening.'

The guy held his smile. A pained politeness.

'I see. Thank you for considering us. Unfortunately we have a restricted membership. We're quite a small club. Just half a dozen tables. And we take new members by invitation only.'

'I've got a referral.'

'Excellent. If you can gain the support of two sponsors we'd be happy to consider your application. May I ask who gave the referral?'

'Friend of mine. John Reed.'

Bombshells. A mainstay of the P.I.'s armoury. Tossed like confetti when the need arises.

And sometimes they fall like confetti.

The guy's face didn't change. Maybe the smile was fading but that had to be muscle fatigue. His only reaction was the hint of a nod, like he was seeing an end to the conversation.

'I don't recall the name,' he said. 'Is Mr Reed presently a member?'

I didn't know if Mr Reed was presently anything and the guy's impassivity seemed genuine but maybe it was his poker training. He might give me the same face if he was hiding a Royal Flush. He stood ramrod straight, ready to take the next firecracker. The only sign we were in conversation was a slight glint in his eye.

But if Reed wasn't a member here, how come he had their cufflinks? Were they a present or had he nicked them?

On the other hand, Reed went by two names in dry cleaning circles. Perhaps the second would ring a bell.

'How about if my friend Mr Cousins puts in a word?'

And this time I saw it. The guy had been over confident. Off-guard. Something realigned in his face and his lips opened and re-clamped before he could stop them. I guess in poker your blank face is held against your own hand. When the opposition smacks down his cards it's no longer needed.

And the guy's eyes too. There was still the trace of a smile but now there was something sharper in there.

Cousins.

He knew the name.

I waited whilst the guy ran calcs and worked plays. It took him five seconds.

'You know Mr Cousins?'

'Just an acquaintance. But I'm sure he'd vouch for me.'

Another pause.

Strategy developing.

'I see. Well, we'll speak to Mr Cousins and Mr...'

'Reed.'

'Reed. May I take your contact details?'

The smile was back. Strained politeness. I pulled out a card. My real name. Real number. Generic details. This card said:

Eddie Flynn
Sales Consultant
Magic Wishes Inc

Harry claims that these things come to him on rainy days.

This UK climate!

The suited guy glanced at the card and slotted it away.

'Thank you, Mr Flynn. We'll speak to your friends. And we hope to see you soon.'

He proffered his hand and I gave it a good shake. His smile didn't change as I climbed down from my stool and walked out.

CHAPTER TWENTY-FOUR
You've got five seconds

We grabbed a late lunch on Queens Circus and took it onto the park. Found a bench by the pagoda facing the sun. I popped a bottle of less expensive fizzy water and ate a sandwich, watching passers-by. Herbie retired under the bench to attack a pig's ear.

I finished the sandwich and sat back with the sound of the river traffic behind me. Herbie finished his chew and came looking for water. I trickled the last of the fizzy onto his tongue. He went cross-eyed. Gave me a look.

'It's harmless,' I told him. 'I forgot your water bottle.'

Excuses didn't impress. He grumbled and flopped down to watch the walkers. Twenty minutes later a shadow blocked the sun and Herbie's grumble became a growl.

The growl intensified. Herbie came up into a stance. The shadow backed off.

'Is that dog safe?'

I looked up.

'He's a softie. Just certain types seem to annoy him. Canine instinct.'

I patted the bench.

'Sit down. He'll feel less threatened.'

The shadow moved and planted itself carefully at the far end of the bench. Tense. Ready to go over the back. Now that the sun wasn't in my eyes I could see that he was still wearing his old peaked beret that was some kind of working class newsboy-look revival that was trendy back in the eighties. The black turn-up jeans and white socks never had been, nor his greasy hair and five o'clock shadow.

Herbie stood akimbo, watching. His back-burner growl kept the guy's eyes focused on him.

'Long time no see, Eddie.'

Eighteen months, specifically. Percy Vallan was an old Met confidential informer of mine whom I'd kept on the books when I moved into private practice. His services were as expensive as they'd ever been – more so if you factored in the psychological price of dipping into your own pocket – but the guy was a trove of facts and rumours related to the current goings-on in South London. When I needed gen on shady people he was the go-to guy. You just needed to go-to the bank first. Percy's call-out fee for basic trivia or a weather forecast was a hundred quid. Real meat started at five. But if his information saved us a week of research, or gave us stuff that just wasn't out there, then stumping up could pay.

'What have you got?' I asked him.

'Coupla snippets.' Percy made a show of relaxing. Turned away from Herbie to watch the river and slide his arm along the back of the bench.

When I'd had as much of his relaxing as I could take I pulled out an envelope and tossed it onto the bench between us.

Percy glanced down and assayed its thickness. Looked unimpressed.

'You got me on a real rush job here,' he said.

'Rush how? You need to make appointments with your memory?'

'Needed to ask questions. Not everything's archived.' Percy tapped his head. It sounded solid.

'Okay. So how about rushing me what you've got. Because the envelope isn't going to get fatter. Unless you want me to push a thank you card in.'

Percy smiled his crooked smile and shook his head. Slowly. Ended up back watching the river.

'Same old Eddie. Appreciation quotient zero.'

'My patience quotient's running pretty low too,' I said. 'I never heard a word from your lips, Percy, that wasn't handsomely paid for. So let's dispense with the favours and appreciation stuff. Tell me about the Double Ace.'

Percy was still shaking his head but he reached out. The envelope disappeared.

'I've known the Double Ace for years. Since the eighties at least. They're a private card club. Owned by Charlie Warren who I suppose you've heard of.'

I had. My eyes opened a little.

"Mad" Charlie Warren had been running a gang south of the river for over three decades. My Met duties had never taken me across his path but we all knew his name. Extortion, drugs, girls and all kinds of rackets in between. His name had lit up in the late nineties after a gang war with the Russians left the streets bloody and the Met scraping up without a single result. There'd been plenty of blood over the years that whispers had linked to Warren. Then in '01 the Met almost collared him after a DS out of Wandsworth disappeared on a search operation down Summerstown way. The team was looking for Warren's meth distribution hub and maybe the DS found it. But he never came back and Warren slipped the net. One down to the good guys. The failure still stung today. Coppers had taken their pensions with promises to take Warren down unkept.

So Charlie liked a hand of cards. I've never been much of a player, didn't get the mystique of characters sat round smoky midnight tables. But I've always admired the hobby choices of the professional criminal. I guess a poker club would satisfy Charlie's proprietorial cravings as much as a gambling itch.

'Is the dining club his?'

'No. That's mostly legit, though one of its board of directors is a pal of Charlie's. The club sub-leases an upstairs floor to Double Ace and Double Ace members get complimentary dining cards so the clubs are tight.'

'Got it. What about Cousins?'

'An interesting name,' Percy said. 'Why are you after him?'

I waited. Percy knew better than to expect to hear Eagle Eye's business. When he realised we were going to sit there all afternoon he slapped the backrest. Question withdrawn.

'The only Cousins I know is Ricky Cousins,' Percy said. 'And if you're asking about the Double Ace then he's your guy – he was a member there till last year.'

'Tell me about him.'

'Not much to tell. Ricky was a freelance: prescription drugs and scam operations; breaking and entry. Minor league. He was never on Charlie's books. But he was sharp at cards and I heard he earned good money round the clubs. Bit of a character. A solid player but not quite professional standard. Just a talent for misdirection. I watched him a couple of times. Ricky was good entertainment: a reputation for bluffing his way out of dog hands. Ol' Ricky had the original poker face. Could be backed into a corner and betting his shirt and still not break a sweat. Of course, real players don't get into that position: when they're backed up they throw in, cut their losses.'

'Okay. Now tell my why you keep saying "was".'

'Because Ricky's not around any more. The story is he made some bad choices one night and took a gamble on a dog hand. Chalked up a big loss to his Double Ace account and did a runner. I heard different numbers. A hundred thou. Half a mill. But even tenner isn't safe money to owe Charlie Warren if you're not good for it.'

'So he disappeared?'

'Done a runner, I heard. Charlie was out looking for him for a while, but I never heard if he found him.'

I pulled my phone out. Showed Percy the snap of John Reed. 'Is this the guy?'

Percy squinted. Tilted the phone. Nodded.

'That's him. Ricky Cousins.' He slapped the back of the bench, which he shouldn't have. Herbie's growl racked up and Percy pulled his feet in. The growling crescendoed and Percy eased himself slowly off the bench and took a couple of paces back.

'It's been nice talking to you, Eddie,' he said. 'Gotta rush before I get mauled. But call me anytime. I'm here to help.'

I pushed my arm out and slapped the back of the bench myself. Thought about it.

'I need a couple more things. Not just memory work. Actual digging out.'

'That sounds very expensive.'

'Another five hundred, to be precise, which is not open to negotiation. And I want results today. You got room in your diary?'

'I don't know. Maybe. Maybe not.'

'You've got five seconds. Yes or no. This five hundred won't be here tomorrow.'

Percy swore and shook his head and tried to watch Herbie all at the same time. But his feet stayed put.

'Well,' he concluded, 'I'm tempted to tell you to go to hell, Eddie. But I've got a little time and I guess five hundred is better than a kick in the backside. I'll call it an investment: good customer relations.'

'Call it what you want,' I said. 'Here's what I need.'

~~~~~

I drove across to Paddington and parked behind the building. Our spots were empty. The agency out earning its rent. Connie clocked me as I walked round and yelled a hopeful greeting but I'd already eaten and a tug-of-war on the leash got us safely past his premises to our front door.

We went in. The lower floors hummed with industry: the Rook and Lye mill, endlessly grinding. I held the inner door for a middle-aged couple exiting the clinic. They thanked me with smiles that suggested a profitable visit.

I put them down as two of Bob Rook's disinterment clients.

Bob currently had a blitzkrieg rolling across the TV and FM stations concerning a financial scandal he'd personally uncovered. The scandal was heinous enough to demand Bob's own dulcet tones on the clarion call voice-over. I had to hand it to him: the ads were good. He'd put in a background of Mars, The Bringer Of War and overlaid it with a voice-over from beyond, proclaiming the irregularities discovered in a swathe of funeral plans opened since 1952. The irregularities equated to an average overcharge of nine hundred and fifty quid per policy in 2012 money, with reimbursements fully transferable to the deceased's estate, heirs and lawyers. Bob's estimate was that upwards of half a million people across the UK had been gypped by their loved ones' demise, and if nine hundred and fifty quid at forty percent commission doesn't sound like a fortune just multiply the number by that magic half million and you'll get the picture.

The adding machines at Rook and Lye and a hundred firms across the country had been billowing smoke for three weeks as they clattered out the accruing profits. And that was the snag: once Bob had let the cat out of the bag the Supermarket Sweep was on. First come, first served. Once the reimbursements were gone they were gone for all eternity, leaving Bob and Gerry the onerous task of making sure the bulk of the claimants came in through Rook and Lye's door. It was their commercial, after all, though if ad. slogans counted for anything they'd sweep the floor. Bob's creative streak had soared to new heights as he worked up their campaign slogan: "Make life a pleasure. Dig up that treasure." And no spade required.

Just a signature on Rook and Lye's form was all that was required to fire up your own personal excavator.

Bob was parking a brand new Porsche behind the buildings this summer on the projected rewards of the dig. Gerry Lye was more circumspect. Still cycled to work, but when the weather turned bad we'd all be squeezing into our parking slots past the rear end of his Jaguar XJ with its LY4 CSH plate. When I first saw that plate I'd been inspired to do my own search but the only candidate I found in the database was BR0K PI which would have worked nicely if not for the fifteen K price tag.

We climbed the stairs to the quieter floor upstairs and I opened up and turned the sign. Herbie trotted to his water bowl then went through and settled into one of my visitors' chairs. I followed and crossed the room to lift the sash. Leaned out to watch the Westway across the Great Western lines. Listened to the hiss and clatter of the city. Afternoon rush not yet begun. I turned things over for a while then eased back inside and rotated my Herman Miller to continue the contemplation. Set the recline angle and got my feet onto the window sill.

The city breath murmured. The rooms behind me were quiet.

Time to think.

I'd moved closer to John Reed the way you drift closer to the edge of a waterfall. Things were starting to move.

John Reed: loner lifestyle, loner job, oddball character, oddball interests. No evidence of roots or connections. No formal identification documents. A guy living below the radar.

Ricky Cousins: small time criminal and risk-taker. The latter urge driving an attraction for card games. Sitting round the table with the big boys at Charlie Warren's club. Gets a kick out of taking the big boys' money but it's only a matter of time before he lets risk trump judgement. Suddenly one day he's in hock to a bad guy and the only way out is to disappear.

John Reed, taking out a flat rental in Bristol. A van and a brush and a new career. No employer scrutiny, no employment records. How the hell Cousins had settled on bill posting I couldn't imagine but my guess was that he'd been in the trade one time, an old day job to supplement his non-taxable income streams. He'd probably been earning enough in Bristol to get by but my guess was that he had other income streams. Maybe his poker skills had been pulling in revenue online, multi-player games where you get to select the opposition and pocket cash on a dependable basis. Cousins might miss the thrill of shadowed faces round a midnight table, but dosh is dosh and my guess was the guy had been accumulating a nice treasure chest whilst he made plans for a more permanent life. Maybe a villa in the Algarve or the Caribbean. Another advantage of his online income: the world was at his fingertips. And maybe his attraction to poking round derelict properties stemmed from his attraction to the newer ones his breaking and entry proclivity had led him to. You couldn't miss the overlap between trespassing to explore premises and breaking in to nick the family jewellery. Maybe burglary was still one of his income streams. Bill-posting, online gambling and burglary: twenty-four hour earning opportunities.

It all made sense.

Except for the thing that had brought me into the affair. Why was a guy with a serious need to stay invisible stalking media celebrities and delivering photographic threats? Even if he was carrying out a little freelance work for the people harassing TownGate the risk would still outweigh the payoff. Staying out of sight was a life or death issue when you were running from Charlie Warren.

I clasped my hands behind my neck and watched clouds drift over the towers beyond the Westway. Listened to a police siren up on the flyover, pneumatic snoring from the visitors' chair behind me.

Cousins should have been lying low and instead he'd been playing games. And whatever his game with Sarah, that camera shot of him at her door delivering his package had been his undoing. The shot had given Bernard Locke the incentive to hire me. And I'd duly dug the guy out.

And once I'd reported to Locke the information was in Charlie Warren's hands within twenty-four hours. Within thirty-six, Cousins was gone.

Hard to avoid the conclusion: the Avon and Somerset Chief Constable was in bed with a London criminal gang.

I grinned. Watched a heavy cloud drift by. Sensed enlightenment just behind its silver lining. Because I'd just hit the key step in the classic investigation checklist: I'd got the strings; I just needed to unravel the knot.

A horn echoed from over the roof – a taxi, obstructed out front on Chase Street. The blast held long and steady. I jumped up and slammed the sash.

CHAPTER TWENTY-FIVE
I could see his future more clearly than he

The sax player was a teenage black woman, gigging to supplement her RCM grant. Tomorrow night she'd be waiting-on over in the West End or stacking shelves at a Tesco Metro for the same purpose. Or maybe she was a full time waitress moonlighting the London jazz scene. Whatever she was, she was good. The rest of her rock-jazz quintet trailed after her like novices as the room held its breath at a Monday evening windfall. The woman reminded me of Brecker, who'd died a year or two back. The same lilting, driven fluency over a funk back-beat. All eyes were on her slim, gyrating figure, including the lead guitar's as he bounced riffs off her with a grin. He *knew*. He got her vibe.

Most Mondays the Podium has piped music and empty tables, good for thinking, which had been my idea. The black musician had nixed that plan, or at least slowed it down, so most of my thinking was done either in the thirty-second intervals or in my subconscious.

I'd a pint of London Pride up on the table and a brindle Staffie snoring below it, and my disjointed and interrupted thinking on John Reed a.k.a. Ricky Cousins had got as far as it was going to without a fresh input. When I pushed the facts this way and that things almost connected. Just not quite. There was no solid narrative that would explain what had happened in Bristol. Like the astrophysicist, the private investigator was always after his Unified Theory. And like the physicist, I worked half the time under the dark possibility that things might not tie up, that the answer wouldn't be reachable. Maybe the threads I'd picked up in Bristol were just strands of separate affairs.

But at each interlude one factor stood out with the promise that it might just link everything.

And confirm the worst of my various theories.

Would put me in the centre.

I held the thread up and tugged but it wouldn't break. You couldn't miss it, once you'd seen it.

The factor that was bugging me was Bernard Locke's photographs that had brought me into this.

The photographs were all connected, but the connection I was seeing was not the one he'd given me.

The quintet crashed to another stop. Applause, then a few seconds of hush through which I could hear Herbie growling under the table. The growl climbed the scale, like one of those sonars that tell you how close the torpedo is. When I looked round a figure was standing at my side. The figure had heard the growling and was staying behind a chair.

'Easy,' I said.

The decibels dropped to standby.

'Sit down,' I said. 'He's cool.'

My visitor was Percy Valan, returned with the stuff I needed. Seemed he'd found the time in his busy schedule after all. I pulled an envelope from my pocket and smacked it onto the table to give us both sight of the motivation. Then the quintet rolled into their next piece and the black lady lifted her sax and Percy pulled a chair out and sat. He stayed two feet out from the table, keeping his legs clear. Reached to plant a manila envelope of his own.

'Five hundred doesn't cut it,' he said. 'And they lifted a fiver off me just to get in here. I should have told them to take a hike. Five hundred is a serious under-appreciation, Eddie.'

'Talk to your union. A deal's a deal.'

'Then you'd better hope it's not the last one. I don't appreciate highway robbery.'

I sort of smiled. It was getting late. I just wanted to know what I'd be taking back to Bristol.

'A thief,' I mused, 'robbed on the highway. How does that work? Which side does the union support?'

'Fuck you, Eddie. I'm still tempted to piss off and leave you to it.'

My smile ignited.

'You could do that, Percy. But that envelope won't be leaving with you now that I've seen it. The best you can hope for is that I'm happy with what's inside.'

'It's all there. You'd better be damn happy.'

'We'll see.'

'And what *is* this?' Percy jabbed his thumb at the stage. 'You listen to this shit? Freaking racket! The only thing worthwhile is the view.

163

That lady's no Count Basie, for sure. Look at her go! If it was all chicks like that maybe I could get interested in jazz. Ratta-ta, ba-boom! Go, hepcats! Groovy, man!' He turned his grin on me.

'Percy,' I said, 'the only thing between you and a ripped-out throat is my foot on my dog's leash. And my foot's getting tired. So how about showing me what's in the envelope before things take a turn?'

Percy glanced down to see how close Herbie was straining. The growls had gone back up the scale so the music just didn't cover them. Percy looked at his envelope. It was within reach but my assurance was good: he wasn't going to take it back. And I'd placed the fat one with the cash well out of his reach.

He shook his head and reached slowly for his envelope. Pulled out photos.

'Have it your way,' he said. 'But I won't always be here when you come begging for information.'

Sure he wouldn't. He'd take a pass on easy money just to spite me. Most of what I'd asked for was in his head, and the pics he was about to show me wouldn't have taken much getting.

'This one,' he said, 'Charlie Warren.'

I looked at the first photo, which had a face I recognised vaguely and could have picked up from a dozen cheaper sources. But it was good to refresh the memory. Charlie Warren glared out from the snap looking as mean as his reputation. I gestured to Percy and he fanned out the next four and I leaned and checked them as best I could in the Podium's lighting.

'I put their names on the back,' Percy said. 'They're Warren's top soldiers.'

'You're solid on that? These are his get-done guys?'

'Solid. This first is Terry Dean, Warren's enforcer. If you're looking for someone to run a squeeze or a clean-up operation then Terry's your guy. Bin with Charlie for twenty years, give or take spells inside. Charlie calls him his Admin Department. If he wants someone's leg broken, Terry's the man. If he wants rivals pushing back, Terry will arrange an operation and be first in the door. And when Charlie needs to talk to someone it's always Terry who fetches them in – and if he needs to make an example of them Terry does the work. He's got this ball-peen hammer and garden snippers, I heard. That's in case you ever meet him.'

The photo showed a lean, hard face under buzz cut hair that covered middle age baldness. A mouth that locked firmly down at the corners, eyes challenging the camera. A face that didn't paper over the owner's nasty streak. If I ever met the guy I'd know him. And the hammer and snippers would be a giveaway.

The next picture wasn't such good quality. Percy had scraped around and brought in a blown up fuzzy image from what looked like a club or formal dinner. Flash-lit sullen faces against a background of suits and waiters. He pointed to a little guy in the centre and gave me a name. Louis Williams. Professional driver. Unpleasant CV, one that made you wonder whether his driving examiner had waived the test and just handed him the certificate.

The next photo was back to higher quality.

'Aaron Grant,' Percy said. 'My cousin's brother-in-law. An ex of mine took the shot at a Christening a couple of years back. Cheeky bitch wanted fifty quid to let me copy it but we negotiated and she made do with a slap and a tenner. But you see the risks I take? To her it's just a Christening picture but if she ever blabs to my cousin or Aaron then I'm toast.'

I looked at the photo. Aaron was another cut from the same tree as Terry Dean. Same temperament. The Christening suit and polite smile just didn't paper over the guy's nature. If word did get back – and one day, consequential on a snippet Percy had provided to me or to ten other P.I.s and coppers, word would get back – then Percy's career as paid informer would be terminated. So I wasn't about to dispute his safety concerns. I could see the guy's future more clearly than he.

I pulled across the final photo. Lousy quality again. A blown-up mess of newsprint pixels.

'I've been digging everywhere,' Percy explained, 'and there's only this one guy over in Bristol linked to Charlie Warren. Martin Kieran. Property developer. I met him years ago. Him and Charlie go way back. Worked jobs together in the eighties. Then Kieran went off to start a property company in the West Country and I lost track. But apparently he's made good money. His extortion and coercion skills have done him proud – a few backhanders and the occasional knuckle-duster work wonders in the construction industry. My contact says Marty's been involved in a couple of heists out Bristol and Cardiff way but he's mostly legit nowadays. But still pally with Charlie. My guy saw them together at a bash six months ago. So he's probably the closest connection you're gonna get over there.'

An old pal in the same business. Making legitimate money with not so legitimate methods. But the main thing was that Kieran was still tight with Warren. Which made him my way in to whatever business Charlie had on in Bristol.

'Anything else?'

'Anything *else?* Jesus, *no!* You already got ten times what you paid for. You think I'm running a charity?'

I pushed the photos and names back into the envelope and reached to hand the cash over.

'Stay cool, Percy. You wouldn't recognise charity if a rough sleeper handed you his winning lottery ticket. And if you're going to count the money do it outside.'

'I'll do that,' Percy said. 'Depend on it.' He snatched the envelope and stood and headed out without another word, thought his head turned to leer at the sax player. Building fantasies he'd never see.

After he'd gone I set the photos up again and studied the face of Charlie Warren's enforcer, Terry Dean. Wondered whether it was the face Ricky Cousins a.k.a. John Reed had seen at the Perseverance Hospital the night he disappeared. Because if Percy's information was right and Warren had found Cousins then Dean would have been the guy in charge of the clean-up. I gave it ninety percent: Terry Dean had been in Bristol a fortnight ago.

When he drove back there I'd know for sure.

CHAPTER TWENTY-SIX
Not quite the guy she thought he was

'Need reinforcements?' Shaughnessy asked.

'Very soon,' I said. 'My crystal ball shows excitement blowing in.'

We were in the front office. Shaughnessy was standing at the blinds, watching the street. Harry was sitting behind the partners desk, finalising notices for serving. Lucy was kicking her heels atop the same desk and I was sipping coffee in one of the visitors' chairs. Herbie and my feet were on the other.

'That's an interesting connection,' Shaughnessy said. 'The Avon and Somerset chief constable in bed with Charlie Warren.'

'Interesting and solid. No other way to see it.'

Lucy was puzzling it over. Unconvinced.

'Sarah and TownGate are under attack,' she said. 'They've got Richmond and his crew playing dirty games and somebody sending threat photos to Sarah. No matter how things connect up it makes sense for Sarah's father to go after the guy threatening her.'

'His reason was legitimate,' I agreed. 'But Charlie Warren has been hunting Ricky Cousins for a year without success. Then the day after I hand Locke his location and alias Cousins disappears. I'm not buying the coincidence.'

'Me neither,' Lucy said. 'But maybe Locke just tipped off Charlie Warren as a convenient way of removing the threat to his daughter.'

'Doesn't work,' Harry said. He continued head-down, shuffling paper, ordering his delivery round. 'Because you'd still have to swallow the coincidence that the guy threatening Sarah happened to be on the run from Warren and that Locke happened to know it. What's the chance of that?'

Lucy kicked her heels some more. 'Yeah,' she said. 'You're right. Even if Locke somehow knew the full story behind the guy who sent the knife photo there are still too many odd connections and coincidences.'

I finished my coffee.

'Coincidences rarely fly,' I said. 'So you flip them round: see them as gold plated links. Then you're starting to see the truth.'

'Let's see how Locke's CCTVs pan out,' Shaughnessy said.

'I'm on it,' Harry said.

The second he was back in from his paper round Harry was going to put Locke's cam. pics through the digital mangler.

I came back to my secondary but not insignificant point.

'We need to get this off our books,' I said. 'As things stand the agency, in the form of yours truly, has been working for the bad guys.'

Lucy shook her head again.

'That wouldn't look good if word got out.'

Harry pushed paperwork into envelopes. Patted them into order. Grinned up at Lucy.

'Don't be so sure,' he said. 'It would probably boost our clientele. We'd have every low life in the city rushing up the stairs.'

Shaughnessy turned from the window and sat down at his side of the desk.

'How are we playing this?' he said.

I planted my mug. Linked fingers behind my head.

'First thing: I need to confirm the situation. Get all the players to check in. That's going to take a couple of days. Then we need to find out what happened to Ricky Cousins after he was snatched, see if we can link Warren to the abduction. Then we confirm that the link from Locke to Warren was more than just an opportunist thing and gift wrap the lot. Hand it all to Avon and Somerset.'

'The big stick approach.' Shaughnessy said: 'Whack the hornets' nest.'

I pushed myself out of the chair.

'The approach has yet to fail,' I said. I whistled Herbie back from his dreams. He rolled and dropped to the floor.

'When the swarm is circling,' I said, 'I'll give you a call.'

'Our desks will be clear,' Shaughnessy said.

~~~~~

I dropped Herbie off with my neighbour Henrietta, working her shift at the dogs' home. Henrietta was busy in the back but Reception knew him and he knew them. He disappeared without a rearwards glance. When his shift ended he'd ride the front seat of Henrietta's

Nissan home, drooling at the prospect of her over-generous cooking proclivity. For me it was an apartment pit stop, a hasty bag pack then a top-up and drive back along the M4.

As I ate up the miles I kicked things around and decided to hold off on another chat with Bernard Locke. We'd be getting together soon but it would be good to have a little more ammunition when we met.

I hit Bristol early afternoon and drove across to John Reed's – a.k.a. Ricky Cousins' – apartment. Parked alongside a van being loaded outside the building. Reed's landlady was supervising. Cardboard boxes and small furniture items were going in. The boxes were filled with the stuff from Reed's flat. Books and DVDs, PC, keyboard. Elsie's cigarette holder semaphored instructions. Left smoke trails. She spotted me, took a last suck and pulled the holder out. Held it, two-fingered. If she was pleased to see me it didn't show, but she was happy to fill me in.

'The flat's up for rent,' she said. 'John's stuff is going in the cellar round the corner until he appears.'

Which could be a while, though I didn't fill her in.

'Very disappointing,' she said. 'John was a good tenant.'

I shrugged. Didn't disabuse her. Her tenant may have been good but he wasn't John Reed. Not the guy she thought he was at all. I pulled out my phone and showed her Percy Valan's photos of Charlie Warren's crew.

Elsie took a look and stopped me as I flicked through them.

'That's him. He came asking about John the day after you.'

The face on the screen was Terry Dean's.

So Warren's enforcer had turned up right after I handed Reed's address to Locke. My guess was that Dean had done more than ask questions. He'd been inside the flat looking for something to confirm Reed's real identity. There hadn't been much to find but when he spotted the poker mag. and Double Ace cufflinks he'd have known.

I thanked Elsie. Commiserated about my "brother's" behaviour. Elsie was resigned. Her problem was fast clearing up. Her guys passed us carrying Reed's multi gym. Stashed it. Went back in for the little that was left. I promised I'd let John know when I caught up with him and jumped back into the car.

I pictured the follow-up after I'd briefed Locke. Worked out the timing: my guess said that Dean was motoring down the M4 first thing next morning; and by the time Elsie bumped into him here at noon Cousins' cover was blown.

And whilst I'd been tidying Friday afternoon paperwork at Chase Street, Terry Dean and his crew were sitting outside this building, reporting to Charlie Warren. Charlie had listened to the evidence and given the green light, and Dean had waited patiently until Cousins turned up from work. Then watched for the chance to snatch him.

Which came faster than they could have hoped.

When Cousins headed out for his exploration of the Perseverance Hospital Dean and his pals followed. And when the white van parked round the back of the derelict site way out in the middle of nowhere Dean must have thought Christmas had come early. It was too good an opportunity to miss. They jumped out and followed Cousins in through the kicked-in gate and it was all over.

Charlie Warren would have received the call around midnight.

Job done.

I'd have been hitting the sack by then, looking forward to a lazy weekend.

Ditto: job done.

I wondered where they'd taken Cousins. Had they driven straight to the disposal site? Or brought the fugitive back to Town for a chat with Charlie?

Either way, Cousins was gone for good.

I fired up the engine. Left Elsie to her removals and rolled out onto the street.

Next step: kick the nest. Send Warren an unwelcome message.

That Cousins was gone but not forgotten.

CHAPTER TWENTY-SEVEN
You must really be the curious type

A search of the Companies House register told me that Charlie Warren's property developer pal Martin Kieran was the sole director of a company called Century Housing, based in Bristol. I drove across the centre and followed my map to a dingy office block by the canal east of the station. A utilitarian HQ. No developments going up nearby. No regional grants pulling businesses in. The company shared the building with a unit that was boarded up and plastered with graffiti, and Century's presence was announced only by its door. No pavement board or parking spot or fancy entrance logo. No public face at all. Companies House had listed them as worth eight million but none of it was evident here. Even minnows like to put up a name plate but it seemed Martin Kieran had other priorities. My guess was that the minnow did the job he wanted. If the director's takings were anything to go by the business was all about paying out. Forward investment not essential. And if Kieran's business methods matched the brief Percy Valan had supplied then eighty percent of its operation would never appear in formal contracts or balance sheets.

I went in. Found a door off the stairwell annex which took me into a tiny ground floor space with five desks and two women working at screens. A glazed door at the back was either the owner's office or the way to the bathroom. The woman at the nearest desk paused at her screen and smiled up. Middle aged, dyed hair, a puffy, flushed face that maybe hinted at a fondness for the rosé and trendy eateries. But she had what counted: a pleasant manner.

I asked if Martin was in, casually, as if popping in on spec to see old Marty was routine. Rosé knew it wasn't, since she'd never seen me, but these buddy-buddy things operate in the background so she never knew. The main thing was that my casual clothes told her I wasn't a salesman. She apologised and said that Mr Kieran was out.

I shrugged it off.

'No prob. Just passing. Just gotta catch him about some planning results.'

'Maybe I can help.'

I smiled. Raised my hands.

'It's kinda confidential. Unofficial.'

'Of course. I see.'

Which she did. Because there was nothing unusual about her boss having quiet chats and unofficial chinwags, meetings behind the scenes. Stuff he didn't burden her with.

'Is there anywhere I can catch him?'

'Did you call him?'

'My phone's dead and my damn car charger's packed in. Guess I'll have to try later.'

'That would be best. Unless you'd like to call from here. He's out on site.' She named the place.

I declined the offer. Said tonight would be fine. Left them to it.

Because she'd supplied what I needed.

Back outside I grabbed my A-Z and found the place she'd mentioned. A cluster of houses along the main road running east out of the city.

I drove that way.

Fifteen minutes later I spotted a board just beyond a hamlet. Century Housing's name up over an idyllic vista of executive dwellings infused with greenery. Behind the board was a fenced-off development of twenty houses. Construction just past the drains and foundations stage. The development would triple the population of the hamlet when it sold, though in monetary terms the area's value would rocket by ten. The site had eaten into an old woodland. What the jargon might label as Green Field. Green enough to suggest the need for a few behind-the-scenes negotiations with the local planning department. I sensed land bought on the cheap, *sans* permissions, then *permissions* suddenly granted. A local official driving a new Jag.

I pulled up and watched. Teams of brickies were working at the far end and an excavator was digging drains along the access road.

I hopped out and walked in through the gate. A sign required hard hats at all times. If I'd had one I'd have worn it. I went with the risk. Walked down the partly laid road to a Portakabin office.

I climbed wooden steps and pushed the door open.

Came into a room with four tables, scattered chairs, filing cabinets and card files. A corkboard with a colour-coded site map.

And three guys.

Taking it easy, sprawled on the chairs. Coffee mugs steaming. Nattering.

Which stopped when I stepped in. Two of the three sat up. Red alert.

The third guy stayed tilted back in his chair with his feet on the table and I recognised the face of Martin Kieran despite Percy's lousy newsprint snap.

The face was broad and taut over sharp angles. Strong arched eyebrows under a brow creased by attitude. The attitude was reflected in the hard-as-nails eyes flanking his boxer's nose. A mouth bent permanently down. Sixty years old with fifty years of mean. Kieran wore a quality suit and open neck shirt but the tailoring didn't hide the man. A businessman only in the schoolyard-extortion sense. Percy Vallan's gen that had Kieran as a pal of Charlie Warren looked good the instant I saw the guy. He stayed back in his chair as the others came alert, though he looked a little puzzled.

The other two were younger, less weather-worn. One of them wore a high-vis. vest and was maybe a legit contractor or foreman. The second wore a leather jacket over tee-shirt and denim and had a glint in his face that didn't flag him as a guy who'd ever hefted bricks. Or worked any other productive job.

I grinned a greeting.

'Helpya, mate?' Glint said.

I ignored him. Spoke to Kieran.

'How's things, Marty?'

Kieran's expression stayed puzzled but he forced in a hint of humour to show he was game.

'How am I?' He thought about it. Then decided not to bother.

'Who the fuck are you?'

'Flynn. Eddie.' I held the smile. 'You don't know me.'

Kieran directed his puzzlement at his cronies now and it was hard to tell whether he was speaking to them or to me. 'Well, Mister Flynn Eddie, you're correct. I don't know you and you don't know me. So what's with all this Marty stuff?'

He switched back to me.

'No point being formal,' I said. 'I'm just here for a friendly chat. Can I call you Marty?'

'Mr Kieran will do fine, if that's no trouble. What are you, a contractor rep?'

I laughed. 'Nothing like that, Marty. You're safe.'

'There we go again,' Kieran said. 'The Marty thing. But I'm pleased to know I'm safe.'

He looked at his buddies again and his buddies laughed and chuckled but once the act was over Kieran dropped the humour.

'What do you want?' he said.

'I've got a couple of questions I thought you might help me with.'

'Really! A couple of questions!' He shook his head, like that would clear things up. Then changed tack. 'Why don't you tell me who you are. Council?'

'God forbid! I'm just an investigator.'

Kieran had been ready to reply but that word stopped him. Stopped them all. We had a couple of seconds of silence as if I'd sworn in church then the atmosphere turned. I guess investigators weren't part of Kieran's business model. His eyes stayed locked onto me but he pulled his feet from the table and rocked his chair forward. Then leaned and dropped his arms onto his thighs to scrutinise me from the ready position. His pals were paying attention too.

'Investigating what?'

'The whereabouts of a guy called Ricky Cousins. You know him?'

If he did, Kieran's face didn't show it. But sometimes no reaction is as good as jumping out of your skin. Kieran should have been puzzling over the name, shaking his head, annoyed by my continued obfuscation. Instead he was rock, and his absolute zero told a tale. I took heart. Turned up my smile, ploughed on. Held up a finger.

'Don't tell me, Marty: you never heard of the guy. Blah, blah, blah. I get it. But I know that you do know Ricky. But that's not what I'm after. What I want to know is do you happen to know where he is? You see, I located him for a client but now he's disappeared again and I'm back to square one.'

My spiel gave Kieran the break he needed to thaw his big-freeze act. Pulled him back into the conversation. His voice was calm, quiet.

'I've never heard of anyone called Cousins,' he said. 'And I'm not happy about you coming in here with this shit and calling me Marty like I'm your best friend or your bookie. So what delusion connects this guy to me?'

'It's not a direct connection. But Cousins is in some kind of trouble with Charlie Warren who's not from this neck of the woods as you know. So, two and two, you being Charlie's man on the ground out west, I thought maybe you'd helped him out. Chaperoned his people when they came down from London.'

'I see. Well we're truly in fantasy land now because I don't know any Cousins and I don't know any Charlie Warren.' Kieran shook his head. 'Some investigator! Running your mouth off with accusations you can't substantiate.'

'Okay, it's a hunch,' I said. 'But my hunches are usually right. And they're telling me that I'm not going to find Cousins and I'm looking at someone who knows why.'

Kieran's eyes stayed locked on mine.

'Who's your client?'

'I'm not at liberty to say. Confidentiality and all that.'

'Stop!' Kieran held up a finger. 'No more games. I asked who your client is.'

'You really want to know? Even though you don't know who Cousins is and have never met Charlie Warren or his dog? You must really be the curious type, Marty.'

But things were starting to evolve. Glint had just stood up. Signals were passing between him and Kieran. The high vis. guy just looked baffled. Probably on the periphery of Kieran's operations, maybe legit. But Glint was starting to move round the table and my focus was there, especially when Kieran jabbed a thumb.

'Sit him down, Stevie.'

Stevie pushed past the high vis. guy into clear floor space.

'Fine,' I said. 'I guess this is a bad time.'

'You've no idea,' Kieran said and now he was on his own feet, coming the other way round.

Reading between the lines I could see that our chat was through. Whatever Kieran knew about Ricky Cousins he was keeping to himself.

Suddenly Stevie moved. Fast. But it was a little too fast. I grabbed the nearest table and rotated it viciously into his path as he came at me and he crashed down over it. The furniture rearrangement opened a gap for Kieran to come directly at me but he wasn't as fast. Didn't catch up before I was out of the door and down the steps.

I strode away fast. Sensed Kieran and Stevie come out of the Portakabin but then Kieran thought better of it, held Stevie back.

I jogged out past the hard hat sign. The sign made sense now.

When I turned at the Frogeye the two of them were still on the Portakabin steps watching me.

I threw a salute, fired up the engine and turned back towards Bristol.

Interesting.

I didn't know whether Kieran had been involved with whatever happened to Ricky Cousins but he'd known for sure that Charlie Warren had been in town clearing up. He'd known about Cousins.

And – the point of the stick in the hard hats' nest – I knew he'd be picking up his phone right now and calling Charlie.

CHAPTER TWENTY-EIGHT
I'd put it down to hallucination

I drove back into the centre and checked back into the Travelodge. Hazeem, my medical philosopher receptionist, had come on shift. He pulled my details up. We had a routine going: he acted surprised and pleased and said "back again?" and I said "just can't stay away" and he found a room at a "special rate". No advance booking needed. The special rate room was a "special room" which had us both grinning because every room was identical unless you counted the mirror-image layouts. What the hotel had was two sets of identical rooms but right- and left-handed, which added the element of anticipation on check-in.

Hazeem asked how long I was staying and I said probably a day or two and we left it at that. When I checked out we'd both know, though when I did check out Hazeem would be in class. But his cheery demeanour suggested that his split of the twenty quid desk tip was reaching him. Sue, the morning girl, was honest that way.

I hefted my bag up three flights of stairs and found this week's room.

324.

Left-handed.

I went in and unpacked. Freshened up. Snapped the cap off a bottle of fizzy and stood looking out over the city. The room actually was a special: its elevation and the alignment with the buildings opposite gave me a narrow view along the docks to the river where the Great Britain's bow nudged eagerly towards the water, ready to sail.

I watched clouds scudding to the south, distant trees stirring, listened to the hiss of cars below me, rush hour building. If Charlie Warren was on the ball his fixer Terry Dean would be across the M25 by now with afterburners lit. With luck he'd overdo it, collect a speed ticket along the way to put him in the mood.

When he got here the waters would start to muddy and I'd see what floated to the surface. My plans were a little vague in that respect but the first thing was to get the players here. The more people in the city worrying about damage to Warren, the better the chance that one of them could be panicked into letting something slip that might point me towards Cousins or build evidence that the cops could follow.

Time passed. I stood and watched.

The glare dimmed as the sun inched round to the back of the building. Traffic thinned and the rumblings coming from my stomach grew continuous. Hunger kicked in. I left my observation post and went to find food.

As I came out of the hotel I spotted bodyguard-cum-covert operative Gary at his post by the bus shelter. I turned away, headed down past the cathedral and towards the Old City. Checked twice to confirm that the guy was still with me. He was.

I searched around and found a Thai restaurant in an unfashionable alley. The place had comfortable decor and snug tables in little crannies and a handful of diners in eating. The proprietor sat me down with enthusiasm and I enjoyed a leisurely meal whilst the light faded outside. Finished with coffee delivered with a jug of cream, heated so that temperature considerations needn't constrain quantity. Coffee as dessert.

I came out and walked a different way back to give Gary a little variety. I wondered if he got overtime. Maybe he was happy to stay on me all night. But it was time to clock off. I didn't want the guy watching me over the next twenty-four hours. We zigzagged a few dark streets and cut back towards the Travelodge by way of the Town Hall and Cathedral. Then I made a sudden move and skipped down a flight of steps to a lower-level street near the hotel. Turned to walk back into the dead end, which was a litter-strewn space between the upper street wall and the surrounding buildings, illuminated only by the street above. It seemed as good a place as any.

Gary came tripping down the steps and turned after me into the shadowed street end. Stopped sharp when I stepped out from a corner.

'Let's do a deal,' I said.

Gary stood still. Grinned unhappily in the low light.

'Here it is: you hand back the job. Tell them you're no longer available. And I don't tell the person who hired you – who I'm still assuming is Bernard Locke – that you've been clocked every time you've been near me in the last few days. Win-win. My privacy. Your reputation.'

Gary was about to reply but then his eyes were diverted to the steps. I walked out and looked up and saw two men in suits coming down at a trot. They hit the street and turned into the dead end to join us.

I recognised the faces straight away.

Terry Dean had arrived in town.

The other guy was Aaron Grant.

Charlie Warren's get-done guys.

Seemed they'd really shifted along the M4. Must barely have had time to grab their best suits before they drove out. But there was no way they'd reached the Travelodge before I went out. And no way they'd guessed I was eating Chinese. Someone had guided them in.

I grinned at Gary.

'Pals of yours?'

The quip was an ice-breaker only. I knew the answer was negative even without seeing Gary's face, which was working hard at staying calm and cool. No quick nods or winks passing between them. Gary hadn't a clue who these guys were.

He looked at them and looked at me then folded his arms and stood back, legs akimbo to see what he would see. Whatever went down was not his business.

'Knocking off time, Gary,' I said. 'Tell Locke I got safely home.'

Warren's stooges walked a little closer then stood at ease. Aaron had a phone to his ear. He said 'Go' and killed the call, stashed the phone. Then they both looked at Gary.

My attention drifted. Snagged on trivia. Specifically whether Aaron's suit was the one in the Christening photo Percy had supplied. Things like that bug you at the most inopportune times. I was tempted to ask Aaron but that would probably drop Percy in it, and a good informer is worth his weight in fivers. I killed the thought. Turned to look at Gary along with Dean and Aaron.

Gary was standing his ground. Waiting to see what went down. But Warren's stooges didn't want an audience.

'Fuck off,' Aaron said to him. He gestured back up the steps.

I grinned and shrugged.

'I can't better that advice,' I said.

'I'm fine right here,' Gary said. 'I'll not interfere.'

Terry Dean joined in. His eyes were locked on Gary.

'No,' he said.

Gary looked at him.

'You're not fine here. Hop it.' Dean jabbed a thumb.

A faint doubt came over Gary's face. I guess looking at Dean had sowed the seed of an idea that this guy was out of his league. But some kind of pride kept his feet planted and his chin up. It was a weakness he shared with the private investigator, though we always add judgement into the mix and that's our advantage: where there's an escape route we scarper. Leave pride to scramble after you. Gary had multiple escape routes. A leap for the broken street lamp by the end wall and monkey-climb back to the top street or a quick dodge round the goons and up the steps or out down the street to the main road.

Or simply take a hint and walk away.

'Gary,' I said, 'you'd better go. These clowns don't want witnesses.'

But that proud streak...

The proud streak opened Gary's mouth and got out the words 'I'll go when I damn...' before Aaron's fist knocked him back into the wall. Hard. His legs failed and dropped him onto the litter.

Not a smart move by Warren's people. Gary would have co-operated eventually and the impatient move distracted Aaron from the main business which was me. As he swung a foot to deliver a kick to Gary's head he didn't see my own fist coming and I caught him a blow hard enough to near-dislocate my shoulder. Aaron's head snapped sideways and his foot missed Gary and he staggered, tripped and head-butted the wall. Now he was down on the floor too.

Appendix to the investigator habit: forget pride; scarper whilst you can; but first, poleaxe the opposition. Gains more ground.

Not that it was over.

As Aaron attacked the pavement Terry Dean jumped in and came at me with a swing I ducked. Then I stepped aside and landed a hard right into his ribs then left- and right-handers on his neck and jaw. This time the right-hander almost did dislocate my shoulder and Dean's chin stubble skinned my knuckles so viciously it cut right through the skin but it stopped the bastard for the vital second I needed to skip round him and jog away towards the main road. Gary was still down on the pavement but he didn't interest these guys now that the action was moving elsewhere. Which I confirmed with a quick glance back. Both Aaron and Dean were coming fast. There's just no way to stop guys like that. Whatever hail of pain hits them they just keep going. It's the only way they know. Finish the job. Worry about the sticking plasters later.

But they weren't going to catch me before I reached the hotel entrance. And wouldn't follow me in. Smashing their way into a barricaded room with the target waiting to hand out more pain and maybe the police on their way wasn't good tactics. They needed to regroup, think things over. Me: I'd just got what I was looking for when I'd poked that stick at Martin Kieran this afternoon. To wit: confirmation that Kieran and Warren were talking; that this whole thing was Charlie Warren's affair, his people who'd taken down Ricky Cousins; and that Warren was getting intel. from Bernard Locke. The players had all shown up and flashed their badges.

So – tactic successful.

Then thirty yards from the main road a black Merc pull round the corner and accelerated towards me. Dean's third guy waiting nearby for the call. So Warren's people weren't here just to give me a kicking. Their package included a ride home.

I shifted into a sprint and passed the Merc before it could react. Heard it accelerate away behind me to pick up Dean and Aaron. But turning or reversing would cost too many seconds. They weren't going to catch me.

Five seconds later I was out on the main road, hotel in sight.

Then I saw another guy jogging up the far side to get a view of the action. He stopped when I appeared. Turned away.

But a second too late.

The light had caught his face.

And almost stopped me dead in disbelief.

Almost. Instinct kicked in, kept my feet moving. I rounded the corner and walked fast towards the hotel. Then diverted into an adjacent side street and found a shadowed recess from which to look back.

A few seconds later Dean & Co's Merc moved slowly past on the main street and disappeared from sight. I stayed in the shadows and waited.

Until the new guy reappeared.

Which he did.

He was walking fast up the far side. Passed ahead of me and continued along the hotel front. I moved out and followed, still telling myself I was seeing things.

But I wasn't.

And my whole house of cards had just collapsed.

The Merc had gone. Just the figure walking ahead of me, crossing over to enter the next side street. I switched places. Jogged to the far side of the road to get a better angle.

As I came up to the corner I heard an engine start and a car rolled out and turned. Moved away fast.

A dark red BMW M3.

One I'd seen before.

Way back at the beginning, when I tailed John Reed home to his flat. The car had been parked outside his building with a guy behind the wheel. I couldn't be a hundred percent sure it was the same vehicle – I hadn't noted the number back then – but this one had the same red alloys and the same custom spoiler on the back, and if there was another vehicle in the country that matched its looks that would be a hell of a thing.

It was the same car. The way things were connecting I was going with the odds on that.

I watched it disappear into the night.

Waited ten minutes to see whether it or the Merc would reappear but the street stayed quiet. The show was over.

The wait gave me thinking time. Time to absorb what I'd just seen.

If I'd taken one of Terry Dean's fists to the head I could have put the whole thing down to hallucination. Sometimes you see stars, sometimes it's faces.

Because the guy who'd jogged up to get a view of the action, who'd driven away in the BMW, was the one I'd been looking for.

Missing in action. Presumed dead.

The artist formerly known as John Reed.

Who was not John Reed.

And not dead.

I'd just seen Ricky Cousins.

CHAPTER TWENTY-NINE
The side of the business they don't tell you about

Eight a.m.

I checked the street from my hotel window. No sign of watchers. I went down and checked the rear exit. Ditto: Dean and his pals hadn't come on shift. I went out into the sunshine and walked round to my breakfast cafe.

My hostess had her usual smile. Asked if it would be my usual order. I said that would be perfect and took my usual window table.

The coffee helped patch over a mixed night's sleep. I'd set up a few basic safety measures before I hit the sack but the measures wouldn't have saved my neck if Dean had come back with serious intent. The best I'd have hoped for was a guarantee that I'd be awake and ready to inflict mutual damage when they came in.

Not the restful night you see in those Travelodge promos.

Though I couldn't complain: you poke a stick in the nest, you expect a reaction.

But sleep had taken a long time to come.

And what had kept me awake was the face of Ricky Cousins.

It was a face I shouldn't have seen. A face that said that this whole thing – my return from London, my chasing round Bristol, my stumbling into Charlie Warren's affairs – should never have happened. Because Ricky Cousins had been absent of his own volition. Not missing. Not snatched from his life as John Reed. Not dead.

And the more I thought about it the deeper the puzzle. Because whatever Cousins was up to he shouldn't have been on that street last night.

And he shouldn't have been at the wheel of the BMW since that was the vehicle that had been watching *him* posing as John Reed up in Redland two weeks ago. So who'd been driving the vehicle then? And where was *that* guy?

Just when the mystery surrounding Cousins had been clearing, when the players in Charlie Warren's little waltz were stepping with the music, the thing had fallen apart. The lights had dimmed and the partners had changed and we were off in a mad tango in a different direction.

The evidence had said that Cousins had crossed Charlie Warren then dropped out of sight, gone to earth living the quiet life in Bristol with a new identity – John Reed – until a smart P.I. brought in on a cock-and-bull story had unearthed him. And further evidence said that the guy had been snatched and was gone for good leaving nothing behind but an abandoned job and a few worldly goods stacked in his landlady's cellar.

The evidence had lined up perfectly to say that Cousins was dead.

But there he was last night, out on the street, resurrected and looking good.

And watching Warren's crew coming after me.

Did Warren and Terry Dean know Cousins was there? Was something going on between them? That was tricky to reconcile with my earlier assumption that they'd killed him.

Or was Cousins not watching Warren's people at all? Was he there for *me?*

Bodyguard Gary had been watching me for sure before his curtains were drawn. Were he and Cousins working together?

And back to question one: how did Cousins come to be driving the M3?

Private investigations abound with this type of conundrum. If I ever write a how-to book I'll put in my top one hundred list of "Things That Made No Sense At The Time". Ask the reader to figure them out. At least the reader won't be groggy from a night's lost sleep and flinching every time they close their hand. I'll put that stuff in too: the stinging knuckles and black eyes, the broken ribs and sleepless nights; the side of the P.I. business they don't tell you about.

On the other hand there's omelettes and coffee and a hostess' warm smile. By the time I'd absorbed those remedies my medical condition had improved sufficiently to let me complete a plan of action that looked good. I was wound and ready to go. The stick-poking might have delivered painful knuckles but it had given me what I needed: momentum. Things were moving.

I pushed a fiver under my plate in a fit of exuberance and was good to go.

Then as I walked out of the door my phone rang and popped the bubble.

~~~~~

'Can you get back to Bristol?'

I was already in Bristol but Bernard Locke either didn't know or was being coy. But his shaky voice got my attention. I asked what his problem was.

'Sarah's disappeared.'

Not shaky. Scared.

I asked what had happened.

'Reed showed up again at the weekend. Sarah spotted him outside her house. So much for your theory that he'd vanished.'

My theory had been solid – until it fell apart last night. But now that the dead guy was resurrected he was everywhere. I didn't discuss the issue. Just asked if Sarah had confronted him.

'She'd more sense. But I went over to Redland to see if I could catch him.'

'No luck?'

'His landlady said he'd still not appeared. But he's somewhere around. Close enough to stay interested in Sarah.'

'Was Sarah sure it was Reed?'

'She didn't get a close-up view but he was prowling round her house again. She assumed it was him.'

'What happened then?'

'She called me again last night. She'd spotted him watching from her garden. I'm in Edinburgh. A conference. I told her to keep her doors locked and avoid risky places. Then when I called this morning she didn't answer. I've booked the first train home.'

'Has anyone been to her house?'

'I asked one of her company people to call in. They've just got back. Her car's outside the house but she's not there.'

'When are you back in town?'

'Not till mid afternoon. But I need someone to start looking for her right now.'

He paused.

'This scares the hell out of me,' he said. 'There's no way Sarah would not answer her door or phone. And if this bastard got to her last night he's had her twelve hours. I can't imagine what might have happened.'

Although he could. Cops have good imaginations. But if Locke was terrified you had to wonder why he'd not whistled up the police. They'd have been round at Sarah's house within ten minutes.

His story was off.

But his fear was real.

I sensed plans changing. Told him I was on my way. Rang off and phoned Sarah. The line rang for twenty seconds then went to voicemail. I cut the line and walked back for the car.

As I crossed the Gorge I made a hands-free to Mark Sewell. He sounded surprised to hear my voice but I cut through his musings and asked when he'd last seen Sarah and when he next expected to do so. Answers: yesterday at the office and this morning at the office. They were due out on a shoot at eleven. No mention of upheavals at TownGate. I guess Sarah hadn't confronted him yet.

I cut the call and turned onto the lane that ran up round the headland. Put my foot down and parked sixty seconds later on Sarah's forecourt next to her Audi TT.

I rang the doorbell. Got nothing. Went back to the Frogeye and grabbed some stuff and jogged round to take a look at the rear windows and doors. All good quality. Decent locks. No way to avoid damage. But needs must: I kept it to a minimum and got in.

I called Sarah's name as I walked through. Got only silence back. Then I arrived in the front hallway and stopped.

The phone table was toppled and its contents were scattered across the floor.

Not good.

I jogged upstairs. Called again. Still silence. I checked the rooms. Nothing. Master bedroom tidy. Bed made up. But the shoulder bag Sarah habitually carried was standing open on her dresser and her phone was right next to it, missed-call light flashing.

There'd been no break-in, which meant she'd gone down and opened the door despite her concerns about her stalker. And once she'd let the guy in the tussle started.

I found a tiny office with a computer and screen that took feeds from the house cams. I brought the screen live. It showed me four segments, three working, one blank. Exterior shots along three sides of the building. The blank segment was probably the porch cam. I grabbed a chair and worked the software. Jumped back through the night at one-hour intervals. The screen stayed blank until ten p.m. when the recording became live. I jumped back to early evening and played the scene forward at thirty-two times speed. Caught Sarah arriving home at six p.m. then going out again forty minutes later. After that there was nothing for a while as the light started to dim. Then at ten p.m. Sarah reappeared, coming in for the night. I slowed things and played forward at normal speed. Watched her walk into the house. Then nothing for a few minutes until the view went suddenly blank.

Someone had come here last night. Lured Sarah to the door and overpowered her. Disabled the camera and wiped the record from just before they turned up.

Locke's assumption was right.

She'd been snatched.

I killed the screen and sat back.

Was this Cousins-related or Warren's reaction to my provocation? Or was it the Stradivarius investigation coming back to her after *that* provocation? Or something else?

The best laid plans... etc. In the shredder right after I'd made them.

Because Sarah Locke was now my sole focus.

And with no way to guess whether she was in imminent peril I needed to find her fast.

But which direction?

Was the lately un-deceased Cousins the route? Or Warren? Or the Stradivarius people?

Not the latter, I decided, though there was a connection between that affair and the other two. The mists were beginning to clear. I was starting to see it.

So: plans revised.

Get to Sarah.

For that I needed manpower and information.

I went back out and folded the Frogeye's hood then sat back on the wing and made some calls.

The early morning cloud cover had cleared and the sun burned my neck, had me twisting this way and that to see my screen.

The temperature was rising fast.
It wasn't responsible for the tension in my chest.

CHAPTER THIRTY
Knock yourself out

My first call-back beamed in sixty minutes later from Roger Daley, our vehicle-trace contact in Swansea. I'd squeezed hard. Told Roger that a life might depend on his finger work.

'My job might depend on it,' he countered. His voice had a tense sibilance that suggested nearby ears.

'Well if they fire you you'll have time to write that book on DVLA you keep telling me about. All the crazy shit that goes down in there. I can't wait to read it.'

'You just wouldn't believe...' Roger said.

I grinned, though mostly with tension. Pictured the view from inside the licensing agency. The excitement. The tales they could tell. But I only wanted one thing right now.

'Okay,' Roger said. 'The M3 is registered to Triple-A Leasing. A Birmingham company.'

Well – I'd known Cousins didn't own the vehicle.

What I didn't know was whether he was relevant to Sarah's abduction. Logic said that her abduction was Warren's reaction to my poking his nest. The opening shot in a scheme to lure me somewhere unsafe. But Cousins had been threatening Sarah right at the start and Cousins was there last night as Warren's crew tried to snatch me. So the guy was right there at the centre of this mess and I wasn't ruling anything out.

Roger gave me Triple-A's registered address and I thanked him and told him to get started on that book. Killed the line. Checked my Birmingham A-Z. Spotted the address on the south side of the city near Bromsgrove. A seventy minute drive that would take me away from where I needed to be. But I'd no immediate lead here in Bristol and waiting for Warren's people to show their hand was too vague a plan.

It was fifty-fifty whether the leasing company was worth the diversion but if I knew who'd been renting the M3 maybe I could get a pointer as to why Cousins had taken over the wheel, and what the original driver's business had been in Bristol two weeks ago. And maybe I'd find something to confirm the hunch that was fast forming. Because the hunch was my real reason for taking the trip.

I drove out of the city and turned onto the M5 north. Put my foot down.

Sixty minutes later I left the motorway and navigated across Bromsgrove to a potholed road on the outskirts. Pulled up outside a dingy workshop with an office up top and vehicle yard behind. Triple-A Leasing's name was up over the workshop door and six old vans were parked in the yard, 90's era Transits and Hiaces, though none had the company name on the bodywork. No cash to spare for vanity touches. Pay budget, get budget. Two jalopies parked amongst them suggested a sideline in cheap private car rentals, though they might just have been employee wheels.

I went in through the customer door and up the stairs. Came out at a counter fronting a cluttered office. A couple of clerks were working screens. One of them spotted me and came over to ask if I had a reservation.

I said I hadn't. Asked for the boss. She went back and tapped on a door and a little guy with straggly grey hair and a worn grey suit came out. He didn't bother with a smile. Business was business. If I wanted cheap wheels this was the place. If I was here to sell something he'd help me back out. He was about sixty and looked as if he'd been renting cheap vehicles since Commers were king. There were no longer any Commers in the yard but there were also no BMWs or any other cars you'd mistake for quality. Just the tired vehicles I'd seen. Steady income whilst the business decayed. If Grey was the owner he'd sell up in five years for little more than the land and building value and retire on a state pension plus perks.

He looked at me.

'Anywhere private we can talk?'

He pursed his lips.

'What about?' he said.

'Private stuff. Sensitive.'

'I don't understand,' he said, though he turned his head towards the girl. She got the message and scuttled back to her desk. Maybe it wasn't the first time sensitive stuff had been discussed.

The guy started again. 'How can I help?'

I stuck with my proposition.

'Better somewhere quiet.'

He stayed puzzled but began to sense that quiet really would be better. He lifted the flap and invited me through to his office. Closed his door behind us. We were in a cubicle dominated by a metal desk set diagonally across with filing cabinets jammed in opposing corners. Ford and Toyota posters on the walls, trade and girlie calendars, the space in between a patchwork of Blu Tacked notes and oil-stained invoices. The only free space was a tiny window with a mesh-enhanced view of the yard and its razor wire.

Grey sat down behind his desk and I pulled out my phone and showed him a pic.

'One of yours?'

The photo was a dark red M3. Not Cousins' vehicle but close enough. Just an internet image for illustrative purposes. But Grey would know which vehicle we were talking about. Any M3 rented out by Triple-A had to be top of their brochure list.

Or more likely: not in the brochure.

He pursed his lips.

'Could be,' he said.

'Could be? How many M3's are you leasing?'

'Are you looking to rent one?'

'Do you have one in?'

'Not presently.'

'Ever? Do you *ever* rent BMW's?'

'I can't say. Just let me know what you want.'

I stashed the phone.

'I need some information on the customer who's renting the car.'

'Which I can't give you.'

Confident now. This was some shit about a car. He gestured.

'Angela will see you out if that's it.'

I ignored his invitation. Turned for a formal inspection of the wall decor. The Ford and Toyota calendars were recent but the Pirelli girlie calendar was vintage. Mid eighties. You could probably do an archaeological dig in here. I turned back and planted a card on Grey's desk. One of my legit ones with the Eagle Eye name across it.

'A private investigator? That's interesting.' He sat back.

'Your M3 customer's in a spot of bother,' I said. 'If I can just pick up his details I'm gone and you'll get the car back in due course.'

The guy flicked my card back onto his desk.

'Thanks, but no thanks,' he said.

I sighed. Checked the wall again. Next to the Pirelli was a Lamb's Navy Rum. 1983. I lifted sheets. White girls tanned to a crisp. Blinding white teeth, ferocious smiles. Those eighties!

'Okay, let's cut to the chase,' I said. 'Here's my leverage: I know the M3 isn't legitimate because you don't own or rent that class of vehicle. A BMW in your yard would draw a crowd. So the vehicle's registered to you only as convenience. From which I deduce that you've facilitated a deception to assist a known criminal. Which criminal has now got himself into difficulties that are about to attract the Law.'

The "known criminal" thing was a guess but the odds were pretty good. I didn't see the people mixed up in the Cousins-Warren thing as legit. Grey watched me with a straight face but there was a new tension there. I clarified things:

'The guy handed you cash to buy the M3. Then you put it on your books and leased it back to him at a penny a week. The reason he needed your help with the purchase was that he couldn't legally buy the car himself for reasons you didn't ask about. But when you rented the car back to him you also didn't check his ID or make sure his license was valid. So when the police follow up on what we give them you're in line for an aiding and abetting charge. And who knows how many of your books they'll go through. Could be a problem if there's other stuff you'd prefer to keep quiet.'

The guy said nothing. I went back to studying his calendars. He broke first. Came back into the discussion.

'So you know all about the guy,' he said. 'Why are you hassling me?'

'Our man has aliases. I need the name and address on his leasing contract. It will probably be phoney, given your due diligence, but we'll check it anyway. We're still looking for background.'

I gave Grey a moment. He was still hesitating. He didn't care tuppence about client confidentiality but he probably cared about potentially unhappy clients. About this coming back on him.

'If you show me that information,' I said, 'I'll hide the BMW hire. So you keep the quiet life. Maybe even inherit the car as a bonus. It's legally yours after all and your client isn't going to need it. Win-win.'

That wasn't the whole picture. The whole picture would have told him that win-win wasn't guaranteed. But Grey was still hesitating: when I turned back he was sitting forward in his chair with a kind of chummy amusement on his face. Like he'd just got it.

'What sort of crime?' he said. 'What's this guy been up to?' He held up a finger. 'Let me guess: he's had his pecker where he shouldn't and you've been hired by his wife or an annoyed husband. And what I'm aiding and abetting is a domestic situation. Pull the other one.'

I said nothing. Looked at him long and hard.

'What?' he said.

'Think about it: do investigators need to run round chasing up aliases and illegal car hires for marital cases? A domestic client needs a few photos. That's it. That's all they pay for and that's all they get.'

I gave him another moment. Then laid it out.

'In thirty seconds I'm walking out, with or without your assistance. And if it's without I'll get the information some other way and I'll make sure your little lease-back scam is in the package when it goes to the police. Because your rental client is in big-time *criminal* trouble and that's likely to be bad news for all his helpers.'

Grey tried to hold the chummy stuff. Threw out a laugh.

'So what's the guy up to? Robbed the Bank of England?'

'Twenty seconds.'

He looked at me, still with a grin. Counted down.

I shook my head and swore. Turned for the door.

'Wait!'

I turned back. The guy stood up.

'This is bullshit. Total bullshit! Lemme look at the file.'

He came round and pulled a filing cabinet drawer open which halved the space in the room. I stood back whilst he rooted out a folder. Then he slammed the drawer back in and slapped the folder onto his desk.

'Okay. Knock yourself out.'

I did. Opened the card file.

Found standard rental paperwork. A twelve month renewable contract for the BMW, recently renewed. The car's date of registration made it just two years old when it came onto Triple-A's books which made the rental pretty good value since the vehicle's monthly rate would barely get you a bicycle. But even that fee was pure profit for Triple-A since they hadn't financed the purchase. And they'd taken a nice up-front payment for sure to secure the deal. Had to be five or ten grand.

But the detail that interested me was the name on the lease.

The name wasn't Cousins.

It was someone called Geoffrey Smith. Address right in this area, back out by the motorway.

That address was the next link in my chain.

I dropped the forms and thanked Grey and left him pushing them back into the folder as I went out.

~~~~~

I drove over the motorway and parked in a sixties executive development a quarter of a mile west of it. Sat listening to the engine tick whilst I checked out the area. The "executive" aspect of the housing had long since faded and whilst driving a vintage vehicle confers some degree of protection against gratuitous vandalism an open top can be an invitation too far. It's the power of the visual.

The houses were a mix of semis and tiny detached units with built-over garages. A draw for the expanding professional class back in the day, but wealth and desirability had been leeching from the area for two decades, leaving neglect, potholed roads and weed-choked pavements, straggly trees lifting paving stones. The sixties bank managers and lawyers had been replaced by tradesmen and retirees, college tutors and inheritance-shackled offspring, families with their minds on keeping the kids away from drug dealers. The rampant greenery still conveyed a suburban cosiness but you'd watch your step at night.

The semi-detached house alongside me was half concealed by wild greenery but otherwise didn't look in too bad a shape. The gutters were tidy and the plastic windows and door looked recent, if soulless.

I hopped out. Took a risk and left the hood stowed. The only stuff worth stealing was either in the boot or the glove compartment, both of which had been modernised along with the mechanics. You could get into both but it would take determination.

I pushed through a metal gate and walked across a garden that was cared for behind its privet hedge but without enthusiasm. A simple lawn and few wilting rose bushes dropping petals. When I rang the bell the door was opened by a pretty brunette.

Early thirties. Slender,

I asked if Geoff was in.

She looked uncertain.

I held my smile. She was uncertain but not confused or in denial. Someone called Geoffrey Smith really did live here.

The way forward is to plant the next stepping stone. I went with a hunch.

'Not home?' I said. 'That's good. Could have been kind of tricky.' I held the smile as if the two of us were in the tricky thing together but the woman didn't buy it. Puzzled switched to wary.

'I'm sorry?' she said.

I handed her a card. Pointed out my name.

'Eddie Flynn,' I said. 'Private investigator. London.'

I held out my hand but she didn't take it. I dropped my arm smoothly. Kiss-off handshakes are part of the job.

'Could I have a word?' I said.

'Geoff's not here.'

'I know.'

Her wariness was growing. She was on the verge of deciding that whatever I was after she didn't want to hear it and was about to slam the door, invite me to call some other time, but I cut her off at the pass.

'There are things you need to know,' I said.

Which got her immediate attention. Her face switched instantly to concern. It seemed Geoff was a guy she wouldn't be too surprised to hear things about.

And if my hunch, which had strengthened on the drive over from Triple-A, was on target there'd be plenty to surprise her.

The woman seemed a decent sort. And the greenery and the rooftops felt homely. Maybe the M3 was a little flashy but the guy had otherwise chosen well. If you wanted the anonymous heart of England this was it.

But my hunch said that whatever story Geoffrey had spun for this woman as they built this nest wasn't the truth, which was why something had snagged in her subconscious. A sense of things he'd never told her. History he'd waved aside. Maybe she'd wondered a few times. So when a private investigator shows up one day it's no big surprise.

'Better inside,' I said.

She hesitated but finally decided that whatever problems I was bringing were better faced than left stabbing her subconscious. She stepped back and I went in.

She took me through to a tiny front lounge. Neat, tasteful. Quality TV screen and hi-fi stack. The guy had a comfortable home. I asked the woman her name and she was happy to tell me it was Fiona. She didn't ask me to sit though. Just pulled out a fag and lit up. Blew a smoke stream that drifted to the ceiling.

'I understand Geoff and you are together.'

'Yes. Or were. You're about to tell me he's been up to something.'

'He's your boyfriend,' I speculated. P.I.s are as good at cold reading as your top flight mediums.

I waited a moment. Looked at her.

'It's not good news,' I warned.

'I've got that. What's he been up to?'

I turned to the window and looked out through the greens and yellows, observed the world from deep in the haven that her boyfriend had thought was secure. It should have been secure but he'd blown it. Let the enemy in. Proof: here I was. If not exactly the enemy, certainly the gatekeeper. The guy had played a risky game and lost, and now I was standing with his girlfriend looking out of his front window.

'You know Geoff's been spending time in Bristol?' I said.

Silence.

Confirmation.

Stepping stone solid. Go for the next.

'I was hired by a client there to check up on his wife.'

I turned back. Fiona was watching me. Took another shallow drag. Leaked smoke.

I took her through it.

'My client's wife had been acting strangely since she visited this area a while back. Her husband became suspicious and I confirmed his suspicions.'

I let the thought rest a moment. Then finished spinning my story.

'It turns out the guy's wife has been spending time with Geoff,' I said. 'The two of them have been meeting up at a hotel just outside

Bristol. It's been a regular thing for the last month or so. But they were careless. I identified the guy inside twenty-four hours through his car and...'

I shrugged. Waited.

Fiona leaked more smoke, deep in thought. Then:

'The bastard,' she said. She looked at me. Her eyes were glinting.

'Sorry to bring bad news. It's the part of the job that never gets easier.'

I held my grim face despite the hogwash. The hogwash wasn't the "never easier" bit, though we deliver bad news often enough. The hogwash was the idea that we'd ever spill the beans to a third party linked to an investigation. When you're chasing errant spouses your main focus is on keeping out of their sight. Collecting the evidence. And the last person you'd brief up-front would be the culprit or their partner in crime or anyone connected to them. But sing a good song and the words don't need to make sense. The subtleties of the investigative process washed over Fiona.

'What do you want?' she said.

She stubbed her cigarette. Her voice was ice.

'Corroborating evidence,' I said. 'Thought I might find it here.'

Normal reaction, when a P.I. shows up asking to dig through your house looking for dirt on your partner, would be to show him the door. But normal reaction, in the blaze of shock and anger, goes out of the window. Fiona didn't doubt for a second that her boyfriend's dirty betrayal had just filled their house with its stink. Maybe she'd sensed that her guy wasn't entirely kosher. And despite the little fiction I'd just fed Fiona my hunch said that her conclusion wasn't far from the truth. Geoff had been living a lie here.

'I need a glance at his stuff,' I said, 'Paperwork and so on. There might be something helps corroborate what the two of them were up to: hotel invoices, fuel receipts, etc. Things that put him at particular locations on particular dates. Link him solidly to my client's wife.'

'Don't you have your own evidence?'

'Plenty. I've a set of photographs and logged sightings. But clients need formal documentation if they're looking to take legal action. Hard evidence smoothes the way for everyone. Avoids any futile contesting of the claimant's case.'

She looked past me out of the window, lost in her thoughts.

'The bastard,' she repeated.

~~~~~

Back outside I sat in the car and searched my A-Z. The house beside me was silent. No indication of the turmoil I'd just unleashed. My hope was that Fiona would hold it together long enough to stick to our agreement, which was that she wouldn't call her boyfriend for a day or two. Better not to tip him off until this was over and he knew he was busted. After that the two of them could have their fight.

I might have felt guilty, wrecking this woman's life on a piece of fiction, if it wasn't for fact that both of them had more to worry about than a P.I.'s slander. If Fiona packed her bags, which she'd said was her intention, it might just save her.

She'd given me an hour to go through Geoff's stuff and I worked slowly and methodically because I wasn't looking for anything as simple as hotel receipts and filling station printouts.

What I was looking for was a mistake, a single piece of evidence that had dropped unnoticed from his messy game. And it took every minute of the hour I was in there but I found it. Pushed away under paperwork in a desk drawer: a single inkjet print that Fiona's boyfriend should have shredded. Just the one mistake. I spun Fiona another story and she let me take the sheet, which saved me having to photograph it and saved her from getting more than a quick glimpse of it, which might have brought questions I couldn't answer.

I'd got what I needed. And far more than I expected when I drove up the M5 to check out Triple-A.

Another stepping stone. Solid and leading onwards. Time to go for the next. Stride out whilst the stones line up.

One more piece of evidence and my hunch would be gold plated.

I stashed my A-Z and fired up the engine. Drove back out, watching the potholes.

CHAPTER THIRTY-ONE
Delivery boy

I drove the A road towards Kidderminster and turned off into a village released from traffic hell by a bypass thirty years ago. The Frogeye was the only thing moving between the few shops and the pub on the main street. The place had probably been this way between the wars.

I took a turn onto a lane and pulled up in front of a terrace of cottages. Hopped out and checked house numbers for the one on the bereavement envelope I'd found in John Reed's flat. Knocked on the door and talked my way into another life. The life in question was that of a fifty year old widow for whom I had bad news – or at least the part of it I was sure about, and enough to explain why she had a private investigator in her parlour.

My story brought questions I couldn't answer but she answered mine with a quiet tremor in her voice and closed the door quietly behind me when I left. Another day nicely messed up.

Bad news and dread. Door to door.

The P.I.'s speciality.

I got back to the car and picked up a missed call from Harry. He sent a pic. through with added commentary.

'They snatched her at just after ten. She shouldn't have opened the damn door.'

'They'd have smashed a window. They were going to take her no matter what.'

I was looking at an image from the erased time slot on Sarah's porch cam. People imagine that computer files are gone for good when you wipe them but all you're wiping is their location information. Until the memory is actually overwritten all the data and pictures, movies, emails and incriminating evidence are still there, waiting for the techie who knows how to find them. Sarah's abductors should have destroyed the drive. Even Harry would have struggled then.

So there on my screen was a close-up of Sarah's abductors.

Terry Dean and Aaron Grant.

Charlie Warren's crew.

'You're a genius, Harry,' I said.

'It's there on the CV. Right under flashy dresser.'

I took his word for it. I'd never seen Harry's CV. When he responded to our ad. seven years ago I was out on surveillance and it turned out that Harry was right there in the area so he joined me for an on-the-job interview. Which ended abruptly after unexpected complications arose. Harry took the action in his stride. Maybe assumed that the guys with coshes were part of the appraisal. When we got clear I asked if he had any questions and he didn't. I congratulated him on satisfying our interview process and he got his jacket repaired and took the job.

'Okay,' I said. 'So now we know.'

'We know something else too.'

Another snap beamed onto my screen.

It formed as a fuzzy half-image then focused.

I took a look.

Grinned.

Obvious, once you see it.

The picture was another from the porch cam. Another wiped frame recovered by Harry's software. But this was not last night. This shot was from three weeks ago.

'I got lucky with that one,' Harry said. 'The cam's on a four week loop.'

I was still looking at the image. And things were snapping into place.

Stepping stones: when they're solid under your feet sometimes they just keep going and take you right across to the promised land.

'This is the delivery?'

'No question. The knife photo's inside that envelope.'

Harry was going by the date stamp. Which told him that the manila envelope being pushed through Sarah's letterbox was the doctored photograph that had pulled me into this affair.

John Reed's nasty communiqué.

Bernard Locke had already shown me a porch cam. snap of the delivery. Reed's face had been on it, a little fuzzy but recognisable.

But Harry's shot was pulled straight from the computer, and this one didn't have Reed's face. This one showed the real delivery boy.

Chief Constable Bernard Locke.

Locke had accessed the computer and pulled out the image, substituted John Reed's face for his and wiped the original footage. Now that I was looking at the original the poor quality of Locke's version was obvious. The frame had been darkened and blurred to cover his Photoshopping job.

'He set the whole thing up,' Harry said. 'Photoshopped that image to implicate Reed and doctored the shots of Reed out and about in the city. Those pics didn't look right to me. Kind of low for CCTV. I played around and found that Locke had distorted the perspective to suggest a higher angle. When you restore them you see that the shots were taken at normal camera height.'

'Locke handed me standard camera shots – from someone watching Reed.'

'You got it, Eddie.'

'Which makes his story of finding Reed through a street-cam. search a load of baloney.'

'My guess: he was given those pics first. Told to find a guy. There was no CCTV search.'

'And the threat to Sarah was just a convenient story to bring me in.'

Harry agreed. 'Someone knew Reed was in Bristol and squeezed Locke to use his police powers to track him down.'

'Only Locke couldn't do that. So he brought me in. Hoping I'd do the job and disappear for good back to London.'

'Can't see it any other way.'

I thanked Harry and killed the call. Squeezed back into the Frogeye.

Another piece of the jigsaw had just slotted home to confirm my theory: Charlie Warren had conscripted Locke to find Cousins, a.k.a. John Reed, and Locke had conscripted me.

And that explained why Sarah had been snatched.

Charlie Warren saw that I was threatening his operation and needed to take me out of the picture.

But his goons had failed last night and Charlie knew I'd be watching for them if they tried again.

So he needed leverage to override my caution, and Sarah Locke was it.

Which meant I'd soon be getting a call from him.
An invitation to his end game.

CHAPTER THIRTY-TWO

Hindsight is always so useful

Two calls came in from Locke as I worked back through late-afternoon traffic on the M5. I let them go then dialled up the voicemails. Both were urgent requests for a call-back. The strain in Locke's voice confirmed that Sarah's disappearance wasn't part of the plan. But when you play with fire...

I deleted the messages. We'd talk when I needed something from him.

A third call came in. I floored the pedal, cleared of a convoy of middle-lane artics and picked up hands-free.

'I'm in a damn fix here,' I said. 'Glad you got back.'

'Is that a script you read from? It always sounds the same.'

Funny guy.

But factually wrong.

It didn't always sound the same. Sometimes I say "Damn Fix". Sometimes it's "Little Problem". Occasionally "Shits Creek". The words vary. No script.

My earpiece threw out a voice like sandpaper over the wind roar. I'd put it down to a bad connection but Zach Finch's voice had sounded that way before mobile phones. He was the kid in class whose voice grated so badly that you longed for the soothing music of fingernails across blackboard.

Zach was my DS back in the Job, the one copper in the Metropolitan Police I trusted a hundred percent. He was still on the force and still a DS and still helped me out now and again. I occasionally reciprocated, but those ops were deeper under cover than a bug in an MI5 agent's rug. The Job didn't solicit outside help.

Today's help was a light chore by my usual standards. A quick dig through Zach's memory. Zach was a Londoner through and through but he'd spent his teens out of town after his parents split and had served his apprenticeship in the Avon and Somerset police. And if Zach's memory banks gathered dust they were never archived.

I summarised what was up. Explained my fix: that I now had an innocent party likely to get hurt if I didn't play things the bad guys' way. Then I told Zach who the bad guys were.

He whistled.

'"Mad" Charlie? What's he up to over there?'

'Chasing down a guy with a debt. The chase ended in Bristol but I seem to have stirred things up again. So Charlie's trying to cork the bottle and he's snatched a third party to lure me in. So I need to get to them before he ties my hands. That might be easier if I know how the pieces fit. I need history: anything Warren was ever up to over here. Any links to Avon and Somerset that might not be kosher.'

A pause. Then:

'What's the interest in Avon and Somerset ?'

'The guy who pulled me into this thing is the chief constable. There's something between him and Warren and I need to know what it is.'

Zach whistled again.

'We talking about Bernard Locke? I sense an apple cart tipping, Eddie.'

'I'm going to kick the apple cart to pieces if Locke has used me to facilitate a criminal act. And if his actions get his daughter hurt he'll be riding the cart to hell.'

'Daughter?'

'She's the third party.'

'Holy smoke. That's Sarah Locke you're talking about! And you're saying Locke's working with Warren but the bastard's snatched her anyway? Sounds like something's going bad over there.'

'It is. Mostly down to me. And no matter that Locke's pally with Warren, he knows that I need to disappear before he sees his daughter again. So I need to know whether he's going to side with the bad guys when I move in.'

'Warren wouldn't get away with harming the chief constable's family.'

'Unless the chief constable's hands were tied. Which they are. Because if something did happen to his daughter he couldn't finger Warren without turning himself in. Which leaves Locke in a corner. His only way out is to see me in Warren's hands.'

'Got it,' Zach said. He thought it through. Checked his files. Pulled out the history.

'Locke was a DI at Bridewell when I was with Avon. Squeaky clean character. Rose up the ranks like he had a jet pack up his arse. But there was one funny incident that came near to touching him – and an even funnier coincidence now you're making connections.'

'A connection to Warren?'

'Could be. You know Charlie: London-based. But he's credited with one caper over in the West Country. Word had it that he was the brains behind a container heist at Avonmouth back in '89. A tobacco consignment worth a million and a half retail. That's three mill. today. Bridewell Organised Crime had had a tip-off and the tip said that Charlie was taking personal charge of the operation. So they kept the Met informed whilst they put together a team to watch the container and close the trap when Charlie made his move. But Bridewell flunked it. Word leaked and the bad guys ditched the job at the last moment. The heist never went down.'

'They find out where the leak came from?'

'No. But common belief was that it came from the Bridewell team. And Locke was running the team. And there was a belief that more operations went wrong when Locke was involved than rightly should have, even if things have a habit of going south in messy ops. But the Warren heist stood like a beacon: the tip-off was a straight inside job.'

'So if that was Locke we'd have him connected to Warren way back.'

'And if there was a connection,' Zach said, 'then Warren would exploit it. Charlie's got a reputation for cultivating his hired help, storing dirt on people who work with him that ensures their future co-operation. Maybe Locke was taking Charlie's money back then and got tangled in his net. Came to regret it later as his career took off.'

'Dirty baggage on his climb up the ranks. Stuff he couldn't ditch. Sounds credible. And the higher the rank the more to lose if the whistle blows. An old hold over Locke might be enough to squeeze him into co-operating with Warren's hunt for Ricky Cousins. But pulling in police resource would have been a tightrope walk.'

'So he gave you a bell,' Zach concluded.

So he gave me a bell. Signed on the dotted line.

Zach's history had just solidified my theory. Locke coerced into tracking down Cousins. Couldn't use police resources but couldn't refuse Charlie's demands. Solution: bring in the private sector. Work up a story about a threat to his daughter and let me loose on the job. He knew I'd recognise his story of using police resource for his camera search as way out of line, but I was out of the system and he had a good sob story to justify his transgression. And I *had* recognised that he was out of line. Wondered about how he got away with even a quiet search. If I'd just been a little more puzzled maybe I'd have dismissed his story as hokum and never touched the job.

Hindsight, always useful.

Like the sky above you when your parachute fails.

I thanked Zach and he told me to watch my back.

Reading from his own script.

I killed the line and went back to concentrating on the road.

My theory was solid. All the threads linked. The stalker and knife photo was a simple lie to bring me in, but the lie had worked well with the fortuitous hostile actions going on around TownGate. So I'd swallowed Locke's story. Taken the job and delivered Cousins to Charlie Warren.

The only oddity had been the fact that Ricky Cousins was alive and well despite his supposed demise at Warren's hands. The only oddity was him spectating as Warren's crew came after *me*.

But that oddity had resolved itself back in Birmingham.

Theory confirmed.

Leaving only the question of how to get Sarah back without putting myself into Warren's hands.

I could see a way but it would depend on me getting hold of one final piece of information.

And Ricky Cousins had that.

CHAPTER THIRTY-THREE
Shrimp special

I parked up at the Law School, well away from my Travelodge and walked a pattern down to the hotel, scanning parked cars and doorways. No sign of Dean or Aaron. Maybe Warren's crew preferred the cover of dark. Or maybe they were still holed up somewhere putting the finishing touch to their plan. And maybe Sarah Locke was tied up in their closet, confused and afraid. At the hotel entrance I took a last look around. Nothing. Even Gary had stood down. Either his day off or sick leave.

Up in my room I worked through a vigorous callisthenics routine to combat the effect of hours wedged in the Sprite. Got my pulse racing and eyes stinging. Finished with a cool-down then propped myself by the open window with a bottle of fizzy water to take in the view. When I showered I took care to keep hot water off my right knuckles where Dean's stubble had skinned them but let it heat my shoulder which was still complaining from the encounter despite the workout. I gave it ten minutes then a final cold rinse shocked me fully awake and I was ready to go.

I grabbed fresh clothes and called Sarah's number. Still nothing. My own phone had two more missed calls from Locke. I played the voicemails. His voice was scared and angry but his messages told me nothing except for the fact that he was back in town and that I needed to pick up my damn phone. I pressed delete, wondering whether Locke was calling on his own initiative or was Charlie Warren's messenger boy. I'd ask him that later.

I exited the hotel's back door and made a quick reconnaissance behind the building. Still nothing. But I stayed cautious. I wasn't ready to be jumped again. I walked back to the car and called in at a deli on the way. The place was just closing, fresh food service finished, but they re-opened their till to sell me a wrapped sandwich and bottle of water. Then I continued up the hill and dropped the supplies onto the Frogeye's passenger seat. Fired up and drove out of the city to a motel car park near the motorway. The place was a fifty-room brick building with just ten or so cars parked outside. The spots would fill up as business travellers eased off the motorway but right now the scarcity of vehicles made the job easier. I spotted the car I was looking for right away under the trees in the farthest corner. A psychological choice, the feeling you'd not be spotted.

I backed in beside a Volvo and watched the building. The place styled itself as a motel but it was a conventional hotel layout. Access to the rooms via a single front entrance. I popped the water bottle and unwrapped the sandwich and settled in.

I'd caught a break this afternoon. I needed pointers that would get me close to Sarah before Charlie Warren fired his next broadside, and two receipts I'd spotted in Geoffrey Smith's Bromsgrove house gave me them. The receipts said that Smith had stayed at this motel for two longish periods recently. And now I'd caught the second break. The car under the trees was Ricky Cousins' BMW. The one rented out by Triple-A to Geoffrey Smith. I'd already figured out that Smith was Cousins but the receipts had got me right to the guy. He'd returned to this roost when he realised that his plan was falling apart. Back to watching the opposition and planning.

I finished my sandwich. Listened to music with the hood up, waiting for Cousins to appear.

Cars trickled steadily in and business travellers crossed to the entrance hauling travel bags and suit covers. Headed out again for expense-account dinners in the city.

Just after seven a figure who wasn't a businessman came out through the glass doors and I watched the intense, goatee-lined face of Ricky Cousins look left and right, checking the car park. When he was satisfied he came all the way out and walked down to retrieve the BMW. I started the engine and tapped the wheel. When the BMW passed I pulled out and followed it towards the city.

The tail was easy in the thinning traffic and I was right behind the M3 when it pulled into a spot in the Old City. I found my own slot and followed Cousins round to a Chinese restaurant just off the fashionable streets. The place was a budget-limited business aimed at the student population, with a fascia in urgent need of a repaint and a tatty, unlit menu display. The silhouettes of a few early diners were visible inside. A waitress greeted Cousins when he walked in. Sat him down. I gave him five minutes then followed.

Cousins was head-down in the menu when I slid into the seat

opposite him. He looked up and his eyes widened and his mouth started to open then closed. A slow reaction for a poker player. But he caught up. Grimaced theatrically and kind of shrugged, like he'd been expecting this. I raised my eyebrows. He didn't respond. I gestured at the menu.

'Go ahead,' I said. 'I hear the shrimp special's good.'

Cousins' face stayed neutral but his eyes were locked onto me. Suddenly the menu didn't interest him. He made a decision and started to get up.

'Don't,' I said. 'Shrimp fried rice is your least bad option.'

He hesitated, half standing. Curled his lip but then sat back down.

'Fuck it is,' he said. 'You seen the shit they serve? Jesus. I dunno why I come back. But they're cheap, and they got a coupla cute students waiting on. I guess that's what brings me back.'

I said nothing.

He opened up his hands.

'Flynn,' he said. 'We meet at last.'

'We were always going to meet. On this side of the grave at least. Though you didn't factor that in.'

He held the leer even if he looked a little scared. His eyes bored into me.

'You're right,' he said. 'This is a fuck up. Shouldn't have happened. This shoulda stayed in Warren's circle. I mean – what's the odds of a private investigator from London Town wading back in? You're quite a wildcard, Flynn.'

'Wildcards turn up. You know it.'

'A million to one.'

'You think you're looking at a million to one fluke?' I shook my head. 'Your arithmetic's off, Ricky.'

He thought about it.

'Well fuck it. I guess you're right. But I can't bank regrets.'

'And regrets are not your thing. That's pretty clear from everything that's happened.'

'*What* has happened? *Nothing* has happened.'

I held up a hand.

'I'm not here to play games, Ricky. I'm here because *your* game has got someone into trouble. And you're my best route to helping them out of it.'

209

'You've lost me.'

'Maybe I have. I'm talking about Sarah Locke. Did you know that they've taken her since they failed to get me off the streets?'

'Sarah who?'

'Second warning. I haven't time for playing the fool, Ricky. You're the centre of this mess and you're the only one can help me.'

'What mess? You've nothing. You can't prove a thing.'

'Ricky: listen. Final warning. Your scheme's fallen apart. So don't get hung up on the proof thing. Charlie Warren won't need proof when he comes after you. And he's the guy you should be worrying about. You won't get lucky twice. So if you tell me one more time that you know nothing then I'm out of here, and Charlie will be sitting in this seat before they bring dessert. And if you run I'll be on your tail. I'll guide Charlie right in.'

I looked at him. Watched the sneer evaporate. He was turning things over. Had been since I'd sat down. Still spotted no upside to this.

I nudged him along.

'Your sole viable option, Ricky is to get on the right train. The one that gets me to Sarah and serves Charlie up on a platter. You're already on Charlie's hit list so you've nothing to lose. You're going to be hiding for the rest of your life but at least you'll *be* alive. They'll get you into witness protection and you can live safely at the taxpayer's expense.'

Cousins looked at me like he was looking into a mirror, hearing what he already knew.

'Witness protection was your backup plan,' I said. 'You're a gambler, Ricky. You knew your hand wasn't foolproof, knew it might end this way. So take Plan B. You might just survive.'

I gave him a few seconds to reach the same conclusion then pulled out the inkjet print I'd taken from his Bromsgrove hideaway. Placed it in front of him.

'If you don't take that train then it's not just Warren who'll be coming for you. You're facing a murder conspiracy charge, Ricky. The cops will dig it all out when they check your computers and you'll go down with Warren. Maybe the two of you can play a hand to decide who gets the top bunk.'

A waitress turned up and planted Cousins' beer. Its arrival passed unnoticed.

'And here's the key point: if you don't help me now, and if Sarah Locke gets hurt, then the cops won't get to you in time to make those charges. And Charlie will have one more kill notched up on his cell wall.'

Cousins kept his eyes on me. A poker face.

'Are we clear?' I said.

And he was. His eyes flickered and finally shied away from the staring match.

The waitress took the opportunity to ask if he was ready to order but he brushed her away.

'Later,' he said.

'Are we clear?'

He looked at me again. Eyes no longer steady. Holding it in.

'Yeah,' he said finally. 'Clear.' He leaned forward. 'And fuck you, Flynn. Mister fly-on-the-fucking-spare-ribs. There's always one that lands. But you'd better believe me: I don't know what's happened to that TV woman, so I *can't* help you.' He sat all the way forwards and his eyes were bouncing round the options, still seeing no safe place to land.

'The whole thing's gone to shit,' he said. He looked at me. 'Thanks to you.'

'That's an interesting way to look at it,' I said, 'by the guy who started the whole thing. And any other time I'd love to come over this table and discuss things in detail but I don't have time. So you're going to help me now or watch me call Charlie.'

Cousins held his hands wide.

'Tell me.'

I pointed to his phone.

'First I need something I can bank. Copies of the pictures you've been accumulating. And that's non-negotiable. If I hear "No" I'm going to call Charlie and walk out.'

Cousins gave it another second but I guess something in my face dissuaded him from stalling further. He went for the compliance option, though his face now had the look of the condemned man's when the hangman checks the knot for safety. He picked up his phone and pulled up his photos and I flicked through them. Pointed out my selection. He sent them across. Still without comment.

'Second,' I said, 'I need to know where they are.'

Cousins started to work up another confused look. I breathed a heavy sigh.

'Warren's people: you know where they're staying.'

This was what I'd come here for. The thing that mattered.

Another hesitation, but there really was no option. Cousins gave me what I needed then pointed a finger that wasn't quite steady.

'You'd better be clear how this went down,' he said. 'I'm helping you out. Helping to put things right.'

I smiled at him. When I talked to the police I'd tell it exactly as it happened. Cousins needn't worry on that score. But the guy was deluded nevertheless. He was putting nothing right.

Then his face relaxed. He tested his beer and grabbed the menu again.

'Shrimp special, you say? I might just try it! How about you, Flynn? Have a drink, at least. On me. You can tell me how the hell you tracked me down.'

He grinned and gestured.

I picked up the inkjet picture and re-folded it. Pushed it into my jacket.

'Enjoy your meal,' I said.

I stood and walked out.

CHAPTER THIRTY-FOUR
Unstable mode

Dusk was coming on as I parked in another motel car park near another motorway. A new development up towards the M4/M5 interchange with a prime view of a shopping mall and a wasteland of out-of-town retail outlets. The motel had a central reception block and two-storey brick annexes stretching out either side with walkways serving the upper floor. The lower doors opened straight onto the car park. Half way along the far block a black Merc E Class was angled up to the building and three ground floor windows were lit up. The Merc was the one Dean and his pals had brought to the ambush last night.

Charlie Warren's soldiers. Billeted and waiting. Looked like Cousins' info. was good.

Dean & Co probably thought they were a smart crew but they'd failed to spot Cousins' camera snapping their every move since they first turned up in the city to watch John Reed's flat. Hadn't spotted the evidence accruing.

I found a spot in the shadow of a steel storage container well clear of the buildings where I could watch the Merc without being spotted. Relaxed with soft music for a while until it was drowned by the grumble of a beat-up Mondeo pulling in alongside me. The car creaked to a halt and its lights died. I climbed out and walked round.

Harry exited the vehicle and worked through some kind of neck exercise to limber up. Then leaned on the roof and grinned across.

'Two capers for the price of one,' he said. 'The Stradivarius *and* Charlie Warren.

He turned to the building. Counted windows.

'That's them,' I confirmed. 'Waiting for the party to start.'

'She in there?'

'Can't rule it out. They've direct access. Could get her in and out. But it's a risk. My guess says she's somewhere else.'

'Any sign of action?'

'Not yet. But it's tonight. They need to close this off. Put Sarah back on the street before the pressure pops.'

'Which means getting you *off* the street.'

'That's the plan.'

'Are we playing along?'

'Soon as they call. They'll invite me for a chat, somewhere quiet. When they go out you can check their rooms, just in case. If she's not there then I'll go ahead with the meet. Give them the slip and a reason to scurry back to wherever they're holding her.'

'You hooked Locke yet?'

'I'm on my way.'

I told Harry I'd be back and left him watching the windows.

~~~~~

Locke answered his door with a ferocious stare. But the ferocity had desperation mixed in. My guess was that he hadn't told his wife that their daughter was missing, maybe planned to keep her in the dark until Sarah was back safe. My guess was that he was feeling the pressure.

Because things were going bad.

'Hell!' he said. 'I've been calling you.'

'Dodgy reception.'

He paused. Selected his words.

'Thanks for coming back,' he said. 'I've not heard a damn thing from her.'

'You wouldn't.'

'Or from whoever took her.'

I smiled.

'Well: that's what I'd like to talk about.'

He stood back and waved away a gaunt woman who'd appeared from a room down the hallway.

'Business,' he told her. 'Just a few minutes.'

So she didn't know. The guy was still hoping to patch this over. Seemed Ricky Cousins wasn't the only one with delusions.

We went into a room and I perched on a sofa armrest and dangled a leg.

'What do you mean?' Locke said.

My last remark had registered.

I waited. Gave him a moment for a sense of bad news to filter

214

through.

'I mean that I'd have expected Charlie Warren to call you. Keep you informed.'

Locke kept a straight face but he was standing ramrod stiff.

'Who's Charlie Warren?'

I held my smile. The denials were coming thick and fast this evening. No-one knew anything. The P.I.'s eternal affliction. When half the bastards I've chased down are being powerboated across the Styx they'll still be asking what's happening.

I said nothing. Just held on to the smile until Locke got the message. Until he spoke.

'What have you got?'

'All of it. Which is why I know that Charlie's been in touch with you.'

Locke waited for more.

'Charlie has Sarah,' I clarified. 'I ID'd his people at her house.'

Locke's face stayed neutral. Maybe a little puzzled. I swung my leg and talked to my foot. My patience was running on fumes.

'Bernard,' I said quietly, 'you're a piece of work.'

He started to speak but I looked up. Stopped him.

'You've put your daughter with some very bad people. And here you are – still playing games.'

I shook my head.

'It's over, Bernard. Best case scenario now is that we get Sarah back unharmed.'

Locke's face tightened, drawing up all the authority his three years as chief constable of Avon and Somerset had bolstered. For a crazy moment I thought he was about to bawl me out or take a swing. But something held him back. Fear, I guess. Fear that this dangerous endgame was on a knife-edge.

Because the only good outcome for Locke would be one where Sarah came back and then the whole thing faded quietly away. But that wasn't going to happen. Not whilst I was still alive. Which is why he was going along with Charlie's plan to lure me in and close the affair.

And he'd just seen that outcome fade. Because I was alert to his scheme.

'What are you proposing?' he said.

'Firstly: to stay alive. Secondly: to get Sarah back in one piece. We're on the same side on that one but your problem is that once your daughter is safe we'll be on very different sides.'

Locke thought it through. Saw the moment of truth looming. The moment where a dirty past of graft and corruption hit the buffers, where a new future was opening up that was no future at all. I helped him along.

'I know the whole thing,' I said.

'And what's that?'

'That you're working with Warren. Or *for* him. It will come to the same thing when the authorities go after him. And I know that your connection has put Sarah in danger. Let's see if I have it: Warren didn't tell you in advance that he was snatching her. But he's reassured you that she won't be hurt. She's just an expediency to help get things sorted. But what if things don't get sorted? What if Charlie doesn't get me?'

Locke glared at me a moment longer but then finally, suddenly, he sagged at the futility of staying with his lies.

'He won't harm her,' he said. 'He wouldn't want the heat. And he's no gripe with her.'

'But he might have one with you when things go south, as they will. So the question is whether, as the flames close in, Charlie blames you for starting the fire. All he wanted was Ricky Cousins found on the Q.T. He didn't ask you to bring in a private investigator. And even if you and I know that that was your only option the nuances of police procedures and limitations will be lost on Charlie. All he sees is that his big-shot chief constable pal has messed him up royally. And what I hear is that Charlie has a way of taking screw-ups personally. He likes to make examples of people who disappoint him. Hurting Sarah to hurt you would fit right in.'

'Warren knows that if anything happens to Sarah I'll crucify him.'

'Would you? Think about it. Turning witness against Charlie would mean turning yourself in. Admitting conspiracy to murder. Your wife would learn that it was your actions that put your daughter in harm's way, and you'd spend the rest of your life behind bars regretting it. So your choice would be to turn Charlie over and go down in flames yourself or lock it all up and live with it. That would be a tricky decision. And if you decided on the *schtum* option Charlie would have the pleasure of watching you holding in your little secret for the rest of your life until it killed you. He'd appreciate the karma.'

'You're overstating the threat to Warren. Right now there's nothing to connect him to anything. And no-one's been hurt.'

Back to denials. I pushed myself off the sofa arm and pulled my phone out. Locke scanned Ricky Cousins' photographic record of the action from Reed's flat to the Perseverance Hospital as I flicked the photos across the screen.

'There's your connection,' I said. 'And you know already what happened to the guy once Charlie had him.'

Locke was looking at a shot taken outside the Perseverance. Reed's features couldn't be made out in the dark, even on night setting, but the implications of an injured guy being hustled out of the rear gate were as clear as the registration on Reed's van and on Dean & Co's Merc. The pictures put it all together.

Locke looked up.

'Who the hell took those?'

'A guy called Ricky Cousins.' I stashed the phone. 'Cousins is the fugitive Charlie had you track down. The pictures show Charlie's crew working their disappearing act.'

'You're not making sense. If Cousins was the fugitive how could he have taken photographs of the operation?'

'That had me puzzling for a while. But Cousins did take the pictures. He took plenty of them. It was his photos that lured Charlie to Bristol in the first place – the ones you used to pull me in. And Cousins documented the whole operation after Charlie's people turned up in the city. How? Because the guy in the street snaps, the one living up in Redland, the guy being hustled away by Charlie's crew isn't him. It's a man called John Reed.'

'But Reed is an...'

'Alias? That's what Cousins wanted Warren to believe. That John Reed was him, hiding under a new name. Only it wasn't. John Reed was a different person. Just a nobody who was unlucky enough to look like Ricky Cousins. Unlucky enough to be spotted by him and selected as the perfect bait. Cousins was tired of running. Saw an opportunity to end the chase. All he needed to do was send Charlie some anonymous pics of Reed living in Bristol and plant clues in Reed's flat to suggest that the guy was him. He figured that when

Warren caught up with Reed he'd take him out quietly, minimum fuss. Minimum risk of come-back. Charlie knew he wasn't getting his cash back so he'd just cut his losses and go for the quick, quiet job. Cousins figured that Reed would disappear without Warren ever finding out he had the wrong guy.'

Locke was staring now. Finally saw it.

'The bastard,' he said.

'If you mean Cousins I'd agree with you. He was happy to have an innocent guy take the fall for his own mistakes. And he ran his plan with cold precision. Stayed close to the action and photographed it all as a back-up contingency, in case Warren ever found out he'd been duped. If that happened Cousins was ready to incriminate Warren with the photographic evidence. Distract him with more pressing matters whilst he scarpered again.'

I jabbed my hands into my pockets. Looked at Locke.

'That's all for tomorrow,' I said. 'Right now we both have a priority, which is getting Sarah back before the shit hits the fan and Warren goes into unstable mode.'

'How do we do that?'

'By outsmarting the guy. He's roped you in to help trap me. So we'll play on that. Tell me how it's supposed to go down.'

Locke took a breath.

'I'm to contact you when they give the go-ahead. Pretext of receiving a message from Sarah giving her location. Charlie knows that the text won't fool you but he says you'll turn up anyway if I offer to come along as backup. Says you'll jump at the chance to turn the tables on his crew.'

I smiled.

'And when I try to turn that table,' I said, 'one of the legs falls off. Namely that you back out, leave me on the spot.'

'Yes.'

'Okay. That's a good plan. We'll stay with it. Except for the leg-falling-off bit. The backup needs to be real.'

I looked at Locke.

He kept quiet. If there was a nod of agreement I didn't catch it.

'It's your only way out,' I told him.

Locke flapped a hand finally. Impatient.

'He's going to call,' I said. 'You need to decide before that happens.'

'Fine,' Locke said. 'We turn the tables on them. How does that get Sarah back?'

'I'll be ready for their ambush and your double-cross,' I said. 'And we'll both make sure I give them the slip, right after bluffing them that I know where they're keeping Sarah. So they're going to go to running to her and you'll follow them.'

Locke clamped his lips. Didn't like it. But saw that there was no other way since Plan A – the one where Flynn disappears – was off the table.

'You guide me in to Sarah,' I said, 'then step back. Warren will never know you were in on it. I'll handle getting her free. And then you're out of it. Warren will have battles to fight and you and Sarah will no longer be on his radar.'

Which wouldn't solve Locke's problem since he'd be on the authorities' radar. His future was a tightrope walk at best. The chief constable had shrunk in the last twenty-four hours. A guy running out of options.

'And your guy Gary...' I said.

He looked puzzled again. Some people never give up.

'He's off the job,' I told him. 'Keep him clear. It's just you and me.'

I left him to it and walked out.

When I got back to the motel the three windows were dark and Harry's Mondeo was untended. I walked across the road into the mall car park and found Harry leaning against a tree eating a banana, watching a TGI Friday's restaurant.

'They went in forty-five minutes ago,' he said. 'I hopped back to check their rooms once they were settled. She's not there.'

It would have been too easy.

'...But they've come equipped. They've some handy looking saps stashed in their bags, and Dean has a duffle with a hammer stashed inside.' Harry grinned. 'My guess: he's got a piece in the glove compartment. They'll be coming prepared, Eddie.'

I grinned back. Private investigation. The whole mix. One day you're serving notices, the next you're ducking coshes and hammers. Sometimes you get both.

I briefed him on my chat with Locke.

Harry's smile widened.

'He's gonna back you up?'

'So he told me.'

'Sounds like I'm redundant.'

I was still smiling. We watched the restaurant. Silhouettes moving inside.

'But you'll be there anyway,' I said.

'Wouldn't miss it.'

Then a customised black Saab 9-3 with spoiler and gold mesh wheels rolled up and parked in a spot opposite the entrance. A guy got out and walked over. Slowly. Concentrating on his phone conversation.

'Well now,' I said.

The guy reached the door and pocketed his phone. I stepped across and walked in thirty seconds after him. The reception stand was unmanned since the maitre d' had taken the guy through. I spotted them moving towards a table half way down where three guys were eating. The guys looked up and their visitor stopped and sat. The lighting and distance were a bit tricky but Terry Dean and his crew were not hard to ID. Nor their visitor, who was Stevie, Martin Kieran's guy at the housing development. I turned and walked back out.

'One of the crew?' Harry said.

'Local hired help. A guy working for a pal of Charlie Warren's.'

Harry thought about it.

'You thinking what I'm thinking?' he said.

I was.

'We might be looking at Sarah's babysitter,' I said.

Harry folded his banana skin and pushed it into his pocket. He was wearing one of his herringbones. Large pockets with flaps. It's an image thing: your favourite uncle up from the country for the antiques fair, though your favourite uncle probably doesn't sport steel-capped shoes. The shoes were Harry's fight against the ageing process. Helped settle disputes before his stamina ran out. He's a practical guy that way.

We watched for another ten minutes then Stevie came back out. Seemed the guy was not that tight with Warren's crew. No invitation to dinner. When I turned, Harry was already jogging away, back over to the motel to grab his Mondeo. If Stevie was heading back to Sarah we needed to stay with him, though if the Porsche shifted out of second gear the Mondeo would need a tow.

The distraction was untimely. We couldn't pass up a chance that Stevie would get us to Sarah but if Harry got delayed I'd be down on manpower when Dean's party kicked off. I watched the restaurant and pondered the odds, counted the minutes.

Then just before ten my phone rang.

'They've set it up,' Locke said. 'One a.m.' He described an abandoned industrial site over from the Temple Meads station.

'Got it. They'll turn up half an hour early to set up the ambush,' I said. 'So we'll go in half an hour before that.'

'Twelve midnight.'

'Have your car handy,' I told him. 'They'll move fast once I've given them the slip.'

'I know what to do,' Locke said. 'Just focus on your part.'

I said nothing. Didn't mention that our plan would become redundant if Harry got to Sarah. I cut the call and went back to watching the restaurant. Terry Dean would be briefing his guys on the plan of action as they polished off their Cajun onions and fajita burgers. Just time for dessert and another beer and they'd be off.

I quit waiting. Walked back to the motel and opened up the Frogeye. Squeezed in and listened to music again.

Dean and his crew reappeared just before eleven. They walked fast across the car park, didn't look right or left, disappeared into their rooms. Two minutes later they were out again and climbing into the Merc. I watched it back out and ease away towards the city. They'd be at the meet site by eleven thirty to beat my own early arrival time which Locke had just leaked to them.

They'd be waiting but I knew they were there.

Which gave me the advantage. Shouldn't be too difficult to hand out a couple of bloody noses then slip free.

Whether Locke would actually follow them when they left the meet was questionable but someone would. And whether they'd take us to Sarah or come straight back here was something I'd no control over.

I listened to the music and tried to calculate odds. My calculations were a mix of speculation and unknowns. Which made them useless. After half an hour I gave up. Fired up the engine and followed the Mercedes down into Bristol.

CHAPTER THIRTY-SIX
Surprises

I cut through a tunnel under the station and came out alongside a derelict site sandwiched between the river and a canal basin. Drove past ten foot boarding and parked on a curve of wide pavement a hundred yards on. The street was deep shadow, streetlights dud from lack of council funds or vandalism. Just the faintest illumination from reflected city light. I walked carefully. A call came in. I took it. Listened. Asked for a call back in fifteen and set the phone to vibrate mode.

The site's perimeter boarding protected a 60's steel and concrete structure silhouetted against night sky. An old mail-sorting complex, due for demolition and redevelopment. A set of wooden gates blocked the old entrance road, secured with a steel chain. I hefted the chain and it pulled free from the gates' cut-outs, securing nothing. It had been sheared and loosely re-draped to look secure. Dean's crew, taking their vehicle in to avoid the risk of passers-by clocking their number plate as they loaded a body into the boot. Foot access needed only a quick duck through a kicked-in panel in the adjacent boarding. Seemed the place got visitors: rough sleepers, druggies, urbexers.

I turned and found Bernard Locke at my shoulder. His face was hard to read in the light.

'Have you spoken to them again?' I asked him.

'No. But they'll be on their way.'

'You got your car handy?'

'I can get to it in sixty seconds.'

'Then let's go.'

We ducked through the damaged panel and came out on weed-shattered concrete. Thirty yards ahead of us was the seven storey admin building that fronted the complex. A ramp climbed up its near side, the route round to the loading docks.

We walked across and stood beneath a wall of smashed windows fronting the derelict shell. Tasted the musty breeze that flicked out from the ground floor. John Reed and his urbex pals would have loved it.

We walked along the building, across concrete split by shrubs, strewn with ironmongery and rotting pallets. Occasional flashes of light from the railway cut through the building's black interior. The front stayed in shadow.

Nothing moved. Blackness and silence. The musty breeze.

No Merc. No sign of Warren's people, though they were here for sure. We both knew it. Both pretended we didn't.

We hit the end and turned back to check out the ramp. Walked up between six foot walls and came out onto the high-level loading yard behind the complex where the railway station lights dazzled us.

The yard was a wide empty space between the building and the railway. Cracked and crumbling concrete. Bushes and rubble. Hand trolleys and a toppled steel drum. We walked towards the building, steered clear of the deep shadows of collapse holes. Arrived at the loading platform. The building's frame was illuminated by the railway lights but the interior stretched away into blackness behind the bays. The breeze reversed and the dank, dead breath flowed over us again. We stopped and looked up at building, eyes and ears alert for movement. But there was nothing. Just the chill, mouldy breeze of an abandoned place.

The gate back to the street seemed a long way off.

The chill would have been a little less chilly if Harry had been somewhere near, scouting for the bad guys. But he'd not caught up. His priority was Stevie and the chance of getting to Sarah.

I flicked on my tac. light and Locke held up one of his own and we climbed up and walked the platform in a charade of scouting for a place to hide, somewhere to surprise Dean's crew when they turned up.

Still both pretending that we didn't know.

I angled my beam left and right, up and down. The light's good for fifty yards, reflected white circles from the steel and concrete interior, glinted back from shattered glass above us.

I turned back, flicked the beam onto a cluster of steel storage containers over by the ramp wall and gave Locke a split-up gesture. I'd check that way. He'd cover the stair tower at the far end of the building.

Then my phone vibrated. I pulled it out.

Locke waited.

Harry.

I picked up. Listened. Told Harry I'd be in touch and killed the line.

I looked at Locke. Our lights brought his face out in shadows.

'We've found her,' I said.

Locke's eyes flashed.

'I've a guy outside the location right now,' I said. 'So the party's over. We don't need Dean's help to get there.'

Locke's torch painted the concrete as his free hand clenched into a fist.

'Damn!' he said. He followed my lead. Looked round. Which I'd never stopped doing. 'Let's get the hell out of here,' he said.

In the ideal world he'd have spoken more quietly but I guess the excitement of the moment got to him. We'd just been handed the way out. No need for the circus.

We turned and walked away from the building towards the ramp. The railway lights dazzled us again. We squinted, watching for holes.

Half way across a silhouette stepped from behind the ramp wall.

We angled our lights together and lit the figure up.

It was Aaron Grant.

Still in his suit but holding a sap at his side.

We split up, angled to left and right to pass him, still aiming for the ramp. Then footsteps crunched behind us and a voice called.

I turned. Caught Terry Dean in my tac. light. Dean had his own torch which dazzled me but didn't conceal the bruises on his face. He had a guy at his shoulder whom I recognised from Percy Vallan's photos. Driver Louis Williams. Williams had a sap too. It tapped against his thigh.

'Glad you made it, Flynn,' Dean said.

I turned and swung my torch to check my back. Aaron was still standing solidly at the centre of the ramp but Locke had walked away into the blackness.

I turned back. Dean and Williams continued to close the distance. Fifty feet. Forty. Williams' sap was still tapping.

Smack, smack.

'You won't believe the stuff I've heard about you,' Dean said.

'Nothing bad, I hope.' Original to the end.

'*All* bad. Ex filth. Pokes his nose where he shouldn't. Good at the fisticuffs. A tough guy.'

Twenty feet.

'We're getting new cards printed,' I said. 'Mind if I put that in?'

'Put whatever you want in. I won't be hiring you.'

'Thought not.'

Dean stopped. Threw a leer.

'Nothing personal. But we don't need private investigators to sort our problems.'

The two of them were ten feet away.

'The question is,' Dean said, 'does "tough guy" mean big boy tough? Or does it evaporate when the real players step in.'

I kept my light in his face.

'I seemed to get by last night,' I said. 'Or is that just a new face-paint fashion?' Even in the harsh illumination his face had colours to match my knuckles.

Dean rocked back on his heels, chin up. Williams continued with the sap.

'You think I noticed the taps?' Dean said. 'You took us by surprise then ran like a pussy.'

'That's a nice way of looking at it. Since you were the guys springing the ambush.'

'We'll now we're springing another.' Dean's hands squeezed. 'And this time you won't be so lucky.'

'Then I'll have to fall back on my P.I. skills. Or your stupidity.'

Dean looked down at Williams. Williams stayed focused on me. Dean still had his flashlight in my face and I still had mine in his. Two cars on main beam, neither willing to give way.

And no room to pass.

Figuratively speaking.

The yard was at least two hundred feet across. And Dean and his pals weren't athletes. More than generous manoeuvre room.

'If you'd just stayed put in London you'd have been fine,' Dean said.

'If I'd stayed in London then Charlie wouldn't have found his man.'

'A good point. Though why Charlie brought Constable Locke into this I'll never know. Chief of Sodding Police for Chrissakes. Charlie's a good boss. Has it well together. He just makes these funny judgements sometimes. Not that I'm gonna mention it to him.' He turned to Williams again. 'Are we gonna tell Charlie he made a pig's ear of this?' he said.

Williams said nothing. Just held me solid in his sight. Not interested in distractions.

'But what's done is done,' Dean said. 'We should be grateful you dug Cousins out. We're just annoyed that you came back. This was none of your business.'

'I smelt something rotten and found I'd been hoodwinked. Which made it my business. I came back to clear up.'

Dean chuckled and looked at Williams again. Williams stayed focused.

'That's a good one,' Dean said. 'There's gonna be some clearing up all right but it won't be you doing it.'

Finally Williams piped in.

'When you get them cards printed,' he said, 'you can add some letters after your name. How about RIP? How does that sound, you piece of shit?'

So this was what had kept him quiet. He turned to look up at Dean and smacked his sap with a new animation now he'd got the card thing out.

I felt a moment's dizziness from the blast of humour. So this was Charlie's plan. Stun me with wit. This was going to be tougher than I thought.

'RIP,' Williams repeated. 'How does that sound? Like BSc or PhD only it's RIP. That's the qualification you're gonna have in a coupla minutes, Mr Big-Shot.'

I grinned.

'Did you make that up yourself, Titch?'

'I'll tell you what I'll make up,' Williams said. 'I'll make up that you'll be wishing you'd been a whole lot smarter by the time we're through with you.' The guy was right in the conversation now. A grin stretched all the way across his face.

I sighed. Kept scanning my periphery. We could have traded one-liners all night but I knew Dean didn't have the inkling. The chit-chat was to establish power. Nothing else. A demo that this was just a day's work for him. He started walking forwards again, closing the distance, and Williams took his cue and stepped out a little wider, sap ready, held forwards and out.

It was time to scarper.

As they closed the last three feet I launched a kick into Dean's groin that he was too slow to avoid and there it was again: the surprise thing. I didn't wait to see his reaction though. I'd already turned and was into a fast jog towards Aaron and the ramp. Dean's agonised yell came loud and clear behind me but there were instructions amongst the pain.

Aaron came into a stance, sap raised, but he was covering a twenty yard wide opening and I swerved clear without any risk of contact and raced back down to the street gate. Aaron came after me faster than I'd have credited though, and the woodwork would slow me down just sufficiently to let him at me. So I pulled up sharp as I reached it and turned as Aaron motored in. He raised his sap but I dived under it and rammed my head into his abdomen and as his momentum took him on past he spun and went down hard against the woodwork. His cosh hand smacked against something nasty, maybe an old nail, and he yelled blue murder. The cosh dropped free and a second later he took my fist on the side of his head, then my tac. light in his nose. He was half up on his feet and scuttling instinctively back as the blows hit him, and the exit hole was suddenly beckoning.

Thirty yards away Dean and Williams were jogging down the ramp. Far too late.

I ducked to dive out onto the street but then a figure shouldered in through the hole to block me. I stepped back ready to defend myself.

Locke. Straightening up.

We stood for a moment whilst Dean and his pal pounded the concrete behind us and Aaron finally found his feet and his sap.

'Sorry, Eddie,' Locke said.

Though he looked more scared than sorry. But he stood solid enough, blocking the way.

'Get out of the way, Bernard,' I said. 'Don't do it.'

Then Aaron's sap caught me a smack on my thigh and even with his injured hand the blow hit the muscle like a fury. Then another belt landed: Williams' weapon whacked between my shoulder blades like a pile-driver and I went down.

I rolled away, seeking the protection of the boarding, but I had two lights illuminating me and two guys who knew what they were doing with their weapons and I took a dozen blows in five seconds that nearly paralysed my arms and legs.

Before Dean called a halt.

His two guys were steaming, ready to finish the job even if it meant having to carry me to wherever the Merc was parked. But Dean was through with larking about, pissed off with surprises and screw-ups. All he wanted was to get the job done. To see me safely in the car and out of here for a drive to a quieter place. The saps would come back out there. Dean's professional sense told him to minimise the blood at this location. Less evidence to tell a tale should there be complications.

So his two guys backed off, though their saps stayed ready, but I was out of motivation. It took me three attempts to get myself up into a leaning position against the gate. My legs were jelly and my arms were on fire. No broken bones but the muscle on my left thigh was spasming and my left arm was numb. Maybe something serious there.

I looked at Locke.

'Bad decision,' I said.

Locke didn't reply. He looked beaten. Like there were no good options any more. He looked like a guy watching the end close in. But if I disappeared tonight then maybe, just maybe... That's what his look said before he turned and ducked out through the gate.

Dean turned and jabbed a thumb. 'Bring him.'

Williams and Aaron got either side of me and grabbed an arm each. I let my legs go, playing for time. I needed thirty seconds maybe a minute, then I'd be good to pull clear, go for the ramp and get out over the far wall into the railway station.

But Dean's crew weren't giving me the chance. They gripped me like a vice and took my weight. Got me walking. Dean was going ahead and talking about "big shot P.I.s" and "clever bastards" though his voice was a bit breathy. I sensed things bugging him. Maybe the thought of the conversation he'd be having with Charlie back in Town. How he'd have to gloss over things, shrug off the job as routine, try to stand upright.

We moved back across the yard to the gaping entrance of the arrivals bay that ran into the building from the ramp end. The

229

flashlights illuminated the Merc twenty feet in.

And a three-by-three metre polythene sheet laid out beside it.

Which was not good.

Seemed Dean was set up to get the job done here.

It was now or never.

I heaved down and back as Aaron and Williams relaxed their grip. Aaron twisted immediately and swung his sap at my head but I was still moving and took the blow on my shoulder as I pulled clear and rolled away. Aaron stepped after me and struck viciously but I flexed muscle and rolled and came upright and his sap smashed into concrete, which must have been hell on his wrist. The distraction took his attention from my fist which landed hard on his temple and slowed him for the second I needed to land a double-fisted follow-up on his neck. He cursed and staggered clear to turn and face me and suddenly the three of them had closed a triangle around me. Three guys. Two saps.

I stood at its centre, grinning the way you do when you're pumped with adrenaline and hurting like hell and trying to decide which way to go when every direction is bad. The triangle was solid.

Dean flicked his fingers and Williams worked a remote, and the Merc came to life behind him, gave us light to work with.

'That was uncalled for,' Dean said. I don't know whether he meant the kick between his legs or the catching them by surprise again. Probably the latter. Whatever it was, he was looking at me with bad intent as he pulled a hammer from an inside pocket. It wasn't the ball-peen I'd heard about but a longer, ugly thing with a claw. For emergencies, maybe.

'Sorry about the kick,' I said. 'Just the excitement of the moment. You'll be fine in a day or two.'

I decided.

Williams and Aaron.

The way out was between them.

I'd take a blow or two but at least it wouldn't be with a hammer. And that way took me back out of the hall, clear of the building.

A good plan if I could coax my legs into more than a zombie walk. My leg muscles were still cramping and I wasn't sure what my left arm was doing but that was my plan.

But a tenth of a second before I acted, Williams and Aaron spotted my body language and stepped closer, cancelling the option.

Then Dean stepped forward to tighten the triangle.

'Don't worry about me,' he said. 'Worry about yourself.'

He raised the hammer.

Just as a wolf whistle split the dark

Dean froze. Turned.

From way down the drive-through hall, barely touched by the Merc's lights, a guy was walking towards us.

Dean lowered the hammer, thinking about more surprises.

'Is this a private party?' the guy called. 'Or can anyone join in?'

The guy continued walking and finally got into better light. Came to a halt on the near side of the Merc so that we were looking at a six-foot three silhouette. A frizz of hair caught the light. The effect wasn't as good as the movies where the lights are arranged so that the shadow gets bigger as it comes towards you but this one looked menacing enough.

'Who the hell are you?' Dean said.

'I'm the guy you don't want to meet,' the silhouette said, 'if you're looking for quiet.'

'He's with me,' I pointed out.

Dean hefted the hammer, looked back at me.

'The fuck!' he said. '*Two* of you?' He shook his head. 'Any more surprises lined up?'

'You don't need any more,' Shaughnessy said.

Dean turned again and stepped back to get us both in his sight. He was still shaking his head. Spoke to Shaughnessy.

'Are you as tough as this guy?' He jabbed a thumb. 'Because he's not so tough.'

'Wait till you wake up tomorrow,' Shaughnessy said. 'Decide then.'

'So what is this? A P.I.'s convention?' Dean was back talking to me. His two stooges had tensed but stayed calm. The odds were still looking okay.

'When you plan an ambush,' I said, 'make sure there's not one waiting for you.'

'This?'

Dean made theatre of his astonishment. Jabbed his thumb again. 'This guy? And you barely standing? You saying you've got us cornered?'

231

His guys were grinning now.

I grinned back. My arm ached like fury and my leg was threatening to drop me onto the concrete but I grinned anyway.

'I can still get about,' I said. 'But my partner's probably sufficient.'

'So he's the hard guy?' Dean snapped his fingers. 'Aaron: check how hard the guy is.'

Aaron widened his grin and strode across, big and confident. Walked right up to Shaughnessy and swung the sap in a fluid movement that was vicious and low, no pause for a warning. But Shaughnessy wasn't waiting for a warning. He'd stepped back and sideways and let lose a straight-arm jab into Aaron's throat that was followed by a pile-driver the guy never saw coming. The sap flew high and came down on the Merc's bonnet whilst Aaron's fluid move continued floorwards. A second later he was eating concrete.

Dean and Williams saw the odds changing a little too late. Dean twisted and swung the hammer back at me but I stepped out of its arc and landed another kick despite my leg, which sent him backwards. Williams was moving in on Shaughnessy, albeit with a little more caution than Aaron had shown. He tensed into an attack crouch, sap circling loosely. Shaughnessy stepped forward, within reach and Williams accepted the invitation, which was a bad idea. As he swung his weapon Shaughnessy twisted and guided the arm and grabbed either side of the elbow. A dull snap echoed from the concrete and Williams coughed out pain and didn't see Sean's fist arcing in. He went down onto his knees using his good arm to stop himself falling onto his broken wrist but Shaughnessy put him on it anyway. Dean was coming back at me, hustling me backwards despite the injury to his groin, and I barely fended off his hammer arm. He adapted, spasmed into a whole-body head-butt, and I pulled my face back in the nick of time and landed a right fist that he probably didn't feel. But then something smacked Dean's temple and that one he *did* feel. Even I felt it. The blow rolled the guy's eyes round like those kiddies' dolls.

But he turned to meet his attacker and you couldn't dispute that Dean was tough. It was the first time I'd seen anyone stay on his feet after one of Shaughnessy's specials had landed. But even if you're on your feet it doesn't mean you're fit to go. When your eyes are bouncing around you're probably making bad decisions. Staying up when you should go down. And you're fighting an opponent who's not moving at zombie pace.

Shaughnessy stepped aside and kicked at Dean's feet.

Dean started to topple and Shaughnessy used the guy's momentum to run him backwards into the side of the Merc. The impact put a dent in the driver's door that looked like a tractor had hit it. As Dean bounced off Shaughnessy caught his suit lapels and landed three fast, heavy right-handers to the head and Dean sat down for a break.

Shaughnessy didn't stop. He stooped and twisted Dean's arm, rolled him face-first into the dust so he could grab the other arm. Pulled out a pair of plastic cuffs and got them onto Dean's wrists and the guy was out of it.

I hobbled across and did the same to Williams, though his broken wrist made getting the cuffs on a damn noisy operation.

We finished up with Aaron, who still wasn't moving.

Forty-five seconds from start to finish.

'Well,' I said, 'looks like they got surprised again.'

'Thought I wasn't going to make it,' Shaughnessy commented. He'd been tied up in Town when Harry drove out. But he'd worked the Yamaha and hit Bristol whilst Dean and his pals were in Friday's. I'd vectored him in as soon as Locke gave me the location.

'Should have come out earlier,' Shaughnessy said. 'I was upstairs, assumed they wouldn't catch you.'

'No matter. I had them covered.'

Shaughnessy grinned.

'How's the arm?' he said. I was massaging my left triceps. The one that was missing sensation.

'I can manage,' I said. 'You take the heavy ends.'

Shaughnessy threw a leer and we stooped towards Aaron.

Got to work.

CHAPTER THIRTY-SEVEN

The cement bag was mainly cosmetic

We finished up, made calls, then left Dean and his pals tied up in the Merc and walked back across the yard. Getting back out through the boarding proved harder than coming in but a hell of a lot easier than getting into the Frogeye's seat. The car wasn't made for people who can't fold their limbs. It took me a while to find the technique, like reversing into a tricky parking spot, but eventually I got my backside onto the seat and my feet on the pedals and I was good to go.

In the ideal world we'd have stayed with Dean to handle the drinks and canapés when the police arrived but the formalities would only slow us. We'd a more pressing place to be.

When the police did arrive at the site they'd release Warren's crew from the Merc and Dean from its boot – which had been Shaughnessy's idea – and the cops would also pull a gun from the Merc's glove box that my guess said had Dean's prints all over it. And they'd want to hear the story behind the saps and hammer lined up on the plastic sheeting beside the car. The implements would tie in with the summary I'd provided to the startled operator, though the part about a contract killing would be hard to corroborate until they dug up John Reed's body. Which might never happen.

But there was enough in the Merc. And fine detail waiting when we talked to the investigating team. Body or no body, Dean would be buried in a mudslide of circumstantial evidence even before Ricky Cousins started talking.

Driving was a little tricky until I got the hang of it but we progressed steadily and I guided Shaughnessy's Yamaha east out of the city and into the black night until the illuminated board of the Century Housing development appeared. We pulled in and parked. Saw we had company. Two guys, standing at the turn-in, arms folded.

We walked over. The guys watched us come. Dropped their arms and took a step forward in unison.

'Whatcha mate? Helpya?'

Big guys. Whatcha was the bigger one. But it was a wide access road. I detoured past them and pushed the gate. It didn't budge. Up beyond I could see lights in the Portakabin.

'Oy! That's private property!'

Whatcha came over to make sure I didn't damage the gate. I turned.

'Are you the night watchman? I don't see a hut and brazier.'

'Never mind who I am. This is private property. So piss off out of here.'

'No can do. We've got business in there.' I thumbed towards the Portakabin.

'You haven't got any business here. I'll tell you again–'

'What's the problem? Someone nicking the bricks?'

'Nonna your business. We've had intruders and we don't want any more. The cops are on their way.'

'I'll bet. Does Marty know about this?'

Whatcha closed the gap. Came up face to face.

'You're getting annoying, pal.'

'Character flaw. Do you have the gate keys?'

'Yeah.' He pulled a key from a pocket and dangled it. 'I've got the key. You wanna try takin' it?'

'It would save a climb.'

Now the second guy ambled over and put his face into mine too.

'Are you thick?' he said. 'Did you hear what we told you?'

I sighed. Took a step back but Thick re-closed the gap. I sighed again. It was the only tactic I had. Shaughnessy was standing back, arms folded. He looked a little impatient but he didn't sigh. He never does.

'Think about it,' I said. 'It's one a.m. in the middle of nowhere. You haven't a clue why you're here but when two guys you don't recognise turn up you know it's not by chance. Don't you at least want to know what's going on? It might save a few tears downstream.'

The two of them thought about it.

'So who are you,' Whatcha said.

'We're the people who've put the light on over there.'

Whatcha and Thick looked at the Portakabin and tried to figure how I'd managed the trick. And maybe they were curious to know why they'd been scrambled in the dead of night. But orders were orders. Secure the gate. They were keeping the key. But the police would be here in five minutes and the seven foot gate looked like the Walls of Babylon the way my limbs were aching. Shinning over had no appeal.

Then a hand closed over Whatcha's fist and he looked round into Shaughnessy's face, which was level with his. He gave a couple of seconds of puzzlement then his mouth opened and let out some kind of gasp and when Shaughnessy stepped away he had the key.

Sean stepped over and worked the key into the padlock. Kieran's guys glared at him and muscled themselves up but they stayed put. I grinned and retrieved the key as the lock snapped open. Tossed it back to Whatcha.

'Thanks,' I said. 'Stay here.'

We went in and closed the gate behind us.

'Remind me never to arm-wrestle with you,' I told Sean.

Shaughnessy said nothing. We walked up the rough road surface and reached the cabin.

The door's squeak was worse than before on account of the jamb being splintered and the top hinge misaligned. I got the thing open and we went in. The office inside was messy. Furniture re-arranged. Cabinets were down, potted plants scattered, chairs toppled.

One table was still standing though and one chair was upright on the far side of it and Sarah Locke was sitting there resting her forearms on the table. It was the first time I'd seen her less than immaculate. Her hair was messed up and her eyes were tired. It had been a long twenty-four hours.

Harry was beside her, leaning against the wall. He had blood drying on his eyebrow and a bruise on his cheek and his jacket and slacks were covered in dust and moisture. I looked at him.

'Negotiation didn't work?'

He shrugged.

'The bastard had locked the door. Took away my surprise option. Had to break the thing in and negotiate with a near-dislocated shoulder.' He shook his head wearily. 'Sixties is too old for this game.'

'You told us,' I said. 'But what's the alternative? A bowling cap and state pension?'

'A desk job would suffice,' Harry said. 'This stuff gets no easier.'

'You'd miss the action,' I warned. 'And paperwork can be tough.'

'You look like you've just shouldered a few doors yourself,' Harry said.

I caught myself. Quit massaging my arm.

'It's fine,' I said. 'I do paperwork with my right hand.'

I asked Sarah how she was. She shook clear of her thoughts and said she was fine. But she was subdued.

'They brought me here with a bag over my head,' she said. 'Locked me in a room with no windows.'

Unpleasant.

'They told me they just wanted me out of the way whilst some business was taken care of but they wouldn't tell me what the business was. That was a little scary.'

'Harry explained?'

'Yes. And he said you were sorting things out, which scared me to hell all over again. You don't sort out these kind of people.'

I thought of the three guys tied up in the sorting complex. Grinned. Then my arm sent a reminder and wiped the smile. It wasn't so much the pain as the thought that it had been a little close. If Shaughnessy had called in a delay on his way down from London I'd have gone ahead anyway. Just Harry as backup. Which would have been fine until Harry diverted to follow Stevie's Saab out here.

Because I'd probably have gone in alone to meet Dean.

Luckily Shaughnessy was in Bristol in time to join the party, and the Terry Dean meet was always going to be one-sided. A game of two halves, at least. First half: Flynn gets stretchered off. Second: he's back in the thick of it as the big guns open up.

And even at the site I'd had the option to call the whole thing off. The plan was to have Dean sprinting back to Sarah on the back of an arranged call coming in from Harry as Locke and I stooged around the complex. The call would have been the phoney news that we'd located Sarah, which I'd make sure Dean heard before I scarpered. But Harry had called before I went in with the news that he actually *had* got to her. So ruse not needed. But the party had been set up and Shaughnessy was in place and it was hard to resist the opportunity to let Locke show us one last time whose side he was on. Hard to resist the opportunity to put Dean and his pals together with their weapons in a vehicle that might yield one or two forensic morsels related to John Reed's disappearance.

An opportunity I couldn't resist.

They could put it on a million gravestones.

My leg cramped. I transferred weight, pressed, stretched muscle. Then my arm cramped. If I just let the muscles go I'd be dancing the polka.

'Have you spoken to your father?' I said.

'He wasn't answering. So I spoke to my mother. She was in bed. Said he was out somewhere. She didn't seem to know what was happening. We talked at cross-purposes for five minutes until I realised that Dad hadn't told her I was missing.'

'You need to talk to him. He has things to tell you.'

Locke would have a lot of things to tell a lot of people tomorrow. The police would want to know who'd pulled me in to track down Charlie Warren's fugitive and I wasn't about to spin them lies, even to save Sarah and her mother. There was no good ending to this for Locke's family.

I heard a thumping from the next room. The plywood floor resonated. I walked through and flicked a switch. A guy was down on the floor beating his heels against the lino. His ankles were clipped in a plastic tie and most of the rest of him was hidden inside a cement bag. I stooped and ripped tape away and eased the bag off. Grinned down at the ghostly figure of Stevie. He coughed twice, blew a storm of dust. Seemed his negotiation with Harry hadn't gone so well. Stevie's hands were secured with more ties. The cement bag was mainly cosmetic.

Harry Green. Pining for that desk job!

'Bastard!' Stevie said.

I didn't know whether he meant me or Harry. Or whether he was mad about the cement sack or the fact that it represented the end of his personal journey through the construction business.

I grinned. Shook my head and left.

Left the sack off only because reaching down would have hurt too much.

We walked Sarah out onto the Portakabin's top step to watch the action down by the gates. Headlights and flashing blues. I wondered whether the two stooges had scarpered. And whether Marty Kieran had turned up and done a quiet U-turn when he saw the welcome party.

As we watched, the gates swung open and the police vehicles passed through and drove slowly up.

CHAPTER THIRTY-EIGHT
After that: nothing

I crossed to the window and tried to ignore the pain in my arm as I pulled the sash up. Stooped to get my head out and my arms onto the sill. Watched the Monday morning rush. A train was accelerating below me on the fast line, heading towards Bristol. In ninety minutes sharp-suited business types would be shaking hands and accepting coffee at meetings across the city. The business week would be up and running.

Life goes on. Voids close.

Somewhere out on the Bristol streets there'd be a guy doing his round, posting bills. He'd drive the same kind of van as the one I'd watched. Climb the same ladders. Over in Redland a prospective new tenant would be looking round the refurbished flat, breathing the same fug from Elsie Flowers' fag holder. The smoke wouldn't quite cover the smell of paint.

Out at the police compound a black Merc would be locked up, waiting for the forensics people to schedule their search.

And in the cells of an out-of-town station Terry Dean and his pals would be waiting for the call upstairs for an executive chat.

I leaned further to catch the rear of the Bristol train disappearing under the Westway. Fifty-fifty there'd be a couple of lawyers in first class heading out to advise their clients to keep schtum. Not that Terry Dean needed guidance.

Up in the Midlands a fiftyish woman would be heading for work bearing the burden of unanswered questions about a brother she couldn't contact. A P.I.'s flying visit and a policeman's preliminary chat had given her nothing of certainty, just a belief that John Reed was gone for good.

Life goes on.

The westerly breeze pushed clouds across the city. The air tasted fresh but bitter.

I watched the world for fifteen minutes then ducked back in and fought the sash down. Went to make coffee.

A while later the others came up. Lucy resuscitated the coffee machine and brought my mug through then perched herself on the roll-top. Her hair had reverted to bright red to match her skirt. Her top was some kind of violet. Situation normal. Harry had changed his jacket. Same style, less dust. He sank with a sigh into the club chair beside Herbie. Herbie lifted an eye then went back to sleep. We'd wake him if needed.

I'd racked my chair back before realising that getting my feet onto the desk would involve more pain than I could tolerate. Maybe tomorrow. I readjusted. Got my right ankle over my left thigh. Grinned across at Shaughnessy as he walked in to tap the barometer. The arrow was on Fair. Moving up.

First day back in.

We'd spent Friday in Bristol helping the police put things together. The thing took all day with a break for deli sandwiches at noon and phone lines running hot to Scotland Yard. There'd be a couple of Met detectives on that Bristol train too, though they wouldn't be riding first class.

Shaughnessy finished his weather check. 'Any call back?' he said.

'Yesterday evening. Dean and his crew and Kieran's man are remanded in custody, charged with the abduction. And there's an expectation of adding John Reed's murder to Dean's charges in the next couple of days. They'll not get a body but the circumstantial stuff, with Cousins' snaps of them snatching Reed, will be enough.'

'Cousins still co-operating?'

'I guess he did the sums. Either scarper and go back to running from an even madder Charlie Warren or play prime witness, back up his photos with court testimony, then disappear into witness protection.'

'None of it helps John Reed,' Lucy said.

I agreed.

'He was just the wrong guy with the wrong face. Never knew what was coming until it hit him.'

Shaughnessy walked over to check the window view.

'Cousins spotted a hell of a lucky break,' he said. 'I guess his poker instincts couldn't resist the opportunity.'

'Lucky as it gets,' I said. 'Having a spitting image living in Bristol might have given him nothing. You can't paste your identity onto someone else unless their own is pretty light. That was his luck: that

Reed was a loner, few friends, no contact with relatives, self-employed. Cousins must have thought he had a winning lottery ticket when he saw how he might work it. Divert Warren's search onto the guy and have him disappear with no ripples. No-one interested. No press coverage. Nothing that might get back to Warren to tell him that his victim was not Cousins.'

'If Reed's landlady hadn't called you it would have worked,' Lucy said. 'Reed's stuff would have been moved into storage and his flat would have been rented out and ValuAd would find another contractor. And Reed's sister wouldn't think anything if she didn't hear from him for a year or two.'

I grinned. Sipped coffee.

'That landlady's something,' I said. 'Who'd have thought she'd get on the blower to chase a missing tenant? Without her interference Cousins would have had his lottery ticket: a look-alike who was a nobody. Minimal official paperwork to remove from the flat when Cousins planted clues pointing to himself. And so easy to leave just the dry-cleaning ticket and Double Ace cufflinks as a bare minimum to give the game away to someone who knew what they were looking for. No chance of Reed noticing that his flat had been disturbed before the bad guys turned up.'

'Cousins shouldn't have left that condolence card,' Lucy said.

'He didn't spot it. Should have. He cleared out all Reed's ID but left the name and address of someone who knew the real person.'

'The guy was under pressure,' Harry said. 'Must have taken him a while to sanitise Reed's flat and plant the evidence pointing to himself. Reed or his landlady could have come in at any moment. And how many people leave addressed envelopes lying around?'

'Still a mistake,' I said. 'And he made another at his girlfriend's house – the woman who thought she was living with a guy called Smith, which had been Cousins' real alias in the twelve months he was running. He'd printed Reed's face alongside his own to confirm the match. Something that wasn't necessary. He should have left everything in his computer and camera. Or at least shredded the print. Though I guess he didn't anticipate anyone turning up in Bromsgrove.

'Did Reed's sister explain the condolence card?' Lucy said.

'What she told me gave me the answer. She and Reed were pretty much estranged. Didn't talk more that once in five or ten years. But she'd left a message when her husband died and it looks like Reed wrote out a card, had it stamped and ready to post before he realised that a card was just a little too cold, no matter how distant they were. So he dropped it into his magazine rack and drove up to the Midlands to pay his respects. Forgot about it later.'

'Does she know Reed is gone?' Lucy asked.

'The police will have warned her. They'll update her when they've put it all together but I don't think she expects to see her brother again.'

'Poor guy. The ultimate Mr Nobody.'

'Everybody's somebody,' I said.

'Cousins really is a piece of refuse,' Lucy said. She slid off the desk and went to watch the trains with Shaughnessy. 'He might just as well have killed Reed himself.'

'To all intents and purposes that's what he did: since Warren putting Reed in the ground was the sole purpose of his scheme.'

'And he's going to get away with it.'

'To the extent that living in witness protection for the rest of your life is getting away with anything. And even witness protection isn't foolproof. Cousins will always live with the thought that he might get a tap on the shoulder one day.'

'Cousins wasn't the only one,' Shaughnessy said. 'Locke was part of the conspiracy even if he was coerced. He knew exactly what would happen to whoever Charlie Warren was hunting down.'

'But it was me who tracked Reed down,' I said. 'Invaded his life and handed him to the bad guys. It's hard not to feel responsible.'

'If Locke hadn't pulled you in he'd have found someone else,' Shaughnessy said. 'And maybe the someone else wouldn't have torn things open afterwards.'

Lucy came back to the desk.

'Does Warren know he got the wrong guy?'

'For sure. Terry Dean would have figured things out on Friday from the police questions. Briefed his lawyer to report back. Charlie knows.'

'Must have ruined his weekend,' Harry said. He was tickling Herbie's ear. Herbie growled contentedly. 'You discover that you've been scammed by the guy you're chasing, see your best people up on a murder rap that's likely to stick, and see heavy action coming your way when the cops focus on you.' He grinned. Tapped Herbie's skull. 'And the icing on top's the collateral damage to Charlie's reputation when it gets out that he's sunk his old pal Marty Kieran.'

'Warren will fight clear of any charges,' I said. 'Reed's murder will stop with Dean and his pals.'

'That's the way it goes,' Harry agreed. 'But Charlie won't dodge the loss of face for being played like fool and dropping a fellow professional in it. That's going to be harder for him to swallow than a twenty-five year stretch.'

Shaughnessy quit with the view and came over to lean back on the desk.

'And the other key player won't see a courtroom either,' he said.

Bernard Locke.

The guy whose dim and dirty past exposed him to coercion when Charlie needed help. Locke had succumbed to the pressure, knowing that someone was going to get hurt. And later had seen my own disappearance as the convenient solution to his problems. But Locke wouldn't be facing any charges.

'If I'd questioned his story a little more closely,' I said, 'I'd never have taken the job.'

'It was a convincing set-up,' Harry said. 'The ready-made story about the threat to Sarah assisted by Locke's nifty Photoshopping.'

'Yeah, it was all convincing. But I had my doubts. I let him convince me that he'd got his pics of the alleged stalker through a quiet street cam. search. And maybe there are coppers who can get into council footage on the quiet, talk them into a little exercise, but not when you're Chief Constable. The guy with all the supposed power is the one who's most tied. Everything he does will attract scrutiny. And his face-recognition story was a little fanciful. I let that get through without a challenge.'

'Hindsight and an unlucky break,' Lucy said. 'If Locke hadn't had his ready-made cover story in the form of routine threats against his daughter and the actions of the Stradivarius people he'd have needed to be much more creative to pull you in.'

'Doesn't bring John Reed back. I'm still kicking myself for not seeing through the bastard.'

'And Locke hasn't come out of it too well,' Harry said. 'All the bad guys have come to grief one way or another. That's something to balance the books.'

Harry had a point. But I was still kicking myself.

Metaphorically. I wouldn't be kicking anything for a few days.

I pushed myself out of my chair and the party broke up. Lucy had jobs waiting for me. Clients to call. Two notice-servings and a legal letter to answer. Fun stuff like that.

~~~~~

By mid-morning I'd made none of the calls. My concentration was shot.

Harry and Shaughnessy had gone out, picking up the jobs they'd interrupted last Thursday, and Lucy was working her computer, sending out demands and fending off utilities companies. Herbie was out there with her. The crunch of biscuits carried clearly through the doorway.

Concentration. Tricky, with your mind wandering, stuck on the question of which direction the black Mercedes had taken when it left that derelict hospital with a shocked and terrified guy in the back. One day you're just living your life, a nobody. The next you're dazed and bleeding in a car boot.

And after that: nothing.

Concentration.

I just had to remember what Harry said: that the bad guys were all taking pain.

Though Bernard Locke's was over.

I guess he'd looked for options and ways out and patch-up opportunities as he drove home from that ambush site – or rather after he found out that the party had flopped behind him – and no matter how hard he'd looked he'd seen no way he could walk into work on Monday and no way to keep the respect of his wife and daughter. When the news had reached him about the police operation at the sorting facility he'd known it was over.

And that's when he took a drive.

They found him twenty-four hours later on Dartmoor. Shut in his car. An old service revolver still gripped in his hand.

Beyond the prosecutors' reach.

Over in Bristol the TownGate offices would be subdued this morning. Carrying on without Sarah. She'd be back in a week or so but then there'd be some more subdued whispering as they heard about the dirty work within their own firm, watched lawyers going in and out as Sarah and Sewell looked for an amicable split.

Though Sewell might find it hard to stay amicable as he pictured what was coming his way when Sarah completed her Stradivarius investigation and handed the criminal arts cadre gift-wrapped to the police and the public.

She'd be back on that next week. Perhaps it would keep her mind off her father.

And off me.

A guy she might wish had never come to town.

CHAPTER THIRTY-NINE
Never trust anyone

Two months later I got a visit.

We came into the building late one afternoon. Stood back in the vestibule whilst Bob Rook held the inner door for departing clients. The happy looks on the clients' faces and Bob's personal assistance with the door suggested that he'd pulled off another compensation coup at forty-five percent, and the fact that he managed to hold his grin after spotting me suggested it was forty-five percent of a big number. Then after his clients had trooped out Bob stayed put to hold the door for me and I realised we were talking seven figures. If a job ever brings Eagle Eye seven figures I'll go right down and hold the door for Bob and grin the hell right back at him. Herbie was unaware of the history but he'd picked up the vibes early on and held his growl as he always did until we were half way up the stairs.

Then as we hit the first landing his ears came up and his tail set off wagging like a wind-up toy. We continued up the last flight and found Sarah Locke standing outside our door. The door can be misleading. Its BACK SOMETIME SOON sign needs interpretation.

The landing was dimly lit since little illumination got through our glass but Sarah's smile lit the place up. The musk of her perfume brought up my own bright smile. Herbie crashed to the floor with his cardiac thing and Sarah laughed and squatted to administer first aid and call him Pretty Boy, which didn't help.

I unlocked the door.

'We'd better carry him in,' I said.

Sarah stood and went through and Pretty Boy effected a recovery that saved the heavy work. He rolled back up and headed for his water bowl.

I closed the door and waited a moment for Sarah to get over her awe and amazement. The reception area is a long room running all the way to the front of the building. It's furnished with Lucy's desk and cabinets plus a hot drinks table and a couch under the window. The couch is mostly for show but doubles as a bed when I wind up late at my jazz club. We rarely have clients sitting there.

247

Sarah "ooh'd" and "wow'd" as she looked around. Like she could hardly contain her excitement.

'Absolutely perfect,' she said.

'It's functional,' I conceded, 'apart from the filter machine.'

I walked her through so she could be impressed all over again by my room, which was also functional apart from the time clock which I'd forgotten to wind, and the potted plants which seemed to be dead. She checked it all out, walked past the cricket posters and got to the window. The view probably impressed her too. Trains and cars. A backdrop of council towers.

She turned back to check out my desk. The roll-top was down to hide the mess. It looked okay.

'Antique?' she said.

'A hundred years old. Same as the clock.'

'It's perfect. Just as I imagined.'

I grinned. The woman had an interesting imagination. Most P.I.s have offices at home, or rent cheap city rooms that look like downmarket accountants' offices. Style is one thing our firm has, even if it's dictated primarily by financial constraints.

I gestured to the remaining visitors' chair. Herbie was already thrashing around on his back on the adjacent one. Staffies are another thing most P.I.s don't have.

I jammed my hands in my pockets and leaned back on the roll-top, still wondering why Sarah would be happy to see me. But her smile was contagious.

'I'd offer coffee,' I said, 'but as I mentioned, the filter machine...'

She crossed her legs. Sat back. Shook her head as she reached to tickle Herbie. She was the first person who'd ever looked comfortable in the chairs apart from Herbie.

'I've been drinking coffee all day,' she said. 'I need detox every time I get home from this town.'

'Then we run on similar lines. When our machine's working we turn out a brew to have you sprinting round the block.'

She looked around from her new vantage point. Checked out the wilting plants and the cracks in the ceiling.

'Absolutely the way I imagined it,' she said. 'Kind of homey. Low tech, but I suspect that's a false impression. I bet you've got all the gadgets.'

'We can handle the tech stuff,' I conceded. 'And everything else. We're fully functional behind the veneer. Just the coffee machine and carpets – those are as bad as they look.'

She completed her visual tour.

'How's Harry?' she said.

'Harry's fine. His jacket cleaned up nicely.'

'I came to thank him for rescuing me.'

'Be careful. You'll have him blubbering.'

'I'll bet he was a tough guy once.'

'He still is. He just complains about it more nowadays.'

She laughed. Tickled Herbie.

'I won't forget that night in a hurry,' she told me. 'I had a sack over my head when Harry crashed in but I heard it all. The door burst open and Kieran's thug went for him and I heard a scuffle then a terrific bang which was Harry, holding the guy against the wall and asking what kind of person locked Portakabin doors when they're inside? Cursing about his shoulder. I could hear the guy trying to fend him off but he was on a losing bet. Harry was just so mad.

'He'd snagged a sleeve,' I explained. 'Something on top of the gate. Harry's tough but he's no athlete.'

She gave it a moment. Then: 'I came to thank you too, Eddie. Despite everything.

'Just trying to clear up a mess.' I stopped there, remembering how the mess had started. Sarah Locke was putting on a cheery face, but her father's betrayal must have knocked her flat. I asked after her mother.

Her face answered my question.

'She's struggling,' she said. 'Can't come to terms with what Dad had done. Not just recently. His old history, when he was an ordinary copper, when they first met. They'll never prove anything now but his ties to Warren and other criminals are clear. Mum is struggling to handle that.'

'I'm sorry it ended that way,' I said.

'Not your fault. My father wasn't the person we thought he was. Maybe he wanted to be but he'd sowed the seeds of his downfall a long time ago. But I'm still struggling to accept that he tracked John Reed down even knowing what would happen to him.'

That had to be the hardest part. But the truth couldn't be avoided.

'I'd like to tell you different but your father knew what would happen. Forty years as a copper told him that.'

She shook her head. Some of the light had gone.

'His mistake was back then. The bad contacts, petty corruption. He just didn't see that he'd never get free of it.'

'Yeah. The higher he climbed the tighter these people's hold. An ordinary copper might brush rumours away but when you're on the fast track to the top the smallest whispers can kill you. Warren watched your father and saw an investment. Waited for the day it would pay dividends.'

She sighed. Shook her head. Managed another faint smile.

'Damn,' she said. 'But I'm sorry he dragged you into the mess, Eddie.'

'Not for you to apologise. His decision, his action, our job description. I'm sorry you had to experience betrayal. His using you as a prop to pull me in. Sending me chasing after your affairs as cover for his search for Reed. I don't think your father saw any choice but he allowed himself to be pushed until it put you in danger, and there's no way to gloss over that.'

'He was always so proud of what I'd done. Where I'd gone.'

'Probably made it harder for him.'

We let the thought float. Her hand tickled Herbie's belly unconsciously. I changed the subject.

'Good programme,' I said.

She snapped back. Her eyes picked up a little spark.

'You had the right to a shout-out in the credits,' she said.

'And thanks for asking but it wouldn't have fitted.'

'I thought all publicity was good publicity.'

'Not in this business. People hire us for quiet and discretion. They want a guy no-one knows. Someone who can operate behind the scenes.'

'Then, from behind the scenes – a discrete thanks.'

'You're welcome.'

I'm not a TV viewer. Wouldn't have spotted the *Exposed* episode if Lucy hadn't raced into the office a week back and pulled it up on Harry's computer. She brought coffee and biscuits through like it was a damn matinee and insisted we sit through the whole fifty-five minutes. Which didn't lack entertainment. TownGate had done a thorough job, pulled the Stradivarius story together and produced the episode within a month. Pushed it out to coincide with their handing over of their dirt on Pauline Granger to the police. The foamy newspaper headlines boosted their audience with the prospect of the rich and respectable going down, and the trail from a criminal arts operation centred in Bristol to an Austrian castle was a cinematographic eye-fest. Helicopter footage. High definition alpine vistas.

The Bardi Stradivariuses had long vanished from Richmond's cellar by the time the police got there but Harry's snaps of the instruments *in situ*, with his close-ups of the interior labels, were evidence enough to bring charges that were going to stick. Granger's operation was going through the forensic mill and though both Granger and Richmond were out on bail the evidence was building. Unless the two of them upped and ran they'd see the inside of a courtroom before the end of the year. Whether the two Strads would ever reappear depended on the Austrian authorities who were besieging Richmond's lawyers in a ferocious campaign to breach his castle's drawbridge.

Photo man Harry had been put on notice that he'd be a key wit. when the CPS took Richmond to court, which wasn't going to help our quiet and discreet image. And then someone had leaked Lucy's name as the assistant who got Harry into the Wallingbury House basement, which might put her on the witness stand alongside him and would finish the firm's quiet image for good. She'd already selected an outfit and hair colour. When the thing came to trial the guys in wigs and robes would need shades.

The best bit of the TV show was when Sarah raced up Richmond's drive to get an off-the-cuff comment from the guy himself. Richmond hadn't taken it well. Attacked her and her crew with a garden rake. The camera was obliterated but its flash memory survived and the team's fighting retreat was caught on a shaky iPhone. The melee was all the British public needed to confirm Richmond's guilt, and word of mouth pushed the follow-up on-demand viewing figures for the episode through the roof.

If Mark Sewell had still been with the team he could have taken another beating from Richmond's rake in the cause of investigative journalism, but the guy's name was not in the credits.

It had been his game that had kept me looking at the Stradivarius affair for an attacker who didn't exist. I hadn't heard the full story but Sarah gave it me now. A simple tale of lust and greed. Sewell had been hot on the trail of the Bardi Strads until he met Pauline Granger in person. That's when his journalistic instincts took a slap-down from his human instincts. Granger had seen the pickle she was in when Sewell first confronted her with his questions and decided that the best tactic was to counter-attack with charm and money. Pauline was an alluring woman. Her charm was more than effective on top of the bucket of cash that was thrown Sewell's way and she pressed her advantage into a full-blown fling to keep the guy on a short leash. And her and Richmond's combined wealth ensured that the cash part of the tryst was impressive: specifically, a million quid delivered to Sewell's offshore account. I guess the exotic talents of the art firm's proprietor were just cream on the top.

So all the other stuff – the attack on Sewell's house, the threat letters and beating – were phoney, designed to build up a credible case for Sewell to shut down the investigation, though apparently Sewell hadn't been told about the beating in advance, so the nuances of the word "phoney" might have been lost on him. But he probably appreciated the good cause, and a check on his offshore balance would have helped as he licked his wounds.

Though maybe he also understood that the beating wasn't entirely phoney. Whilst the carrot part of the affair must have tasted pretty good – maybe Sewell even thought he and Pauline had a real thing – the stick was real, encouragement to play along and make sure the investigation was buried fast. A warning to stay in line.

The *Exposed* episode didn't mention Sewell but Sarah confirmed that word had got out within the industry, and the police were going after her partner over the million-quid payoff. If Sewell ever got back into the business he'd be producing soap powder commercials.

'It was nice to see Richmond's holiday home,' I said. 'Got me thinking about a walking tour through Austria next year. That scenery is something.'

Sarah smiled.

'Impact television,' she said. 'It puts you right there.'

Then she sat forward in her chair.

'But I didn't come here just to thank you.'

I waited.

'We've kicked some ideas around,' she said. 'And one we really like is a fly-on-the-wall inside the investigation business. I'm talking a mini series at least. Pilot and four episodes, maybe eight or ten. The day-to-day life of a private investigator. It would be a killer. And I was thinking maybe your firm. We could come in for six weeks and you'd never know we were here. Just one guy with a compact camera. The public would go crazy for it. And we'd be looking at high six figures for your cut on the first series alone.'

I pushed myself away from the desk and grinned down at her then turned and grinned at my Time Recorder clock up on the wall. I reached out, pushed gently down on the lever, and the stamp went "ping". I was still grinning as I turned back to her and she sensed the message.

'That's a nice offer,' I said. 'We'd earn more from the fly-on-the-wall than from the actual investigation work.'

She stood. Came over.

'By a factor of ten. A reality P.I. would top the charts.'

I didn't doubt it.

I held the grin. Waxed creative.

'How about Lucy selecting the clients?' I brainstormed. 'Maybe writing the scripts? Who knows what scrapes we'd get into?'

She broadened her smile but she was hearing my message.

'Thanks but no thanks,' I said. 'Not our style. We're cosy the way we are. Mostly unknown and unappreciated and getting by.'

'It's a once-in-a-lifetime opportunity,' she said.

'I don't doubt. But we don't need opportunity. We do this for a living. There's no reality version. Just us, our clients and their third parties and it works out nicely that way. Quiet and confidential. Regular cheques.'

She sighed. Pushed the lever down herself. It went "ping" again.

'I thought you'd say that,' she told me. 'But if you ever change your mind I'm just a phone call away.'

'Got it. And if you really want to go with the series there's a hundred other firms. Most of them would be considerably safer to be around. Less costly in camera equipment.'

She nodded. Her smile was resigned but warm.

'You've got my number,' she said.

I said nothing.

She turned to give Herbie a last tickle then moved towards the door. I held it open and she touched my arm.

'I like you, Eddie,' she said. 'Very much.'

'In the interests of full disclosure: that's mutual.'

'I actually wondered whether we had something going back there.'

The night in Bristol. The suggestion of a nightcap at my hotel. The byway left unexplored.

'But you pulled away,' she said. 'I was a little puzzled. Then I realised.'

I tugged at my own memories for the explanation.

'You didn't quite trust me,' she said. 'You thought I might be one of the bad guys.'

'I didn't know you,' I said. 'That's different. I was reserving judgement. P.I.s are cautious that way.'

'That's a better term: reserving judgement. But if you had no reservations?'

'Then my mini bar would have been yours.'

'You said there was no min bar.'

'There you are,' I said. 'Never trust anyone. Until you know them.'

I thought of the devastation that just had wrecked this woman's family.

'And even when you know them,' I said. 'Sometimes not even then.'

I held the door open and walked her to the stairs.

THE END

ACKNOWLEDGEMENTS

Firstly, thanks to any readers out there who've been patiently awaiting the publication of this book. Writing books is not my full-time occupation and last year (2020) saw a long delay to the start of this next chapter in P.I. Eddie Flynn's casebook as other work took priority. Whilst the 2020 Coronavirus pandemic put many people at home with time on their hands, and should have presented me the opportunity to get the next book out, it was not to be.

The good news, if you enjoy the P.I. Flynn stories, is that the next book is already in production.

Thanks to my wife for checking the early version of *Dog Waltz* and providing invaluable feedback. And thanks to Lyndon Smith and Miles Manning, former Metropolitan Police detectives, for running their eyes over some of the technical aspects related to the story's police operations. As with all such advice, the author first asks for help then tampers willy-nilly with that advice to make reality fit fiction, though my intention always is to present stories that are plausibly aligned with the real world.

Travel restrictions during the writing of the book prevented a detailed check of the geography contained in the narrative. It's some years since I visited Bristol and where research and memory don't quite cover the gap I hope readers familiar with the locations will forgive the distortions of their city as it was – or perhaps wasn't quite – in 2012.

BEHIND CLOSED DOORS
Michael Donovan

Family feuds, booze and bad company. Teenager Rebecca Slater's walk on the wild side has taken a downward spiral. And now she's disappeared.

But her family don't seem to have noticed. Wealthy, private, dysfunctional, the Slaters deny that their daughter is missing – even as they block all attempts by Rebecca's friends to contact her.

So the friends contact a private investigator.

Eddie Flynn is good at finding people. And he's good at spotting lies. It doesn't take him long to see through the Slaters' denials. So he digs around, and isn't too surprised when some unpleasant people come scuttling out of the cracks in the Slaters' perfect world.

But for these people the teenager's disappearance is part of a plan. One that's too important to be threatened by an investigator with more persistence than sense. So it's time for the investigator to disappear...

Winner of the **Northern Crime 2012** award, *Behind Closed Doors* has been acclaimed for its departure from the norm for British crime fiction...

'Donovan refreshingly breaks [the tradition] with remarkable success'
Cuckoo Review

'Eddie Flynn is part Philip Marlowe, part Eddie Gumshoe, a likeable wisecracking guy but with a temper when roused ... humour ... violent confrontations ... well recommended.'
eurocrime

www.michaeldonovancrime.com

THE DEVIL'S SNARE
Michael Donovan

They call them the "Killer Couple". Accused of killing their daughter the Barbers have been on the run from public opinion for two years.

But the Barbers are still fighting. And if their high profile campaign to clear their name and get their baby back has made them rich that was never their intention.

Meanwhile a failed prosecution hasn't dampened the media's hunger for revelations. Their investigators are on the job, moving towards an exposure that will spotlight the Barbers as the killers they are. And now a dangerous vigilante has joined the fray: if the system can't bring justice he'll mete out his own.

P.I. Eddie Flynn doesn't read the tabloids. Shuns limelight. Trusts only in facts. But can't resist challenges. When the Barbers come to him for help he pushes judgement aside and signs up. His mission: keep them safe and find their child.

Sounds like nice, solid detective work. Until Flynn realises that his clients are hiding something...

'A slick, dynamic mystery.'
Kirkus Reviews

'Escapism at its best'
Postcard Reviews

'... complicated ... wonderful ... brilliant. I recommend anyone ... to try this book. [It] will haunt your days and nights.'
Georgia Cuthbertson, Cuckoo Review

www.michaeldonovancrime.com

COLD CALL
Michael Donovan

In the black of night the intruder breaks into the victim's house armed with a knife and garrotte. Her body is found thirty hours later, a mass of stab wounds, a deadly laceration round her neck.

Is this the Diceman, killing again after seven years lying low? Or does London have a copycat killer?

P.I. Eddie Flynn has been out of that world since his failed hunt for the Diceman let the killer go free and cost him his job in the Metropolitan Police.

Now, with the new killer on the rampage a bizarre phone call from his dead victim drags Flynn right back to centre stage and a new hunt. But this killer – copycat or not – takes a P.I.'s interference personally.

So now he has a new focus for his madness.

"Chilling ... crafted with style...
wild nightmarish scenes."
Bookpleasures

"Masterful... If you haven't been
introduced to Eddie Flynn yet, be prepared"
Red City Review

www.michaeldonovancrime.com

Made in United States
Orlando, FL
03 December 2024

54815786R00161